KV-638-510

THE SECOND JEOPARDY

Roger Ormerod

CONSTABLE CRIME

Constable London

First published in Great Britain 1987
by Constable and Company Limited
10 Orange Street, London WC2H 7EG
Copyright © by Roger Ormerod 1987
Set in Linotron Palatino 10 pt by
Redwood Burn Limited, Trowbridge, Wiltshire
Printed in Great Britain by
Redwood Burn Limited, Trowbridge, Wiltshire

British Library CIP data
Ormerod, Roger
The second jeopardy
I. Title
823'.914 [F]   PR6065.R688

ISBN 0 09 467970 3

M 74789
F

M 74789

NEWPORT BOROUGH LIBRARIES

0353465

RARY Tel. NEWPORT 855245

The second jeopardy

Harry Hodnutt finds it demeaning to ask the police for assistance. Having just served a sentence for jewel theft, he now finds himself haunted by the death of Angela Reed. There is no denying that it was he who involved her in the jewel robbery, but he was found not guilty of her murder. Now the man who claims to have been married to Angela is threatening Harry's life.

The police offer assistance, though not in the form Harry expects. Virginia Brent, daughter of the Assistant Chief Constable, seems more likely to be a liability. Yet they share the same objective. Harry will be safe only when the true murderer is found, and Virginia claims a personal interest in that Angela was her sister.

Together they pursue leads that scare even Harry. Only with an army of his fellow toughs would he have gone near Sean O'Loughlin, master-criminal extraordinary. But Virginia, naïve, forthright and determined, does not hesitate, though she still needs Harry's protection. In their partnership they discover more than the truth, they learn understanding of each other.

But it is Virginia who produces the only possible solution.

Roger Ormerod, who lives in Wolverhampton, is the author of over twenty novels of suspense. He recently received high praise for his *An alibi too soon* from Harriet Waugh in *The Spectator*: 'I am glad to announce that the detective novel is still alive and well in Mr Ormerod's skilful hands . . . he ranks among the few English crime writers who can still construct a traditional detective novel in which the ending does not come as a wet squib.'

1

Detective Sergeant Tranter leaned back on the park bench and tried not to laugh. 'You, Harry?' he asked. 'Don't make me laugh.' Then he did.

Harry Hodnutt was bending forward, staring at the path and tearing a blade of grass to pieces. 'All *right*.'

'What's he going to use? An anti-tank gun?'

'It's not funny.'

'Damn it, you're even bigger than when I saw you last.'

There was silence. They both knew their last meeting had been four years before. To be precise, four years three months and five days. It was on that day that Sergeant Tranter had said to Harry: 'I am charging you with robbery, and with the murder of Angela Reed.'

The sergeant pursed his lips and stared at the scuffed toes of his joggers. 'So what is it, Harry? Don't tell me you're asking for police protection.' He glanced sideways, then quickly back again.

'Not that.'

'And why me?'

Harry turned his head. He had a face that had looked too often and too close to flying fists, and knuckles to match. There was no expression on his face. Expressions had difficulty getting out.

'You're my friend.'

'Me? I arrested you.'

'All the same.' Harry nodded ponderously. 'Just wanted a bit of advice.'

Nothing changed in Tranter's relaxed posture, but inside he'd stiffened from big, flat feet to the ruffled nape of his corrugated neck. A lot of his work relied on instinct, and he'd have said that

Harry Hodnutt, for all his bulk and lumbering strength, was incapable of cold-blooded violence. Get him annoyed, and maybe it'd be a different story. Tranter, who was too close to retirement, had no intention of checking it out. But Harry was cold-blooded at that moment, almost monosyllabic with it, and he had been calmly discussing violence. But against himself. That was what the sergeant had found laughable. Yet . . . and this was not amusing at all . . . it could so easily become inverted.

'Now let's get this straight,' he said, licking his lips and sucking at his moustache, not looking at Harry. 'You tell me this character as good as said he's going to kill you.'

'Not in so many words.'

'You told me . . .'

'He skated round it.'

'But you got that impression?'

'Thassit.'

'And so . . .' Tranter knew he had to handle this tenderly. Harry was quite capable of thumping Tranter into the ground – might even enjoy it. And Harry wasn't noted for a vast intellect.

'And so,' said Tranter, clenching his fists, 'you're telling me this because one day you're going to come along to the station and ask for me. And tell me you've hit somebody a bit too hard, and what you want to know from me, right now, is the law on the subject.'

'You crazy or somethin'?' Harry moved his massive shoulders and made it a simple question.

'Whether you could plead self-defence.'

'Why'd I want to do that?' Harry got to his feet and stretched. Normally he stood six feet three inches, but stretching he seemed to reach to the trees, his chest expanded, his head sank between his shoulders, and he yawned. 'If you ain't gonna talk sense,' he said, 'I might's well gerroff. I thought you'd help. Seems I was wrong.'

'Now wait a minute, Harry.' Tranter was half on his feet. Harry reached forward and put a hand on his chest and eased him back again. The spread fingers completely covered the motif: Love And Peace, on the sergeant's track suit.

'You're tired, Sarge. Sorry I troubled you.'

'Harry, I apologize. I got it wrong. Sit down again. Who is this idiot who's had the nerve to threaten you?'

6

Harry stared down at him. The fact that he hadn't simply turned and walked away indicated concern. Tranter knew that. Concern, not worry. It would take a lot to worry Harry. But Harry was frowning, which meant he was thinking, and that could be a serious matter.

'You'll listen?'

'All ears.' Tranter nodded. He was interested, anyway, as the whole thing sounded way off beam.

'All right, then.'

Harry sat. Tranter offered a cigarette, but Harry shook his head. Tranter watched a thrush worrying a worm from beneath a rhododendron, and waited.

'Tells me his name's Fletcher,' said Harry at last. 'Vic Fletcher. Sat opposite me one evenin' in the Cross Keys, me just sitting there with a pint and nothing to do. I'd been out a fortnight by that time. Nothin' coming along . . . you know.'

'None of your old mates with a job for you?'

'Somethin' like that.'

'Don't let 'em con you, Harry. Nicking cars, waving plastic guns . . .'

'For Chrissake!'

Tranter glanced at him. The voice had been bitter, angry, when Tranter had only been ribbing him. 'Advice, Harry,' he said gently.

'I'm stayin' clean. Do I tell this or not?'

'Tell it then, tell it.' Tranter might have been soothing a child.

The look Harry threw at him was as angry as his tone. Too many people assumed he was dim, and he was fed up with it. He shook his head, and gave it a few seconds.

'This Vic Fletcher,' he went on at last, 'he just started talking. Like a blasted professor or somethin', all about life and its meaning and people's responsibilities to society . . .'

'Big words, Harry.'

'What *he* said.'

'Philosophy, it's called.'

'I bet it is. Anyway, on he went, and all I did was get bored. Then he started chuntering on about justice and how it's falling down on the act, and how it was his duty – oh, some crap like that, you know – duty to step in when justice flops on its face.'

'Sounds just like my Chief Super.'

'If you can't be serious . . .'

7

'Honest. He says things like that. We spend months getting in the evidence, and the jury brings in a not guilty . . .' He stopped, slapping his knee. 'There I go. Sorry, Harry, nothing personal. He wasn't talking about you.'

'Maybe not your boss, but this Vic Fletcher was.'

Tranter stared into the distance. A woman was walking her dog. He couldn't have said what pedigree the dog possessed, but the woman was packed with it.

'How d'you know that?'

'He mentioned the murder of Angela Reed.'

'Did he now? Did he indeed?' Tranter lit a cigarette. All of a sudden it had ceased to be amusing. 'So he knew you?'

'Must've done,' said Harry moodily.

'And you realized that?'

'I'm not a complete fool, Sarge.'

'No.'

Harry, the sergeant knew, was no worse than a naïve and trusting fool, with the social conscience of a Labrador puppy. He had always allowed himself to go along with any wild scheme that promised action, and if the law stepped in to slap his knuckles, then that was part of the game. It evened things up for Harry, so that he could emerge from prison all purified and free to start again. Tranter hoped that anything Harry had in mind for starters after his recent prison term would occur on somebody else's patch. It had always been a messy business, arresting Harry Hodnutt.

'I knew he was up to something,' Harry claimed. 'But I played it cool. Waited. To see what happened.'

'Didn't actually screw his neck till he told you what his game was?'

'Didn't need to. He told me in the end.'

'And what was it? Is it, rather.'

'He kept cropping up, like he was following me. Kept spouting the same old rubbish about conscience and retri–whatsit.'

'Bution.'

'Yeah, that. Then he came out with it, and why he was haunting me. Sort of apologizing, you know. Said: Harry – we were on Christian names by then, Harry and Vic – says Harry, you do see what I'm getting at? All prissy. And when I said no, he said if the law wasn't goin' to hand out the penalty, then he'd have to do it,

8

and he was sorry and all that, but it wasn't his fault the death penalty's been abolished, and he never believed in abolishin' it, and he hoped I'd see it his way.' He stopped, panting. He'd memorized it, and the effort had been exhausting.

'Wants putting away.'

'No Sarge, he's got a point.' Harry frowned. There was room on his low forehead for only one frown line, but it was a deep one, and impressive.

'*Somebody* wants putting away. You didn't thump him? Didn't tell him to get out of your life?'

'He told me who he is, and that made a difference. He's her husband, Sarge. Angela Reed's husband.'

Tranter swivelled on the slatted seat. 'She didn't have a husband.'

'Oh yes she did. Him. They'd bin married six months. He says. Kinda kept it quiet.'

'Then why the hell didn't he come forward . . .'

'Says it's irreverent.'

'Irrelevant.'

'Yeah. Says I oughto've got life, whatever her name. And it just isn't right that they let me get away with it.'

'On the murder there was no direct evidence. You were found not guilty, Harry. It clears you. You can't be tried for it again. It's called double jeopardy.'

'He told me that,' Harry said eagerly, pleased to find the two of them agreeing. 'Just them words. Said I could safely tell him the truth – that I'd killed her – and nobody could touch me now.'

'Except him?'

'Thassit. Except him. He said it kind of elected him to do it, on behalf of justice.'

'Did he say how he was going to do it?'

Harry screwed his toe into the path. 'No.'

'Or when?'

'Nor that.'

'He's playing on your nerves. Waiting for you to crack.'

'Guess so.'

'You don't look nervous to me.'

Harry turned his battered face and grinned. It was really the only expression that ever managed to break free from the maze of bumps and knobs and distortions, and it lit up his face, like a

9

crumpled rose opening to the sun. 'Oh I am, Sarge. Really I am.'

The woman with the dog strolled past again. She could possibly have been in her late twenties, but every year had added something. The dog could have been an Alsatian, and it clearly adored every inch of her from toe to the top of her proud head, from walking pumps to knee-high stockings, to knickerbockers, to the blouse with the cape flaring over her shoulders, past the easy, confident smile to the smart, wide-brimmed hat tilted on her auburn hair. There was a hint of arrogance in her stride, more than a hint of confidence. She did not glance at them, but the swing of her hips indicated that she'd seen them, and had noted that they'd seen her.

Harry's eyes followed her, then drifted off. He said casually: 'That's him, there.'

'That's who – where?'

'The chap pretending to be a gardener, hoeing that patch. That's Vic Fletcher. It's why I asked you to meet me in the park, to get a good look at him.'

'*That* is Vic Fletcher?' Tranter stared. 'You could eat him for breakfast.'

Harry said nothing.

Fletcher would have been half Harry's weight, the sergeant guessed, and perhaps five years younger. Put him at twenty-five to Harry's thirty. He was slim – thin – in tight jeans and a T-shirt, no muscles enlivening his arms, no width to his chest. When he turned, aware of Harry but deliberately not gazing at him, Tranter saw a crisp, short hair trim, ginger hair, an incipient beard trying to disguise a weak chin, and a fleshy, soft mouth. Fletcher moved away, the hoe luring him behind a stand of shrubs.

'Looks vicious to me,' said the sergeant. 'I bet rabbits move aside when he hoes round 'em.'

'So what d'you reckon?'

'Start running if he shows you his knuckles.'

But Harry had been speaking the truth about his nerves. He was placidly patient. 'Seriously, Sarge,' he said gently. Somehow, a gentle and thoughtful Harry was more upsetting than a violent one.

They both knew that any number of weapons could even out the physical differences. Any dark night would suffice.

'Well . . .' said Tranter, drawing in his last lungful of smoke before resuming his jogging. 'If it was me, and I knew I hadn't killed Angela Reed . . .'

'Go easy with them ifs.'

'And if I didn't plan to leave the district . . .'

'All my friends are here. You're here, Sarge.'

'So I am. If it was me, in those circumstances, I'd do my best to find out who *did* do it.'

'That's how I figured it. But you know me. I ain't no great shakes at reasonin' things. I wouldn't know where to start. I'd need help, sort of. You know what I mean. And if you lot couldn't find out who killed her . . .'

'We had you, Harry.'

'So what d'you suggest, Sarge?'

Tranter got to his feet, stretched, bent and failed to touch his toes, straightened with his face red, and said: 'Tell you what. I'll ask around. I'll see what I can do.'

Then he trotted away on another circuit of the park, his small pot bobbing in front of him. Harry shrugged. He hadn't expected much, so he wasn't disappointed. He looked round for Vic Fletcher but couldn't see him, so headed for the nearest exit, limping slightly. Harry was inclined to be over-trusting in his relationships. This did not extend to the police in general, but he'd always trusted Sergeant Tranter. With Tranter, he knew where he stood.

The woman with the Alsatian strolled back, seated herself on the same bench, and searched in her shoulder bag for a dark brown cigarette, which she lit with a small lighter shaped liked a .22 automatic pistol. The dog settled at her feet. She blew smoke at the empty sky and waited. She was a woman who could wait well, who could make a decorative exercise of waiting. The impression was that the surroundings, carefully landscaped by an artist, had been waiting themselves for exactly that poise, that angle of the fine-boned face, that alertness – even in repose – to bring life to the composition. The air was still, not breathing. She belonged.

Two minutes later, Sergeant Tranter completed the circuit. He collapsed, puffing, beside her. She waited patiently until he could speak, knowing that she could give him fifty yards in a hundred.

'That was him,' he managed at last.

'He looked nothing more than a tough layabout to me.'

11

'Deceptive. You'll have to make up your own mind.'

'I said "looked",' she pointed out gently. 'Nice smile, though. What did he tell you, Paul?'

'That he's being threatened by somebody called Vic Fletcher, who's a groundsman here, or who's borrowed a hoe for the day.'

'I saw him. He was clearly observing you both. Threatened, did you say?'

'Fletcher claims to have been Angela's husband.'

'Husband?' She looked down as she tramped out the cigarette end. 'Well now.' The hat shadowed her face. He couldn't tell what she was thinking.

'Which'd give him a legitimate claim, if he's planning revenge.'

'If that's what he's planning.'

'I'm not sure you ought to interfere, Virginia.'

When Virginia Brent smiled, her rather prim, even severe, mouth spread across her face as though eager to display its agility. Her lower lip, almost too full and verging on the sullen, stretched to match the upper one, and together they headed for her ears, the result pouching her cheeks, slanting her grey eyes, hoisting her eyebrows. It lasted only a moment, a passing comment on the sergeant's remark, dismissing it as naïve and reminding him that he had no authority over her. Virginia Brent possessed an inexhaustible capacity for interference. She called it curiosity. Secretly, though she never expressed it aloud, she knew she was an addict. Her god was logic. Everything, she would tell you, had a logical explanation, once you had all the facts together. Illogical behavioural patterns irritated her, until she managed to hammer them into sensible logic. No mystery could be allowed to remain so. This one had haunted her for four years. How dared the sergeant call it interfering!

So she flashed him her smile, and Tranter looked away, blinking.

'Tell me about him,' she said.

'Harry? Oh, he's just another toughie, who knows nothing else. Always had to fight for his crust, like the rest of us, and as he's none too bright, how else could he do that except with his fists?'

'He got six years for armed robbery, Paul. A gun, that means.'

'He also got full remission, and he always claimed it was a toy, though we never managed to find it.'

'All the same . . .' She pulled at the dog's ear, and he

12

grumbled affectionately. 'So you'd call him a thug?'

'Not that.' There were facets of Harry's character that baffled Tranter, who hadn't a subtle nature.

'He was supposed to have unloaded Angela from the car at that lay-by, and killed her. Would he do that?'

'No. We know he didn't do that because she put in a 999-call, after he'd left her.'

'So she did. I was forgetting.' She moved a hand negligently. They both knew she had not forgotten one detail.

'He was believed to have driven away, thought better of it, driven back, and *then* killed her.'

'Would he have done *that*?'

Tranter lifted his shoulders. 'I never believed it, but that was how he was charged. It just doesn't sound like Harry. I didn't go for it.'

'And neither did the jury,' she reminded him, reaching for the dog's lead and getting to her feet. 'Where does he live?'

'I'll take you . . .'

'No. It's got to be alone. Where, Paul?'

'You won't like it.'

'Do talk sense, please. What does it matter whether or not I like it? The address, please, or I'll have to waste time searching the pubs.'

Paul Tranter gave her the address, and watched her walk away. There was now nothing provocative about her stride. It indicated clearly that Virginia Brent had a new purpose in her life.

He hoped she would take the Alsatian with her, but doubted it. She was a proud and independent woman, and would consider that to walk dark and dangerous streets with a dog at her side would indicate a need for protection. She might even feel that she was putting the dog at risk. No, she would walk alone. Her confidence would be her protection. She would probably feel afraid, because she possessed abundant imagination, but it would not be evident. She would rely on her intuition, her alertness, her reactions.

All the same, he decided to put a tail on her. No . . . he changed his mind. He would do it himself. Her father would kill him if anything happened to her.

But in the event, he lost her. In those poor streets she was invisible. She became part of them.

It was just as well he knew where she was heading.

13

2

It was late September, but autumn did not burnish Hanger Lane. No sered leaves rustled in the gutters; no copper glinted in the sun. Rumour had it that on one midsummer day a ray of sunlight had reached as far as the wharf, but no natural growth had reflected its warmth, so it had never since ventured there. Now any remaining light from the depressed sun was absorbed by the soot-encrusted high wall on one side of the lane, and was lost in the eyeless shell of the derelict warehouse on the other side. A gentle breeze drifted dust between the grey cobblestones of the wharf, and a sour green glow was reflected from the surface of the turgid canal. It was sufficient to outline the shadows of the old, rotted narrowboats, lying half-submerged, and the only one still on an even keel.

On the deck of this narrowboat Harry Hodnutt was engaged in evicting half a dozen hippies, who'd taken possession in his absence. He was doing this with good humour, standing in the bow where only one at a time could get at him. He was hurling them into the water, shouting out encouragement.

'That's it, laddie. Your arm ... whoops!' Splash. The algae split open. 'A lady! Naughty, naughty. There we go!' Splash. 'Next please. Ah, feet is it? Watch yourself!' Splash.

The locals had a fear of the canal. One immersion, it was believed, could bring on the most terrible diseases. In practice, the submerged cycles and prams and old bedsteads were the greater hazard. You could almost walk across on them.

Virginia was watching from a deep doorway, her back pressed hard against an ancient, heavy door. She wondered, vaguely, whilst watching Harry's performance with critical approval, what might be behind that door. She was wearing a man's shirt, suitably dirty and too big for her, and a drab, brown skirt, once pleated, now merely crumpled. Her legs were bare, her feet in sandals, one of which had a broken strap, producing an awkward shuffle when she moved. One hand held a beer can and a smouldering cigarette, the other scrabbled at the wall, partly in response to the action on the boat, partly because she'd forgotten the detail of dirt behind the fingernails. Her shoulder bag was

14

canvas, one corner torn.

High up, and opposite to her, Sergeant Tranter stood on the only piece of solid floor he could find, and peered anxiously through an empty window frame of the warehouse. He couldn't make up his mind. Was that really Virginia?

Harry completed his operation and hitched his jeans. Green-coated shadows were crawling on to the towpath opposite. 'An' don't come back,' he shouted. One of the two ladies of the group, the one with God Is Love across her scrawny chest, called back: 'Get stuffed,' and gave him the fingers. Harry laughed, wiped blood from his chin, and turned.

A woman was slopping towards him across the cobbles, one hip slightly forward from the other, gesturing with a beer can.

'Not another!' said Harry, sighing. 'No room at the inn, love.'

'It's you I want.'

'Can't afford it. Bugger off, eh?'

'I want a word with you, Harry. Sergeant Tranter sent me.'

He stood, looking down at her. It was just possible to detect the mass of untidy and greasy blonde hair, from which a headscarf had slipped to her shoulders, the red slash that was her mouth, the dashes of mauve-pink across her cheekbones. It seemed un-likely that Sergeant Tranter had sent this woman, and yet . . . she knew Tranter, she knew Harry's name.

'Permission to come aboard, skipper?'

It was an original canal narrowboat, which had been converted. The difficulty was to decide to what it had been converted. The only real change was that it was lower in the water than when it had travelled with a full load. This was because there were multiple holes in its bottom, and it had triumphed over the other rotting wrecks only because it had settled on something solid and level. The water was a mere six inches beneath the floor inside.

Harry laughed. 'Aw . . . come on then.'

The floor, at least, was more recent, but nevertheless it creaked beneath Harry's feet as he led the way down the six steps into his living quarters.

'Hold on, I'll light up,' he called back.

He was fitted out with propane gas. A mantle popped and spread mellow light into far corners of his meagre cabin. It was singular – a living quarter. It was all in there, a chair and a table

15

and a bunk bed at the narrow end. The smell of rotting wood was overwhelming, and the tattered curtains must have been launched with the vessel.

Harry moved to the far end, keeping his head low, and sat on the edge of the bunk, knees sticking up like steeples. He was wordlessly offering her a retreat behind her, should she need it. She came down the steps, one sandal flopping, drew the chair away from the table, banged her beer can on the surface, and sat with her knees spread, the skirt hanging down between them. Now, once he'd got past the heavy blue eye-shadow and the curtains of mascara, Harry could detect the colour of her eyes. Grey. Fixed on him.

'Brought your own beer?' he asked.

She made a gesture, palm lifted from the table surface then flapped down again. 'It's full of sand. I might have needed something heavy.'

Nothing changed on Harry's face. There was a certain charm about his rugged ugliness, she decided, and the line of his mouth indicated no cruelty. His eyes were brown, deeply-set beneath heavy bushes of eyebrows. And they were looking right through her.

'Who are you?' he asked quietly. 'What d'you want?'

'I think perhaps it's what you want, Harry. May I call you Harry?'

'If you like.' He didn't ask what he should call her. The implication was that the meeting might be too short to make it a necessity.

'What's this about Sergeant Tranter?' he asked.

'He told me you need help. The Angela Reed murder. I've got a similar interest.'

'Help from a woman?' It was a polite question.

'You'd have to pay a man. I'm free.'

His eyebrows moved. 'What similar interest?'

She sighed. He was inflexible, not to be drawn out by pleasantries.

'You did a snatch job,' she said. 'A jeweller's shop. You had a companion, who was not arrested, and you've never given his name. I'm interested in the jewellery. It wasn't recovered and it's not come on the market. If I can find it, then I get ten per cent of the insurable value. If *we* can find it, Harry, we might also find

16

the person who killed Angela Reed.'

He was silent. He reached up and pulled his nose, scratched his ear. He detected a creak beneath his right foot and thumped the deck with his boot, to see whether it would go through. She watched him working it out, and gave him time, trying not to imagine what might be floating a few inches beneath her own feet, and gradually, as she relaxed, the assumed character flowed away. Her shoulders straightened, her legs came together and stretched out, crossed at the ankles, her mouth, which had seemed hard, softened.

'Can't offer you a drink,' he said at last. 'Sorry.'

'It's all right.'

'No cocktails or gin and tonics.'

She raised her eyebrows. 'And I thought I did it well.'

He shook his head. 'Round here, at your age, it's all jeans and spike heels. Disco wear.'

'Spike heels,' she whispered.

'You're dressed like an old woman with make-up like a teenager. You were right about the beer can, though. Could've needed somethin' heavy. I'd keep hold of it if I was you.'

'For the trip back?'

'In case I decide to toss you out on your ear. Now . . . what the bloody hell's the game?'

There had been no change in the pitch of his voice. It was low and steady. But an edge had crept in. The wooden walls tingled with danger. Harry, she reminded herself, could be a very aggressive man. She managed to keep her eyes on his, and shrugged.

'All right, I made a mistake. You don't need anybody's help. You're just a big, independent slob, with only one use for a woman.'

'So now we know.'

Still not taking her eyes from him she swung the tatty canvas shoulder bag round and prodded her left hand inside it, produced her pack of brown cigarettes, and her dainty automatic pistol lighter.

Harry laughed. 'A pea shooter! You're frightenin' me.'

'A lighter,' she said, flicking it. 'You mind if I smoke?'

He made a gesture, his huge hand flitting like a bat in front of her. 'Can't get it outa the curtains, though.'

'You're lovely, Harry,' she said. 'Why the hell're you living

17

here? Tell me that.'

'D'you know how much I get from the Social Security?'

'Nevertheless . . .'

'Tell me what you're after?' he demanded in a flat voice, and she felt that this was a turning point. A reasonable response, and he'd accept her, might even confide in her. But he went on before she could say anything. 'And don't tell me it's the jewellery snatch, 'cause I'm not a complete fool. That was nothin'. A few thousand in it. Ten per cent of nowt, that's what you'd be on. Not come on the market, you said. Load of cr . . . rubbish. Quartz watches and cheap jewellery . . . don't kid me. So let's have it, Miss Whatever-you-are. What's the game?'

'They said you weren't too bright, Harry. They said you were an ugly tough. You're not ugly, Harry, and you're not dim.'

He eyed her steadily for a moment, then stared down at his feet. She'd spoken with sincerity, with an air of pleased discovery. He could get to like her, he decided, a heavy decision because Harry was wary in matters of trust and friendship. He looked up. She was speaking again.

'That day you were arrested . . . remember it? From then on, you were on remand in custody until your trial came on, then in prison for four years. So you wouldn't know what was going on. Right?'

'It's right that I don't know what you're on about.'

'The same day that you did the jeweller's in the High Street, at about the same time, in Trinity Street, which crosses the High Street . . .'

'I know the town.'

'In Trinity Street three men, plus a driver, pulled a bank job. A good day for it – the tills were full of wages money. They cleared a hundred and twenty thousand pounds, Harry. In cash. Ten per cent of that is twelve thousand. I've waited four years for you to come out, and now I've got a chance. I think those two robberies were connected, and in some way connected with Angela Reed's death. So we team up, Harry. You find your murderer, and I find the money.'

He brooded on it. Harry, brooding, was like a giant bullfrog, all set to pounce. He raised his eyes, staring at her through the fringe of his bushy eyebrows.

'You know too much about it. Who are you? Insurance . . .'

18

'I'm on my own. My name is Virginia Brent. I was at your trial, Harry, in the balcony. I've read your trial transcript, to refresh my memory. I've read your statement.'

'You're police.' His eyes glinted.

'No. My father's the Assistant Chief Constable . . .'

'Ha!'

'And Paul Tranter's my godfather.'

'Ohoh!' He tossed it back at her with scorn.

'So I've got access . . .'

'That money,' he cut in. 'It'll have gone by now. Spent. Salted away. No . . . spent, you can bet. Not a chance, and if you know so much, you oughta know that.'

'Harry,' she said, 'don't you think the police know what they're doing? They had ideas about who'd been on the job. They put in undercover men, used every informant they knew, and nobody, just nobody, started spending money freely.'

'An out-of-town team . . .'

'But no.' She smiled. 'That's the point, you see. If, as I believe, the two jobs were linked, the jeweller's and the bank robbery, then it was local. Because *you're* local, Harry. You've come back *here*, to this town, because this is where you belong. And there's just a possibility that your mate on the jewellery job was local, too, and the whisper around was that he could've been the bossman for both jobs . . .'

'What!' he almost burst out. 'Charlie . . .'

He got to his feet abruptly, forgot to duck, and banged his head. He sat down again. She was smiling.

'You tricked me into that,' he grumbled.

'Not tricked. But it's a start. Charlie, you say?'

'You *are* police. You'll go dashin' off to the sergeant . . .'

'No, Harry. He agreed to put me in touch with you. He knows I'll tell him nothing. He might help us, or he might not.'

'Why should I trust you?'

'I'm trusting you.'

'I don't see that.'

'Harry, don't be slow. It's obvious. Angela Reed was killed at that lay-by, and there was only one person who could've known she was there. You. You said you left her alive. But she was killed with violence – she had a half inch hole in her forehead. *You* can be violent. So I'm trusting you not to kill me. Would it be so very

19

difficult, Harry? Here and now! And if we work together, at any moment – any time you feel I've let you down – you could pick me up with one hand and break me into little pieces. So I'm trusting you. I propose to spend a lot of time with you, Harry, and I don't want to be on edge every second.'

He was watching her with what might have been a smile, but if so it was too shy to break free. His head was shaking, dark and floppy hair flying, dispersing his thoughts.

'I don't know what to make of you,' he admitted.

'What've you got to lose?' She leaned forward encouragingly. 'You've served a sentence for the jeweller's shop job, and you were found not guilty of murder. You've got Vic Fletcher at your back. Why not give it a try?'

He jutted his lower lip, and showed his teeth in a wry grin. 'And tell you personal secrets that nobody else knows? That's what you're after, I reckon.'

'This loyalty of yours, Harry! It's splendid. But people take advantage of loyalty—you owe them nothing.'

'Friends,' he murmured.

She thought, then, that she had perhaps made a mistake. Had Harry, with an outward appearance that would not be seen as attractive by most women, ever found a relationship with any deep meaning to it? Friendship, then, would have been his ultimate experience, and he'd treasured his friendships, nurtured them. How sad, then, that these had so often been abused. It had been too easy to take advantage of a trust he squandered so selflessly. And she had denigrated his friendships! He would now have every reason to reject her.

'The police know about Charlie Braine,' she said quietly.

'If you know . . .'

'Your contacts were investigated. No, not by me, Harry. I told you, I've got access to inside information.'

'Not that again!'

'That again. And it seems to me I know more than you do.'

'Not about Charlie, you don't.' He was fierce in his claim.

'One thing,' she told him gently. 'There's one thing you obviously don't know. You haven't been to see him? At his place?'

'No. Kind of . . . you know . . . embarrassin'.'

She didn't understand what he meant by that. 'Then you can't know that Charlie Braine went missing on that day, the day you did the jeweller's. Missing and never heard of since. Alive or dead.'

His eyes looked startled, and something moved ponderously behind the battered façade of his face. He took a whole minute to absorb the information, to lay it beside the presence of Charlie Braine in his memory, to assess it, to accept it.

'I didn't know that,' he mumbled.

'So there's more to it than you thought,' she pointed out, leaning back to make it casual and in no way a victory. 'Why don't you tell me all about it, Harry?'

The gas mantle was roaring. He half rose, reaching forward to adjust it down, flapped his palms on his flanks, said: 'Have a job getting the mantles.' Then he sat down again and rubbed his face vigorously with his rough palms. Eventually, his eyes once more met hers. He said nothing, simply stared at her.

'Trust me, Harry,' she said.

With those words she realized she was not committing him, but herself. If he trusted her and offered his friendship, he would be presenting her with the full extent of his emotional wealth. It was a responsibility she hadn't expected to encounter. The thought warmed her. Impulsively she leaned forward, not aware that her face was glowing, her eyes revealing her eagerness.

'Come on, Harry. It ought to be fun.'

Harry smiled. 'Yeah. Could be. When do we start?'

'What are you doing tomorrow?'

3

'Tell me once more, Harry,' she said, like an excited child demanding a fairy story.

'For Chrissake! Not again!'

Harry was uncomfortable in the car's passenger seat. This was no reflection on the expertise of Mercedes, only in so far as they'd clad their seats in tan leather, and because he was aware that his jeans and denim jacket had long since ceased to be merely dirty. The luxury of a 380SL sports car was not part of Harry's lifestyle. He feared to soil the seats, aware that leather would absorb oil or grease, and she was beginning to impress herself on him as a woman who wouldn't hesitate to buy a new car if the seats were soiled.

'Again!' she said. 'And do stop wriggling. Every time you tell it, new details creep in, and you never know when they could mean something.'

'If you've got covers for the seats . . .'

'Stop worrying. We'll get you a new suit . . .'

'No!'

She glanced sideways. 'If you say not, Harry.' She powered round a tight corner. 'Or perhaps you're nervous?'

'I'd feel better behind the wheel,' he admitted.

'Then we'll make it a chauffeur's uniform, and everybody'll be happy.'

Harry wriggled again, but this time with genuine unease. Virginia (and he still could not bring himself to call her that) was beginning to unsettle him with her personality. She overpowered him. She completely took for granted his involvement with her plans, and seemed to expect to draw him into her existence with a casual snap of the fingers. Clearly, her existence was better than his, so what had he got to complain about? This she did not say aloud, but her attitude shouted it. Her awareness that he might be hesitant was evident only in the occasional ribbing she used when he indicated reluctance. But Harry was impressionable. She impressed him with her energy and enthusiasm, and her boundless confidence. Impressed and disconcerted him, because she was clearly impetuous. She might even have meant that crack about the chauffeur's uniform.

'I don't like driving with an automatic gearbox,' he countered.

'It's all they fit on this model. Tell you what. We get the uniform and we'll let you pick your own car. Match the colours.'

'I'm not having you spending . . .'

She was smiling when she turned to glance at him. 'But Harry, I didn't mean *buy*. You, an expert with the wire coathanger and the hot-wiring, and you're talking about buying!'

'Watch the road.'

'I am. *And* the rearview mirror. He's still there.'

'Let me drive, and I'll drop him in a couple of minutes.'

'Don't be so impatient, Harry. Why drop him? We're only going to see Cynthia. Perhaps Vic Fletcher knows Cynthia.

D'you think so?'

'Maybe. Look, don't you think we ought to be serious about this?'

She said nothing, concentrating on the road. Vic Fletcher, tooling along at a reasonable distance behind in a battered Metro, could have been left standing by the Merc. But Fletcher was uninteresting to her. Harry was the interest, and she was aware that they were not yet at ease with each other. If he'd only known it, her flippancy was a sign of nerves. Very few people knew that. But she was nervous of Harry, afraid of his basic self-reliance and his independence, which might well come between them. So far, she hadn't worked out how they could meet at a mutual point that satisfied both.

As arranged, she had picked him up in the square that morning. She was wearing grey tailored slacks, a pink jacket over a white blouse with a frilly neckline, hardly any make-up, and with her own hair chestnut and loose over her shoulders. He'd barely recognized her, and had been reluctant to get in the car. He'd been more at home with the slut of the previous evening, and she wondered whether she'd now made a mistake by springing it on him. But he would have to learn that there was money behind her, and influence. The sooner he accepted it the better, because they would probably need both.

It came as a surprise to her to realize that she was already considering their relationship in a context of continuity.

So she drove in silence as she worked out what tone to use that would relax him. It was he who broke the silence.

'You were kidding about your father being the Chief Constable?'

'Assistant. And I wasn't.'

'And Sergeant Tranter ... your...' He gulped. It was beyond his imagination.

'Godfather? Yes. Paul Tranter and my father are old friends. The only difference is that daddy bounced up the ladder and Paul didn't. Paul's a street policeman, and proud of it. Daddy's a politician. You know what I mean?'

'No. You've turned the wrong way if you want to meet Charlie's wife.'

'On purpose. Driving around. We've got to work out how we're going to operate.'

23

'But for God's sake . . . I'm an ex-con.'

'I know it.'

'Does your father know about . . . this?'

'Yes.'

'And approves?'

She laughed. Her nose crinkled, and her head went back. 'No. Nor does Paul Tranter. But we'll keep 'em guessing, you and me.'

Harry bored on, getting it clear in his mind. 'They're thinkin' I'll get you into trouble?'

'Harry, you're marvellous. Paul said it for both of them. He said you'd been led into trouble all your life, and he didn't want me leading you astray again.'

'And that's what you're doing?' asked Harry solemnly.

'I've got a feeling that something like that might happen. If so, I'll feel better with you around.'

Harry threw back his head and laughed. The car rocked round a corner. He shouted: 'Steady!' She eased her foot from the throttle.

'Now tell me again how you met Cynthia.'

'Cynth,' he said. 'That's what I always called her. You'd need to get to know Cynth.'

'It's what I intend to do. Tell me how you met her.'

She slid the Merc through the S-bend created by a humped-back bridge, and slowed in order to drift into a lay-by. With the engine cut, she leaned back, eyes half closed.

'The disco, Harry. From there.'

They were ten miles out of town. With the car silent, the only sounds were the rustle of the stream behind them and the distant thrum of a harvester. To the left the hedges pushed close, weeds rampant at their feet. It was a small lay-by, with barely room for two cars, and intended to provide a passing place in this narrow, high-sided lane. A hundred yards ahead a more important road crossed it. The stop sign was just visible.

Harry glanced round, but Vic Fletcher's car did not appear. He settled down to tell it again.

He'd been chucker-out at a disco, where things had a tendency to roughen up. In this capacity he'd heaved out a lanky drunk, and the woman he was with went at Harry with a spike heel in one hand and claws in the other.

24

'Had to give her a bit of a tap to quiet her down,' he said, 'but I'm not too good with the women-folk, so it sorta put her outa circulation, so we took her into the office and when she came round there was a right mouthful she gave me, so I said I'd take her home. The trouble was she'd come out with a woman friend, and now they'd split up, and her husband wouldn't be pleased to know she'd picked up with a feller. So I took her home, me driving her car, 'cause of the spike heels, and when we got there – this place of his, twelve miles outa town – it was all a bit of a washout, 'cause hubby had been spraying a Granada and didn't know she'd been out. That was Cynth.'

'And that was Charlie Braine, with the spray-gun?' She knew it by heart, and was only waiting for any new detail.

'Yeah. But o'course, she'd still come home with a feller. Me. So Cynth covered, sayin' something about look who I brought to meet you, Charlie, as though I was a gift from heaven. So what, says Charlie, eyeing me up and down, and she says he can drive, Charlie, really drive, and he can handle himself.'

Virginia had noticed that, in the telling, he'd slipped back into his natural vernacular. 'But you didn't know what you were getting into.'

'Not straightaway. Cynth'd got me caught. That was Cynth for yer. Like a spittin' cat at the disco, and a purrin' one then. Independent as a cat, too. But you could trust her, providin' you didn't cross her. Then . . . whoo-hoo! Ever tried holdin' a spittin' cat? That was Cynth. The clip on the jaw, mind you, she'd forgotten it. Standin' there, rockin' on her heels – which was somethin' in those shoes – with her hands behind her and her bottom lip in her teeth, nothin' but mischief in her eyes . . . she handed me over to Charlie, who said he reckoned he might have somethin' for me. And you know what that was.'

'Stealing cars for him.'

Harry nodded. He was now well set into his story and absorbed with the narrating of it. In concentrating, he attempted to recall his impressions of that time.

'O' course, I'd figured he wasn't legal. I mean, that place of his . . . you'll see it. A big shed with a corrugated iron roof and a back way out that used to be a railway line. Kinda secret, that back way. Yeah, it was hot cars. I pinched 'em and he sprayed 'em, and he had some weird character I never met who worked the

garages and supplied log books to fit. I did that for three flamin'
years, and got to like it. Pride in the job, that was it. High-class
stuff we were on. Charlie got the log books from his soft-footed
contact, got the orders from somebody or other, and sent me out
to pick up the heaps. To order. Not any old unlocked car, y'see.
It'd gotta be the right car of the right year. Took some doin', I can
tell you.'

She drew on her cigarette, nodding. 'I can understand your
pride, Harry. Get to the jewel robbery.'

'Well yeah. Will do. That was Charlie movin' up in the world,
with big ideas. Reckon his cough was gettin' worse, him with a
spray-gun in his hand all day. Look at him and you wouldn't see
it, but Charlie'd got grand schemes, and you couldn't know it
behind them overalls, all stiff wi' paint, and the knitted hat on his
curly hair, with a bit of a tinted fringe round the edges. But then
he comes out with it. He was fed to the eyeballs with cars. Him
and me was gonna do a jeweller's, he says, so there I was with a
gun in me hand again, but not a real one this time.'

'Hold it,' she said crisply, grabbing his wrist. 'That's new.
Again, Harry? Not a real one this time. When *was* it a real one?'

'You don't wanta hear . . .'

'Oh, but I do.'

He stared out at the tangled hedges. 'That was way back. Some
fellers raked me in. A warehouse. Stuck a gun in me hand and
said look ugly, so we didn't haveta rehearse, and in walked the
fuzz, and the top man says drop it, which I did, only I never got
the hang of the safety catch and it went off and blew me big toe to
hell and gone, so I could hardly hoof it away into the distance.
That got me my first stretch inside, and what we gotta talk about
it now for I dunno.'

'Background,' she said comfortingly. 'No need to get worked
up.'

'Sure. So now you know. You'll have noticed the limp . . .'

'I noticed.'

'So you'll know why I told Charlie no guns for me, and I finished up with a plastic thing, feelin' a right idiot.'

'But you went along with it, all the same?'

'Sure. We were mates, weren't we? Mind you, I was more
friendly with Cynth than with Charlie, though not quite mates, if
you get what I mean.'

'Precisely, Harry.'

'Though it'd come close now an' then,' he said with fierce pride.

'She wouldn't be able to resist you.'

'If you don't wanta listen . . .'

She turned a solemn face to him, a whisp of hair shading one eye. 'Of course I do. The jeweller's, Harry, please.'

'In the High Street . . . you know that. We went to have a look at it. Case the joint, said Charlie. High Street! That was a great idea, to start with, crowds of people, cars, buses, traffic lights . . . oh, great. And we hadda go an' see it on early-closin' day, when it was quiet. But Charlie said that'd be great, just see if it wasn't, and we went in and did it on the Friday. I wanted to do the drivin', but no says Charlie, 'cause the driver'd have to run out first an' get the car goin', there bein' only two of us and me, I'm no good with the running, so Charlie said he'd drive. So on the Friday we did it, me with a bit of plastic in me fist, just to look frightenin'.'

He stopped, seeming to be depressed by the memory. Virginia said nothing. This was the third time he'd been through it for her, and there, every time, he paused. She knew what it was. Until she'd pointed out the coincidence of the bank robbery at almost the same time, he'd not examined his memory with any criticism, but now he was realizing that there had been something out-of-phase, even farcical, in the jeweller's shop set-up.

'We parked,' he went on, slapping his knee. 'Edgin' along the kerb in the traffic, on double yellows, and before we got to the shop door the horns were goin', and Charlie hadda stop and give 'em the sign, 'cause Charlie was always a right clown, and there were two of 'em in there, this old geyser and the girl, rigid as soon's they saw me, and it was only plastic. Charlie had this white plastic bag with his shooter in it . . .'

'You said a real gun, Harry? You're sure of that?'

'So he said. A real gun, that this feller who pinched the log books had found on one of his jobs. Sure. Why not? Charlie wasn't gonna shoot anybody, but they didn't know that, so they shovelled the stuff in, sparklers all over the floor and Charlie crunchin' his feet on layers of plastic watches, and then he says that's it, an' runs outa the door, me backin' up and him headin' round to the driver's seat . . .'

27

'Seven thousand, two hundred and forty pounds, Harry, that was the insurance assessment. Your Charlie might've fenced it for two thousand. He'd make more than that re-spraying a single Jag you'd stolen for him. Think of that.'

'You said it before.' His voice was harsh and impatient.

'Just wanted you to realize.'

He had realized. The whole job was a screwball, and he'd been taken, lumbered. 'And this ten per cent of the big job you spoke about, the bank haul. Twelve thou', that'd be. How much of this car we're sittin' in would *that* buy? A third? Oh, I know cars. I've pinched everythin' that runs on four wheels. Had *you* realized?'

She was silent. Nothing in her expression changed, simply the sharp chin rose, stretching the line of throat and neck into a smooth, progressive curve. Harry glanced away quickly. She was watching the vapour trails of a superjet, heading for a home landing at Birmingham International. Straight as a . . . straight as Harry, she thought, Harry who was either silent or honest. He didn't understand deceit. That was why he was angry when each repetition of his story destroyed more completely his faith in friendships and his belief in Charlie. She knew that. She was ashamed to know it, because she had not been fully honest with him herself. As Harry had sensed. Feeling it, he was reluctant to go on.

Eventually she spoke with encouragement. 'You stood in the doorway, with your back to the street, and Charlie ran out . . .'

'It was all hell out there,' he said. 'Traffic backed up and stuck, and way back somewhere a police siren goin', and I heard the engine fire and Charlie's door slam and his howlin' tyres. O' course, in front he'd gotta bit of a clear run, so he was away, and me standin' there like a fool, listenin' to him go. He was using this Escort XR3 I'd picked up for him. Picked it out special. Gotta be that car, and black, but he'd done it up in two colours, red an' green, to confuse the fuzz he said . . .'

'Harry, I didn't understand this before. How was two colours going to confuse anybody? Lots of cars are two colours.'

'But not down the middle.' He was eager to display Charlie's ingenuity. 'One side red, the other side green.'

'You mean . . . *meeting* in the middle?'

'Yeah. Meetin' over the bonnet, over the top, down the boot.'

'And that was supposed to confuse the police!'

'You see, people one side o' the road would see a red car, and people the other side a green un . . .'

'But Harry . . . oh, Harry, it would shine out like a homing beacon. It's crazy. Now wait . . . think . . . did you see which way Charlie went? He'd get to the traffic lights at Trinity Street . . .'

'Well left, o' course. We'd planned that. Whatever the lights, he could've forced his way inta the stream.'

'And turning left, he'd go uphill past the Mercantile Bank on the other side of the street, at around the time three men and a driver were heading away from the bank downhill with three canvas bags of currency, and every police car in the area would be chasing a red and green Escort that couldn't be missed! Didn't I tell you? Didn't I say? The two jobs must have been co-ordinated. The jewellery job was a fake, Harry.'

She had clutched his arm. He looked down at her fingers, surprised at the strength of her grip, surprised too at the delight in her eyes, the life in her face.

'Sure,' he said. 'Well yeah, I suppose so.'

'And haven't you thought . . . Harry, I'm getting to know you, and I bet you wouldn't let yourself think Charlie had deliberately abandoned you. Go on, admit it.'

'Mates, we were.'

'No, that was you and Cynthia.' Her eyes sparked. 'Harry, it was deliberate. He didn't want you in that car. He was a decoy for the bank job, running a big risk, in a car he'd deliberately made noticeable, and he didn't want you with him in that. He thought you'd simply turn, and disappear in the crowds.'

'What . . . me with my six feet three and the limp and this face?'

'He'd think that. Hope that.'

He nodded. She had to watch his eyes, she had learned. No good watching that face. And in his eyes there grew a deep pool of relief, that the answer had been provided and was pleasing. 'Well yeah,' he said, and still smiling she turned back to face forward, and face the possibility that she had been afraid to recognize.

With the evidence growing that the two robberies were linked, it was increasingly possible that Angela's murder was linked with both. That could make it a faceless and vicious removal in

29

the course of a crime, the prospect of which made Virginia wince. Her deity was logic, which could be exercised only if emotion and passion were involved. Logic ran out of impetus in the face of cold and callous elimination. But she was committed. She could only pray that Angela had died for a more noble reason.

'If this Fiesta hadn't been parked right behind Charlie's,' Harry was saying, but again she turned to him.

'You did say a *black* Escort?' she asked.

'Charlie's? Yeah, black he ordered, and black he got.'

'Then why in heaven's name did he spray it red and green?'

'I told you . . .'

'No. Think about it. He wanted a stupid two-colour car, for the police to have a go at. You got him a black one. Then why did he re-spray *both* halves? Why not simply one half, say yellow or pink or something, then he'd have a black and yellow car, or whatever?'

'I suppose he thought . . .'

'It would take only half as much work.'

'. . . he'd do both halves.'

'But it's nonsense. Assuming he expected to get back to his place in due course, by way of that back road you spoke about, he'd re-spray the whole thing as soon as possible. Any colour he liked. So why spray both halves of the car in the first place?'

'Maybe,' said Harry, a little disturbed and puzzled by her intensity, 'he just *wanted* it red and green.'

'In which case, why didn't he ask you to pick up a red Escort or a green one? Tell me *that*, Harry.'

'I don't think it matters. Let me tell you about . . .'

'Matters? It's off-beat behaviour, so of course it matters. There has to be a reason Charlie did that, and if we can find out the reason, then we might be on our way to finding the murderer.'

'Oh sure,' he said. 'If you say so.' Though what the connection could be between a two-colour car and the death of Angela Reed, who'd become involved so casually, he couldn't see.

'So tell me how you met Angela,' she said, sighing at his lack of response.

'She just happened to be there, in the little Fiesta parked right behind Charlie's Escort. What else could I have done? People had seen that thing in me hand, and there was screamin'. Nowhere for me to go, so I went to that car, and it was blind luck the passenger door was unlocked, and I got in and scared her into driving me here.'

He was speaking in a defiant voice. The police had disbelieved, or pretended to disbelieve, his story. So now he deliberately condensed a half hour journey to one clipped statement.

'Here, Harry?'

'As you damn well know.' He nodded heavily. 'Why else did you pull in at this particular lay-by, if you didn't know?'

'Of course I knew. I wanted to see if it'd upset you, sitting here in the lay-by where she was killed.'

'It isn't that upsetting me.'

'I know, I know. Sorry, Harry, it was a stupid trick. Let's get out and walk, shall we? Stretch our legs, while you tell me all about it.'

He looked at her for a moment in puzzlement, then shrugged massively and opened the passenger's door.

When she joined him he was stretching, examining the lay-by critically with his head lowered.

'It's changed.'

'Has it?' she asked. 'Let's stroll along to the crossroads.'

'The bin's gone. The litter bin.'

'Yes. It wasn't a litter bin, Harry, it was a road-grit bin. They've put it the other side of the bridge.'

'That explains it then.'

'There wouldn't have been room in a litter bin, would there?' she asked reasonably.

'What . . . oh yes.'

'That's where her body was,' she reminded him. 'In the bin. It was May, so it was empty of winter grit. Let's walk up to the road. You hadn't finished your story.'

4

The air was motionless, heavy with the musty smell of hay. The departing harvester had left an empty husk of silence. Harry fell into step beside her, his feet heavy and hard on the tar and pebble surface. The lane was narrow, the banks high. He noticed

31

that she was examining the grass verge each side, but said nothing for a few moments, until she deliberately tramped through a few yards of weeds on the right-hand verge, kicking her way through the tangled mess left by the summer's growth. A dust of seed rose round her legs, casting fawn shadings on her slacks.

'There'd be fewer weeds in May,' she said, 'but at that time they would be growing fast.'

'If it matters.'

'Perhaps it does.' She stopped at a five-barred gate, beyond which the stubble of the wheat stretched ahead and away, rising towards the hills. 'You were saying? The Fiesta,' she prompted, resting her arms on the top bar.

He leaned over it beside her, staring at nothing, his mind in the past. 'I got in and scared hell outa her, and she drove me away. Twenty or so she'd have been. Nothing to her, thin as a shaving and five feet nothing in her socks.'

'Socks?' She nudged him. 'You saw her in her socks?'

'A figure of whatsit. In the car she was a whisp of nothin'. I showed her the gun an' said drive, and she laughed. Couldn't believe it, I suppose, so I stuck my face at her, and that did it . . . she drove. Only not as fast as I'd've liked, so I kind of snarled at her and offered to break her arm, and she said how'd she drive with a broken arm, and just went on drivin', following the smell of Charlie's burnt rubber. Cheeky, she was. She was gettin' at me all the time. Said was that a stick-up, an' I said it was. So she said where's the loot then? And I hadda say my mate'd got it, and that got a good laugh, and all the time the police cars were streakin' past with everythin' going, and she just drove. After a bit she said I wasn't frightenin' her with me toy gun, so I threw it outa the window. By that time we were drivin' outa town, but I said nothin', because we was headin' this way, which suited me, and she was all chatty, like we were goin' on a picnic or somethin'. Trouble was, I never did get the hang of frightenin' women . . .'

'How was that, Harry?'

'Dunno why. No challenge to it, you see. P'raps that was it. Try breakin' the arm of an Irish navvy, that's a challenge. Women . . . you daren't touch 'em, they'd snap like twigs. So there's no heart in it. She musta seen that, 'cause she said where could she drop me, and were we headin' for my place and was I gonna ask her in for a drink? I shoulda taken time to smack her bottom, but when I'd got her to head for the lay-by...' He jerked his head back towards the Merc. 'By that time I wanted to be on me own.'

'Something special about that lay-by, was there?' she asked idly, aware that Vic Fletcher's Metro had now quietly slipped into it and was parked behind her Mercedes.

'It was where I used to park the cars I'd got for Charlie. Nice'n quiet there, so I could walk up to the phone box and check with him that it was all clear, before drivin' them in.'

'Show me this phone box, will you.'

He heaved himself upright and led her the few yards to the junction. The crossing road was wider, but still minor, and was the only direct link between the township of Porchester, itself small, and the tiny village of Harley Green, where Charlie had had his spraying shed.

'The phone booth's up the hill to the right there, just round the bend. Can't see it from here. So when I dumped her in the lay-by...'

'Dumped her?'

'Alive, damn it, and yellin' blue murder at me an' calling me a thievin' skunk. When I dumped her there, I told her there was a phone box less'n a quarter of a mile away, but I didn't tell her which way. Get it? She'd gotta guess, which'd give me a bitta time to drive a roundabout route to Charlie's. But she musta guessed right first time, 'cause I ran bang smack into a police trap, which meant she'd rung a 999 call and told 'em, and I needn't have wasted my 10p.'

She turned from him and began to pace slowly up the hill towards the phone box. When he caught up with her she spoke quietly but intensely.

'You haven't mentioned *that* before. You gave her money?'

'Aw hell! I'd got her out of the car and was headin' round to the driver's seat, an' I said she'd better phone for a taxi and she screamed at me that she hadn't got any money, and I tossed her a 10p piece.'

'Her shoulder bag was on the back seat. There was money in that. But Harry – there was no tenpence piece in the pocket of her jacket when they found her.'

He lifted his shoulders like the two halves of a drawbridge, then allowed them to slump. 'So she lost it.'

'Have you ever seen a police search? They'd have found it. Be-

33

lieve me, they would, anywhere in the lay-by, the road up here, the phone box. They'd have found it.'

'Don't know what you're on about,' he grunted. 'She must've phoned for a taxi.'

'No taxi firm got a call.'

'So she phoned somebody else . . .'

'Ah yes. But who? She wouldn't need money for a 999 call. So who would she phone, when she'd phoned the police about her car and about you and the hold-up, and they'd said: wait there? Who would she want to call, I wonder, with her tenpence?'

They walked five more steady paces. He said at last: 'So you don't believe me.'

She paused long enough to punch his arm. 'I thought we'd got that clear. I believe you, Harry. The whole thing depends on you, and if I'm not going to believe you we might as well pack it in. Is that the phone box?'

The idea of painting phone booths red is so that they should stand out. This was one of the old design, cast-iron body and small glass panes, but it wasn't standing out. It was set back against a high wall of natural stone, beyond which was clearly private property, and beyond which there was also a rampant ivy root, which had drooped its feelers over the wall and clad the booth in an almost impenetrable screen. It was unvandalized, possibly because the vandals hadn't found it. When she went inside and lifted the handset she got the dialling tone. She fought her way out again.

'Well endowed with graffiti,' she commented.

'I used to phone Charlie from here.'

'So I see. A bit of the graffiti's yours.'

'Eh?'

'Just above the phone. CB 297 it says. Was that Charlie Braine's number?'

'Well,' he grumbled, tugging at his thicker ear, 'I kinda forget things like numbers.'

She laughed, and thumped his arm again. He wished she would stop doing it. Virginia had more muscle than she was entitled to, and sharp knuckles.

She stood back, straddled her legs, and put her fists on her hips. 'She walked up here, found this phone booth first try, called the police, then used your tenpence to phone somebody else, and didn't wait here, as she was asked to, but walked back to the lay-by and waited there. I wonder why she would do that, Harry, go back to the lay-by? Officer Graham, who came to pick her up, didn't see her. She wasn't waiting here. Nor at the lay-by. Perhaps she was already dead, Harry, already tucked away in the grit container. If so, it was very quick work. There wouldn't be *time*, you see. Officer Graham got a radio call and drove straight here from Porchester. Five miles, is it? Angela wasn't anywhere to be seen, so it was reported back, and the patrol car was called in. It was two hours later they found the body.'

It sounded like a rehearsed speech. To Harry it sounded pre-pared, as though she'd waited only until she had all the facts demonstrated to her – and to Harry himself – before throwing it at him. Because it meant that Harry was the only person who'd known where Angela Reed was! Because Harry might well have turned back, regretting that he hadn't disposed of her at the lay-by when he had the chance, and aware that Charlie Braine could cause her car – and therefore the only connection between Harry and Angela – to disappear under a new coat of paint. And because Harry, who'd claimed he'd wasted time on a roundabout route, might well have used that time in killing her.

'You think I done it,' he said, nothing in his voice, nothing in his eyes.

'I didn't say that. I've already told you . . .'

'As good as.'

'You have to face the fact, Harry, that if nobody knew where she was, then all that's left is a casual passer-by, who stopped and killed her. She wasn't raped. Nothing like that. Just attacked, and left with a half-inch hole in her forehead. That's what we've got to argue round.'

'We?'

'Because you're the only one who knew she was here.'

'If she got her tenpenn'orth, what about the one she phoned?'

'Well yes – that hypothetical person, who'd have had to move like a flash of lightning to get here before Officer Graham. So . . . we have to find that person. Come on, Harry.' She took his arm, allowed her fingers to rest in the crook of it, and began to walk him back to the car.

'Funny,' she said, 'that she'd trouble to walk back to the lay-by. It must have been painful.'

35

'How so?'

'The road surface. Look at it, gravelly and rough. No nice smooth pavement to step on to. Not much grass.'

'Why painful?'

'Didn't you know?' She gave his arm an admonitory shake. 'She wasn't wearing any shoes. Just tights. They never found her shoes. Not in her car, not where they searched.'

'But she *did* have her shoes.' His step was slowing. 'I was driving away, and she shouted: my shoes, you big oaf, my shoes! So I slung 'em outa the window. Couldn't work the pedals with them things underfoot.'

She drew him to a halt and turned to face him, where she could watch his eyes and at the same time prevent him from walking on.

'Something else you didn't say before,' she said quietly.

He fluttered a huge hand in front of her face. 'Details, details.'

'What were the shoes like?'

'Shoes. I just heaved 'em.'

'Try.'

'Oh . . . I suppose . . . pinkish, I think. Those spike things like Cynth wore.'

'Stilettos, Harry. We call 'em stilettos. It could be why she kicked them off for driving.'

'Right then. So she wore 'em to walk up here to the phone and back, and didn't have 'em . . . afterwards. So what?'

'That head wound, that's what. It was thought it could've been caused by a stiletto heel. The shape and size of the wound was right. That seemed to mean another woman's heel, if Angela didn't have *any* shoes. But if she had them, it could have been done by one of her own. She was wearing her pink skirt, and her tights didn't show any signs of wear on the soles, no tatters as she'd have had with walking on this road, and no grass stains. So she got back to the lay-by . . .'

'You know an awful lot.'

'Got back to the lay-by, still wearing her shoes,' she pushed on. 'And perhaps one of those shoes killed her. *One* of them, Harry. It's possible that *that* one would have been taken away – who doesn't know about fingerprints?'

'You didn't get all this from police records.' His voice was deep.

36

'But why take away both? Tell me that, Harry.'

'Strikes me it's you who ought to be doing the tellin',' he said stolidly. 'All this business about what she was wearing. *Her* pink skirt, you said. Like as if you knew what clothes she owned. And all about her tights. How would you know that?'

'I told you. I've got connections.'

'Hah!' It was flat contempt.

She knew then that she could no longer hold back from him. It had been a mistake to lie to him about her interest. She had assumed he would understand a money motive rather than an emotional one. But at the beginning she had wanted from him no more than information. She had been using him, as had all his past acquaintances. But now the situation had changed, and she knew she needed him. He had to be told, even if it complicated their relationship, might even destroy it.

So she stared up into his lumpy face and his miserable eyes, and told him.

'Harry, I knew about the skirt and the tights because they were returned to me. I was the one who arranged the funeral, and I was the one who went along to her little flat and examined the clothes there, because I knew her exact wardrobe. I was her nearest living relative.'

Daughter? thought Harry. No ... impossible. Aunt and niece? But Virginia didn't seem auntish. 'You're her sister?' he tried.

'I'm nine years older,' she told him, dodging a little because it was irrelevant. 'So now you know. I'm not doing this for the jewels or the money. I loved her, as simple as that. She was wild and she was always in trouble, but she always came to me. Except that last time. I want to know why, whether I let her down somehow, and ... oh, for God's sake, Harry, I just loved her.'

His eyes were clouded with distress. For her? For himself ?

'You should've said.'

She made a hopeless gesture.

'Thought we were kinda partners,' he told her. '*Why* didn't you?'

'Would you have helped . . .?'

'Hah!' he said, a gleam peering through the screen of his eyes. 'I think I see. If you're her sister, then you'd have *known* she was married. She'd have told *you*.'

'Of course she would.' Her lower lip was caught in her teeth.

'Then Vic Fletcher's not . . .'

'Of course not.'

'Then he's got no *reason* to talk about killing me.'

'No reason at all.'

Then she waited for him to think it through, wondering whether he'd need prompting. He reached up and rubbed his face vigorously, and when he lowered his hands he was grinning.

'So *that's* the reason you didn't tell me. If I'd known they wasn't married, I wouldn't have needed to find out who killed her.'

'And I wouldn't have been able to persuade you to help me,' she said, leading him on and dreading his response.

'Don't know about that.' He eyed her up and down with stolid approval. 'I always like to help a lady.'

'Could be dangerous,' she warned him, but her heart was racing.

'I'll break an arm and a leg.' But he was talking about Vic Fletcher again.

She took his arm, jerking it for his attention, restraining him because he seemed intent on reaching Fletcher as soon as possible.

'You see,' she explained, looking sideways up at him, with such mischief in her eyes that he persuaded himself he could now see she was Angela's sister, 'Harry, you're not out of danger, simply because Fletcher's got no claim. There's me, you see. And with or without your help I'm going on with this . . .'

'With my help.'

'And if, in the end, we prove that *you* killed Angela, then it's not Fletcher who's going to kill you. It's me.'

She was laughing up into his face. His eyes glowed back at her.

'You and who else?'

She wriggled her shoulders, swinging on his arm to his stride. 'Just me, Harry, just me.'

Then Harry was serious, because he'd seen beyond her laugh and into her eyes, and he'd realized that she meant it.

'Let's go and see Cynth,' he said.

'She of the stiletto heels,' she agreed, and the moment was gone so completely that Harry thought he'd imagined it.

They walked side by side down the hill and back to the lay-by. Not touching now, not speaking. She had been surprised by his perception, and by his ability to penetrate so quickly to an understanding of their new relationship. But she felt that something had gone from it. His enthusiasm, spurred by Fletcher, had led him to accept her assistance when he'd needed it. Now it was she who needed the assistance, and she was uncertain whether she'd used the correct approach with him. Making a joke of her intention to kill him, if she proved his guilt, had been intended to tell him how certain she now was of his innocence. But Harry was basically a serious man. He had understood something of the determination in her intention, but had turned away from it.

As they came in sight of her car, she saw that Vic Fletcher was sitting in it, behind the wheel.

Harry stopped in mid-limp, making a soft growling sound in his throat. Her fingers clutched his arm. 'No, Harry.'

'Let me break him apart . . .'

'Where's the challenge you spoke about?' she said softly. 'He's no stronger than a woman.'

He began to move forward again, and she noticed how he had changed. The bulky pace, now with the limp barely perceptible, had become a lithe movement that poised him on the balls of his feet, his shoulders were loose, his chin ducked low, his hands grappling into something between a clutch and a bludgeon.

'He got me into this,' he said thickly. 'He shoulda let it die.'

She made no move to follow him. 'Harry,' she said. 'Harry . . . no.'

He stopped, and turned. Every bump on his face seemed to have hardened. 'Say it.'

'Not like this,' she said quietly. 'Not with violence. If you scare him off altogether, we'll never know why he was after the truth. Think, Harry. Let him go. Frighten him . . . but no violence.'

His expression did not change, but a muscle eased here and a tension softened there. His eyes gleamed, then he tossed his head. 'If I touch him, it'll be violent.'

'Let me do it.'

For a moment he seemed unresponsive, then he moved aside. 'It's your car.'

She walked past him. Fletcher was sitting back with a hesitant grin on his face. She took a second to register him in her mind. A

39

weak, secretive man, she decided, who would preserve his secrets. They moved surreptitiously behind his weak eyes, but their substance remained hidden. The pale grin hid a fear of Harry that was deeply seated, so it must have been important to him to make this gesture of defiance. Sitting there, he was telling her that he wasn't going to be shaken off, that he'd be there at the end. What the end might mean to him was his secret.

'Get out of my car,' she said, her voice thin, its edge honed.

'Nice bit of machinery,' he said, but he was already opening the door.

'We'd prefer not to see you again,' she told him.

'So what's in it for you, lady?' His sneer was paltry, his lips being unable to handle it. He stood beside the car, watching warily as Harry approached with ambling intent.

'Can you walk back to the phone?' he asked her quietly.

'If necessary.'

'Then call an ambulance, but don't give your name. This character won't be able to speak for a long time.'

'Going,' said Fletcher, raising his palm in protest. 'Just going.'

Which he did, so rapidly that Virginia had to raise her voice, for it to reach him. 'You wouldn't, Harry, would you?'

'Just watch me.'

The Metro fired up, and Fletcher managed to force it into a wriggle and a squeal of tyres as he took off and passed them in a cloud of dust. Only when he was out of sight did they allow themselves to laugh, she with her hand on his forearm, he with his head thrown back.

At that moment, Fletcher was no more than a laughable irrelevance. It was perhaps a mistake for them to take that attitude, but it drew them a little closer.

5

'Show me the back way,' she said, settling into the passenger's seat and offering him the chance to drive.

He slid behind the wheel, notching the seat back. 'If I'm going to dirty your seats, we might as well make 'em match.'

At the crossing he drove straight on, though the lane ahead

was not signposted.

'It doesn't really go anywhere,' he explained, 'only to the old brickworks. Something to do with clay, somebody said, but it ran out. Whatever . . . the place closed, so it's quiet up here.'

The tar and gravel soon gave way to a rough, broken surface, through which shone the red and gold of broken, fired bricks. The brickworks had supplied the surface for its own approach road. She found herself wondering which had come first, the works or its road. Harry was taking it quietly, his eyes darting around as the hedges fell away and the surroundings revealed themselves as barren. The exploitation of the available terrain had been ruthless.

'What're you looking for?' she asked.

'Habit.' He turned his head briefly, grimacing. 'I used to bring the cars up here, an' I didn't want to be spotted. But it was a choice spot for courting couples.'

'Not very romantic, is it?'

'They didn't come for romance,' he said lightly. 'They came for nothing more'n sex.'

She looked at him with raised eyebrows, smiling in amused surprise.

'They used to have their own sidings,' he went on, 'with points and things, but Beeching finished all that, and they had to carry on with lorries. That's the actual works, though you can't see the kilns, and there's a big quarry the other side, half full of water now.'

The buildings were no longer a firm conglomerate, gaps in their continuity breaking the pattern. Two chimneys still stood, one at an impossible angle, and she did, in fact, catch glimpses of beehive shapes that could have been kilns. He was steering around its left side, where the levelled loading area was still channelled with sunken steel rails, clogged with brick dust. He ran the wheels along one set, then swung right to the level, grey line of hardcore. The steel rails came to an end, and they were driving along the bed of the abandoned twin-track railway. Long ago the rails and sleepers had been salvaged. The surface was rough, but firm.

Harry dropped back to twenty. 'Hell on the suspension,' he said.

She could see that this would indeed provide a secret

41

approach. At times they ran along cuttings, and even on the level stretches the hedges were so rampant that the car was well hidden.

'Why're we going to see Cynth?' he asked, his tone casual. 'And don't tell me it's because she used to wear them spike things.'

She eased back in the seat. The suspension was thrumming away, the Merc showing off by smoothing it out. 'They were all the go, four years back. Going out, now, though. No, it's not that. Cynthia's husband disappeared, and Angela died the same day. Two robberies, which must have been connected. It's too many coincidences, Harry.'

'You're not tellin' me Angela was mixed up in the robberies. She was *there*, and I jumped into her car, that's all it was.'

'I know, I know.'

'If she was your sister, you'd know what she was like.'

She gave an easy laugh, but there was enough wrong with it to attract his attention. 'She was capable of anything, that's all I can say. The world had gone wrong, and she was searching round for something she could do that would show she was rejecting it. Why not a bank robbery? To her, it might have seemed that all their money was obtained at the expense of the proletariat.'

'Who?'

'Those who don't have any.'

'That's the reason banks get robbed,' he told her. 'People who haven't got any want some, and that's where it's kept, in banks. None of your fancy words and ideas. Just 'cause they want it.'

'To Angela it would've seemed a romantic and exciting gesture . . .'

'What I should've done,' he said, glaring ahead, 'was to give her that good spanking I spoke about, and sent her home to daddy.'

'You think that would've worked?'

'Amateurs!' he said with scorn. 'They're ruining the whole scene.' He glanced at her. 'Anyway, how could she have been involved?'

'I take it you know how far we've got.' She prodded him in the ribs. 'You're not concentrating.'

'Looking for the gap,' he assured her.

The trouble was that there were no significant bends and no grades to guide him. It all looked the same, a disappearing per-

42

spective of grey hardcore, and the gap in the right-hand hedge, which Charlie had kept reasonably clear, had had four years to realize it should not be there. It had welcomed nettles and docks, and a flush of rosebay willowherb was standing naked, now that its fluffy clothing had been blown away.

'That's it,' said Harry. 'I think.' He stopped the car and got out, trampling some of it down. 'Yes, that's the bungalow. Don't reckon we can get the car through, though.'

Virginia didn't reckon he could persuade her to get through, either, not with all those nettles. She climbed out to have a look, lifting herself onto her toes.

They had passed the village of Harley Green, Charlie having had the good sense to select a reasonably isolated building for his re-spraying business. She was looking down on the property, the railway line having been run along an embankment just there. The track Harry had used to bring in and take out the cars was still visible as two depressions through humps of miserable grass, running directly down to the shed.

It had been a smallholding at one time, the shed possibly having housed chickens. A sagging wire-netting fence ran along both boundaries of the property, flanked by a farmer's pasture on one side and a sluggish stream on the other. The bungalow itself was small, possibly two-bedroomed, red brick with a shallow roof of slate. The shed, Virgina saw, was larger than the bunga-low. It would have accommodated three cars, she guessed. The end facing the railway line had double wooden doors, one sag-ging badly, so much so that it would no longer close properly.

'I can't get through this, Harry, and I'm not risking the car.'

'No sweat.'

Before she realized his intention he had her up in his arms, and was plunging through the undergrowth. She was on her feet again before she could protest. The effort had not even affected his breath.

'Let's walk down quietly and have a look in his workshop,' he said, a hint of anticipation in his voice, and now, on what was almost home territory to him, he led the way with confidence.

'Harry,' she said, trotting to catch up. 'I never knew ... did you live here?'

'With Cynth and Charlie? Lord, no. I was in digs in the village. A Mrs Thomas. I useta do her garden for her. We had some smashin' roses. I think we can squeeze through the gap in the doors.'

She had been keeping an eye on the bungalow, checking whether they were observed. But there was no movement. The bungalow, judging by the general dilapidated appearance of it, could have been deserted, but there were curtains at the windows, and beyond its corner she could just see the green rear of a small hatchback.

Harry thrust his shoulder through the gap in the doors, pausing to put a hand to the sagging one. It groaned open a further reluctant foot. She followed him inside. He was standing with his hands on his hips, looking round. The light was poor, there being no windows or skylights. He was waiting for his eyes to adapt.

It was not the same as he recalled it. Gone was the pear-drop choking tang of the paint, the light from the bank of floods in the roof, the concentrated beam from Charlie's working spot, the hiss of the spray-gun, the phut of his compressor, the scattered strips of masking tape, the crumples of masking newspaper Charlie had used. There was no life in the building, no purpose to it.

Harry realized that he'd been eager to get inside. Part of his life had circulated inside this building, for three years. He'd assumed he might recapture something special, because ... yes ... there had been a sense of adventure to it, a whiff of danger, and with every car a feeling of relief and triumph that once again he'd pulled it off. Now there was nothing. It was a vacant shell, its corrugated iron roof ringing with nothing more than empty memory. There was a sad desolation to it, a musty and stale deadness in the air.

The workbench still ran along one side – hadn't it been bigger? – the abandoned spray-gun lying on it with dead paint clogging its nozzle, beside it two empty cans with four-inch brushes in them, the thinners long since evaporated. Beneath the bench more cans, probably still full of acrylic car paint in every available colour. Scattered on the floor were empty cans. Morosely, he kicked at them, rebounding them from the walls. One rolled to Virginia's feet.

She stared down at it. Water-based wash, it said on the side. Dilute only with water. Cardinal Red. 'Harry,' she said, but she got no further.

A narrow side door was kicked open, intruding a shaft of brilliant daylight. The figure was a silhouette, but could be detected as a woman, short but sturdy. Also obvious was the silhouette of a shotgun.

'Didn't I tell you!' she screamed. 'Keep away from me, you bloody witch.'

It was Virginia she was facing, and directly at Virginia that the shotgun was pointed.

'Cynth!' bellowed Harry, to distract attention, then he had flung himself at her, one arm raised to deflect the gun.

As he hit her the gun fired, the charge thundering into the iron roof, lifting a portion of it for a second before it flapped back. The gun skidded across the dirt floor as the two locked bodies sprawled together after it. Cynthia was a fighting, biting tigress, snarling and spitting and screaming as Harry tried to subdue her. 'It's me, Cynth,' he choked, trying to prise her fingers from his throat. 'It's Harry, Cynth!' as he tried to tangle her flying feet and knees in his legs. He caught her wrists, spreadeagling her. 'For Chrissake, Cynth, it's me.'

Then they were struggling again, rolling in the dust, her arms round his neck, her face buried in his, both their legs flailing as each tried to stabilize their situation. Cynthia raised her head. 'Oh Harry, Harry love!' she cried out, and the struggling went on.

Virginia, having rescued the shotgun and expertly ejected the cartridges, watched them, and realized that Harry had come back to a big welcome.

Eventually they scrambled to their feet, still laughing, she with tears streaming in channels through the dust on her cheeks.

'Harry!' she choked.

Then he lifted her with his right arm round her waist, and her left one was round his neck. Her feet were six inches from the ground.

'Cynth,' he said, 'I'd like you to meet Virginia Brent. Virginia, this is Cynthia.'

It was done with immense formality. Virginia wondered how he'd look in a dinner jacket and black bow tie. Magnificent, she decided. But her attention was concentrated on Cynthia.

She saw a woman of about her own age, which was thirty, but slimmer, shorter, barely five feet three inches, the waist and hips emphasized by the tight fit of her jeans. A slim blonde, was Cynthia, the bleached blondness that grows out. It had not been corrected for some time. In spite of the fact that she was still laughing at the joy of their reunion, when Harry put her back on her feet Cynthia slumped. The weariness was implanted. The greyness in her complexion was not entirely from the dust the welcome had stirred. Her eyes, too, lacked any sparkle, and eyeshadow served only to emphasize their depth, and did nothing to hide a despair that had lodged there a long while. Virginia thought there could also be fear, in the line of the lips and the quivering at one corner of Cynthia's mouth.

There was certainly suspicion. Cynthia made no move to shake hands. Her head was tilted when Virginia offered the shotgun, then the two shells, one fired, one not.

'Sorry about that,' she said, looking past Virginia's shoulder and not sounding sorry at all.

'You get intruders?'

'You'd be surprised.' She turned back to Harry. 'When'd you get out, Harry?'

'Two or three months.'

'And you didn't come to see me!'

'I thought Charlie was here.' He flexed his fingers and stared at the result. 'Didn't know he wasn't around.'

She squeezed his arm. 'That's no excuse. If he had been . . .'

'It would've been embarrassin', Cynth, you know that.'

She seemed not to be able to stop herself from touching him, and shook his arm impatiently. 'I don't see that.'

'Embarrassin' for Charlie,' he explained. 'He left me standin' there, Cynth. Outside the jeweller's.'

'I know.'

'Well then.'

She was silent. Her arm fell to her side and she shrugged. Her face was thinner, he thought, no life in it now. There was an awkward pause. This would have been the obvious moment for her to invite them to leave the dreariness of the shed for a cup of tea in the bungalow. It didn't seem to occur to her.

'It was only yesterday,' said Harry, 'that I found out he didn't come . . .' His hand moved, embracing the confines of the shed. 'Home,' he mumbled.

'So you *did* come to see me,' Cynthia cried. Her voice held too

46

much excitement; it overflowed the comment. She was tense, Harry realized.

'As soon's I could,' he assured her.

'And brought a chaperone.' Her eyes were bleak when she turned to face Virginia, who grimaced.

'My chauffeur,' corrected Harry, and Virginia knew he had it in hand.

'I thought,' said Cynthia, who'd not even heard his remark, 'that you'd have news of Charlie.'

'I know less than you do.'

'He just didn't come back, Harry. Something terrible must've happened to him. Must have.'

He was watching her moving about, three paces one way, three the other, as though afraid to be too far from him. Her arms were crossed, hands cupping her elbows. Harry watched with his worried frown.

'You said "come back" Cynth. Sounds like you knew where he went that day.'

'I know now. You were on trial, and you'd gone out with him. Of course I knew then. Charlie! What the hell did he think he was doing? An armed robbery, they said on the news. A two-coloured car. Of course I damn well knew it was him. I'd seen the car, in here. And seen what he was doing to it. Of course I knew, you big fool.'

She was becoming agitated. Harry felt at a loss, and searched for Virginia in the shadows, but she was quietly prowling the perimeter, touching this, sniffing that, observing everything.

'I didn' quite mean that, Cynth,' he said quietly, humbly. 'I meant, did you know he was on somethin' special when he left?'

'A feeling,' she threw at him.

'What sorta feeling?'

'What's the matter with you, Harry, coming here and throwing out your questions?'

He scratched his chin. 'Thought you could help. I rather wanta meet Charlie, and ask him why he left me on the pavement and dropped me right in it.'

'But you'd be embarrassed,' she threw at him, pausing with her legs spread, her palms together in front of her mouth.

'*He* would,' he pointed out. 'He'd be embarrassed here, if you was in on it. Meet him on his own, and he'd only be bruised.'

'Hah!' she said, flinging down her arms.

'You said you had a feeling, like,' he reminded her. 'Before he left. I thought you was out for the day, at your ma's.'

'It changed.' She was impatient. 'Ma phoned. I can't remember. But I didn't go. It was all different, somehow. I came in the shed here. Different. Didn't smell the same, and Charlie was on edge, the brush in his hand, and he wouldn't go on with it till I was out of the place. It was all different. And I watched him drive away with you, Harry, up on the old railway track. *That* was different. I'd never seen both of you together in one of his cars.'

'You're right there, come to think of it,' he conceded, praying for Virginia to intervene. He didn't know what to say next.

Cynthia herself rescued him. 'He didn't phone. If he'd got stuck, I reckoned he'd phone. I spent the whole day outside, with both doors open, to here and to the house, so that I could hear both phones.'

'Both?'

'Different numbers. Didn't you know *that*, Harry? Ex-directory for the one in here.'

'Always wondered why I always got him, first ring, never you.'

'So now you know. Any more questions, Harry?'

The welcome, he realized, had become exhausted. Her voice was brittle.

'Sorry, Cynth,' he said, and there must have been in his voice something of the sympathy he felt, because she suddenly gave a choked sob and threw herself at him. Her cheek came opposite his chest. He clutched her to him, feeling her shaking, and the desperation and despair in her outpouring of emotion.

'There, there,' he said, his great hand spread against her back, feeling stupid and awkward and inadequate. And then, when her sobs became sniffs and the tension had gone from her, he held her away from him and lifted her chin with his forefinger. 'I'll find him for you, Cynth. I'll find him.'

She stood back, grimaced a faded smile, and thumped him in the chest. 'And if you do, you can just tell him from me, Harry, that he can drop dead as far as I'm concerned, and if I ever see him again I'll have his eyes out.'

'Why would you do that?' Harry was baffled, not questioning her ability.

'It must've been a woman,' she said fiercely. 'What else could it've been? He'd been acting strange for ages – months. You can't tell me . . . it must've been.'

'He wouldn't have dared.'

'How right you are, mate, how bloody right. But Charlie was a coward. Didn't you know that? He wouldn't have dared tell me.'

'That's how you know?'

She nodded decisively, lower lip caught in her teeth. 'It's how I know.'

'By what he didn't say?' He was worrying at it.

Another nod, even more decisive. 'Exactly. What he didn't say, when he left me, was "see you". He always said see you. That time he didn't. And he didn't see me again.'

Harry tried to laugh, but it came out wrong and got itself bounced around by the corrugated iron roof.

'Oh come on, Cynth . . . you women, you never use any sense. Charlie! Never. You know he thought the world o' you. Couldn't talk about anybody else. He'd've said somethin' to me. Sure to've done. And there was never a hint. Heh! Somethin' else. If he'd gone off on purpose, you'd know. He'd have taken his clothes and things. Did he do that, Cynth?'

She looked at him firmly, then down at the toe screwing patterns in the dust, up again. Now there was hope in her eyes. 'No, Harry, he didn't.'

'You see. He was intendin' to come back to you, Cynth.'

'But Harry,' she whispered. 'In that case, something terrible *must* have happened, or he would have come back.'

And Harry, faced with the two alternatives that had haunted her for four years, could think of nothing to say. Then Virginia was at his elbow and offering the only possible comfort.

'But if he *intended* to return, Cynthia, that's surely the most important thing.'

Cynthia stared blankly into her eyes, then slowly she seemed to relax, and she nodded.

Virginia put a hand to Harry's arm. 'Harry?'

'Yes, yes,' he mumbled. 'We'd better be off. See you, Cynth.' Then he looked away. It had been an unfortunate choice of exit line.

It seemed ridiculous to Virginia that they left by the same gap in the double doors, walking towards a deserted railway track and seen off by Cynthia silently, instead of a farewell from the front door. But neither Harry nor Cynthia seemed to feel it unusual.

Virginia said nothing until they reached the weed barrier. Then she spoke. 'I can manage . . .'

'Nonsense,' he said, and picked her up again, plodded through the tangle, and placed her carefully on her feet. 'Could get to enjoy that,' he said.

She made no comment, but stood and looked at the car. 'D'you reckon you can turn it, Harry?'

'If you'll shout me round.'

They managed to get the car round and she climbed in beside him.

'Where now?' he asked. 'Reckon *that* was a waste of time.'

'Not at all, Harry. Can you take me to a stream? I need water.'

'Cynth would've given you a drink.'

'Not to drink. Any sort of water.'

The car was rumbling along, its exhaust puttering a protest at the depleted speed.

'There's the quarry, if that'll do.'

'Possibly. And it wasn't a waste of time. I think I know why your friend Charlie painted a black car two other colours.'

And Harry, who had been deeply affected by Cynthia's distress, registered his disappointment in Virginia's apparent lack of feeling by saying. 'Well . . . good for you.'

He said it in a dismissive tone, which sent up her eyebrows in surprise, until she realized why. Then, for a moment, her sight blurred.

6

The difficulty, Virginia decided, was that Harry was becoming enmeshed with old friends and acquaintances. His emotions were involved, but not hers, and she was being left out in the cold, watching and observing but feeling nothing. This was not what she had wanted. She had a feeling that Angela, whatever her faults of impetuosity and ridiculous enthusiasms, and with her spirit packed full with crackling emotions and warm, deep compassion, could not have lost her life in a cold and casual manner. Even her death would have been involved with emotion. It therefore followed that the understanding of it would also entail a feeling for the emotions involved, and Virginia was concerned that she was encountering ones that were outside her experience.

Harry shamed her with his naïve perception. He was turning out to be more sensitive than a large and ugly man had any right to be. She had assumed his assistance would have been mainly physical, but it was beginning to seem that she was wrong in that.

'Did you hear what she called me?' she asked, probing his understanding.

'Bitch or witch. It wasn't personal.'

'That shotgun was damned personal.'

'I don't think she'd have fired it.'

Damn him, she thought, you could never tell from the tone of his voice what he was thinking. 'You don't *think* she would? Don't tell me she's always been unpredictable.'

Harry concentrated on his driving, at a time when it wasn't needed. 'She's not crazy, if that's what you mean. Just . . . well, she sort of always *felt* things pretty strong. All love and kisses, or scratches and kicks.' The stacks of the two chimneys were now visible. 'You still want the quarry?'

'It's water I want, so we'll try the quarry. Harry, don't you realize, she was expecting a woman. Cynthia was. Bitch or witch, that's a woman. And she was talking about her Charlie having gone off with a woman. Surely they can't be the same person! I just can't see Charlie's woman coming to visit Charlie's wife.'

'Charlie's woman my ass,' he said angrily. 'Charlie didn' have no woman. He was *proud* of Cynth. Couldn't talk about anythin' without coming out with something like Cynth says this and Cynth says that. Y' can always tell, if they're proud of the missus.'

'She'd be a handful.'

'Kept life interestin'. Or so he said.'

'He told you she was a handful?'

'Didn't need to tell me. But he did say she kept life interestin'. Mind you, he was drunk at the time.'

'In vino veritas,' she said as he drew the car to a halt.

51

'As you say, if it's not filthy.'

He sat back. They had reached the point where he was about to turn off the hardcore and into the old loading area.

'But Harry,' she said, 'if your Charlie thought so much of her how would he feel if he got the idea she was seeing another man?'

'What . . . Cynth?'

'Would he challenge her with it? Would he tackle the man and warn him off, perhaps beat him up?'

'Heh, heh, you're getting fancy ideas. Charlie wasn't like that. Kinda shy. Quiet like. Nothin' violent for Charlie.'

'Are we talking about the Charlie who charged into a jeweller's with a rod in his hand?' she asked, her voice delicately poised.

'A rod?' He laughed. 'Where've you been? And *that* Charlie, I'm telling you, was scared sh . . . outa his wits. Didn't I say how he was dropping things an' trampling on 'em? He'd really got the shakes. It don't alter what I said. Charlie wouldn't face Cynth, if she *did* have another bloke, nor face *him*. He'd be sorta . . . I dunno, shocked and disappointed, like she'd let him down. It'd be like walkin' into a club and finding your wife doin' a strip on the stage.' He pointed. 'Look, we turn left here, if you want the quarry, round the back of the buildings.'

Before he could slip his foot from the brake to throttle, she touched his arm to restrain him. 'Let's talk it through. So Charlie wouldn't have cut up rough. What would he have done?'

'Ask yourself. Suffered.'

'In silence? And not reacted? Wouldn't he, perhaps in retaliation, have found himself another woman? Wouldn't he have tried to find someone else he could walk with, on his arm, and feel proud that she was there?'

'And all this,' he said, squinting at her against the sun, 'is based on what he might've thought about Cynth and another man? It's a bit much, ain't it?'

'Remember how you met her? The disco. You threw out the chap she was with. And that was three years before the day of the robberies. A lot can happen in three years.'

He slid the car into motion. It permitted him to keep his eyes from hers. 'The trouble with you,' he informed her, 'is that it's all damn theory. You want everything to fit into little pockets of cause an' effect. Nothin's like that. People don't do anything 'cause it's the right thing to do at the right time. They do daft things. So reasoning'll get you nowhere.'

He was telling her that her god of logic was a false prophet. She lifted her chin. 'I'll remember your advice, Harry.'

'And anyway ...' There was no sign of triumph in his voice. 'That feller I threw out was only the one she was dancin' with – if you can call it dancin'. She'd come with a woman friend. Remember?'

'I remember. So my reasoning is all a load of rubbish, and Charlie would have been heading back to Cynthia after the robbery?'

He nodded, then stopped the car because the abrupt downgrade facing them was steep, and would have been impossible to negotiate if the surface had been wet. It was clear that the reason for the closing of the brickworks had not been any shortage of clay. Everywhere she looked there was the red smear of clay, still, after all these years, predominant. They had dug into a hillside, then down and outwards, forming a bowl into which the approach, at the head of which they were now parked, had dipped at a progressively steeper angle. Now it was impossible to see the depth to which the pit had been quarried. The clay-surfaced ramp ahead of the car proceeded for only fifty feet before it dipped into the brown surface of the water. There was no sign of any green growth, no weed, no algae. The water lay like a sheet of burnished bronze, beyond it, in an arc, a cliff of red earth.

'We can walk down it, now it's dry,' said Harry. 'But don't try paddling. They say it's two hundred feet deep. The first thing they teach the kids in the village school is that it's full of ghosts an' ghoulies, to keep 'em away.'

'Let's walk down, then, and have a word with them.'

Harry shrugged, and got out of the car. She stood the other side, hitching the strap of her bag on to her shoulder. 'Don't look so miserable, Harry. I've got a reason.'

'I'm not miserable. Inside, I'm singin' hymns o' praise. It just don't show. You going to be all right in them shoes?'

'Safer,' she assured him, 'than with you carrying me.'

They walked down to the water, heavily on their heels and leaning back. It was not until they reached it that she was able to dispel a disbelief that it was genuine water. No breath of air stirred its surface. She crouched and touched it with her finger. It was water.

'Harry,' she said, demanding his concentration, 'Charlie used a black Escort that day. He asked you to get him a *black* one. Then he painted it red one side and green the other. To confuse the police, he told you, but it now seems certain it was to attract police attention, because he was probably working as a decoy, as an accomplice with the bank robbers. His job was to draw off the police, and try not to be caught himself. It seems he was successful, because he wasn't picked up.'

She paused. Harry stared out over the water. 'Nobody's arguing.' His tone indicated that his agreement was in suspension.

'But there was the question of why he painted both halves of the car, instead of just one half of it.'

'*Your* question. Me, I'm saying nowt.'

She bit her lip. He was not responding, and she was a person who needed encouragement. Sometimes, she was well aware, her surface confidence was false. Self-criticism had a tendency to intrude, caused by an ability to see more sides to an argument than her own. She now needed Harry's support, his agreement, to point her along one specific corridor of thought. But he seemed still to be upset by Cynthia.

'All right,' she conceded. 'My question. I thought that if he'd only wanted a two-coloured car which would stand out, he could have asked you to get him a red one and paint half of it green, or paint it psychedelic or something. You *do* see what I mean?'

'Oh sure, sure. I just thought . . . .' He moved his shoulders almost impatiently, but Harry was tired. He'd exercised his brain too much that day already, and brainwork was exhausting. 'I just thought he'd kinda not worked it out . . . sorta nervous about what we were going to do. I told you – people do daft things.'

'You heard what Cynthia said, though. It was a special job. He wouldn't go on with it while she was there. He was being careful, not careless.'

He attempted to squeeze his nose into a more elegant shape. 'That's true enough.'

'And the smell was different, Cynthia said. And Harry, she told us he was using a brush.'

He turned and looked at her. 'She did, too.' Now she had his interest.

She smiled up at him. 'I saw cans that had contained a water-based paint. I don't know what that is. Probably something like whitewash with pigment in. One was called Cardinal Red. And on the bench were two empty cans, each with a four-inch brush in it. Dry, of course, but they could have had water in, and not paint thinners. So I took one of the brushes.'

She produced it with triumph from her shoulder bag. It was a four-inch brush caked solid with green paint.

'Did he ever use a brush on his other cars?'

He shook his head. 'Just the spray-gun. Maybe a fine brush for touching up.'

'And I thought ... perhaps after all this time ... it might still wash out,' she concluded in triumph.

'Let's have a go, then.'

He took it from her and crouched at the edge of the water. He hadn't thought it through, but he could see she had something. So maybe she was giving an impression of coldness, all brains and no feelings, but at least she could use her brain. He dabbled it, he splashed it around, he sprayed himself with water, and slowly to the surface there rose a smear of green. He withdrew the brush, rose to his full height, and slapped the bristles on his palm. It was still a solid lump, but it left a green stain.

'By heck,' he said, 'you were right.' His face suddenly burst apart with a grin. 'So what?'

She found, to her disgust, that she was almost dancing to the flood of light from his smile. Why could she not hide her emotions more secretly? 'Did he ... and think about this, Harry ... did he say anything about the weather?'

'Now you mention it.'

'What?'

'Hoped it wasn't goin' to rain.'

'There you are, then. It would have washed off with the rain. But you see what it means, Harry. If he intended to drive home, which he wouldn't do until he was certain he was in the clear, he wouldn't have needed to go to such trouble, using water-washable paint and two separate colours. His spray-gun was waiting, and he could have changed the car to any colour he liked in his own time. He wouldn't have needed to colour *both* sides, Harry, not if he *intended* to re-spray it. With a red car, he could have sprayed half of it green, and then when he got home changed the whole thing to brown. Or blue. Or black. But he painted both halves of the black Escort, by hand, in paint that would wash off . . . and what would he get by washing it off? A red and green car would become a black car in a few minutes. Not in hours, which it would take if he'd *sprayed* it red and green.'

She was watching his expression with her head tilted, and gradually the confidence had faded from her voice. 'What's the matter?'

'I know what you're saying, that he didn't intend to go back home.'

She nodded, her eyes anxious.

'Well . . . why wouldn't he plan on driving home, and hosing it down when he got there?'

'If he planned on driving home, Harry, it would've been by way of the railway track, after he'd managed to get clear of police traps. He could have hidden out in the buildings here to be certain. And once home he'd know he had time for a complete respray, so he wouldn't have needed to play around with water-based paint. He was an expert sprayer. He would have done a proper job on it, a two-colour *spray* not a hand painting. The only possible reason for using washable paint has to be time. He wanted something he could get rid of in minutes, and while he was a long way from his spray-gun.'

Harry considered what he recalled of Charlie. He'd had pride in his work. The two-colour job had been tatty and dull, he now remembered. Not Charlie's style at all. 'Maybe you've got something.'

'Right. So look how he was fixed. A two-colour car, red and green. He'd only have to dodge into one of those places with a car wash, and he could drive it out black. *That's* why he painted both halves, Harry. He wanted to switch to a car that had no trace of the colours red and green on it. A kind of completely fresh start. He had no intention of going home. He had the jewellery shop haul, which might or might not have been worth much, and his share of the bank robbery in due course.'

'You sound sure of yourself.'

She nodded. 'That was why I tried to reassure Cynthia, by saying he was surely intending to go home.'

He shook his head. 'Feminine logic.'

'It did no harm.'

56

'But you're sure he wasn't?' He jerked his eyes at her. 'Off with another woman?'

'Why not? And why couldn't that other woman have been Angela?'

'Oh bull . . . There's no connection.'

'No?' She took the brush from his fingers and tossed it into the water. 'Then how, do you suppose, did she manage to find the phone booth so quickly? Because she knew it was there, that's why. She had used it before to phone Charlie, to tell him she was waiting. She *knew* that lay-by, Harry. Perhaps they'd used it for their meetings, there's room for two cars.'

'Stretchin' it a bit.'

'She phoned me, Harry, a month before it happened. All excited about this man she'd met. Wouldn't give his name, but he was dishy, she said.'

'Not Charlie then.'

'And one strange point . . . she said he had a tinted fringe round his hair, and when you mentioned spraying . . .'

'That's Charlie! His woolly hat came down just above his ears.'

'. . . I had a feeling. I knew.'

'Intuition,' he grunted, still not fully convinced. 'It was a casual meet. She was parked there, outside the jeweller's, and I got in.'

She took both his arms in her hard fingers, so that he had to face her. 'But *was* it casual? Think about it. He was your friend, but he left you there, stranded. He didn't want you in the Escort, because that was where it started getting dangerous. And also because he was going away and didn't want you to know where. But he left you an escape route. Angela was right behind him, with her passenger's door unlocked. It's just the sort of thing she'd have loved. If you hadn't pounced on that door, I'll bet you she'd have pipped her horn and invited you in. Charlie was looking after you, Harry. Why d'you think she was so casual with you? She knew who you were, and that you wouldn't harm her. What went wrong was that she expected to leave *you* in the lay-by, and you left *her*. She couldn't help ribbing you, because she knew she was safe. Charlie would have told her all about you. But she took it too far, and you were annoyed.'

'That I was.'

'So you see. Don't you see, Harry? Even at the last, he was thinking about your welfare, you big fool.'

She was surprised and confused at the pleasure it gave her to present him with this. Behind his attitude had been the constant thought that Charlie, the man he'd trusted, had left him standing in the doorway of the jeweller's shop. But now she had given him new faith in Charlie. No . . . she had restored the old faith. And perhaps the reserve she felt between Harry and herself had been based on the loss, his fear of venturing into a new situation of trust. So perhaps that could now be swept away.

Judging by the irradiation of his face – it glowed, it flamed – she was correct. Judging by his sudden hoarse shout of laughter and joy, his natural trust was bursting free. And if his hands were anything to go by, clasping her one each side at the waist and swooping her high until he laughed up at her, kicking and screaming, his release was centred on her.

He put her down. 'Idiot!' she said, flustered and touching her hair.

'Well, how about that!' he said.

They walked back up to the car, her hand on his arm, matching him stride for stride, almost assuming a limp.

'So Charlie was off and away,' he said in wonder. 'What d'you know! The devil.'

'And with Angela, don't forget that.'

'It's the only explanation,' he agreed.

'And then you took her car away from her.'

He grinned down at her. 'No wonder she was mad at me.'

'You split 'em up, Harry. They lost contact.'

He stood at the driver's door of the Mercedes, looking at her across the hood. 'So maybe I did that.' He was abruptly more sober. 'So she didn't turn up at their meeting place.'

'What is it you're trying to say, Harry?'

'It rained later,' he said stolidly. 'Not while we were doing the jeweller's. That was around two o'clock. But by four it was raining.'

'Washed the car . . .'

'Not that.' He turned, and stared back at the way they'd driven in. 'Look at that. We came in, doing a steady right turn round the buildings, then right again onto the old railway.' No sign of his careless voice, she noticed. His words were carefully chosen. 'So if you were coming to the quarry you'd do the same. Steady right round the factory, then a sharper right to the ramp down to the quarry. Just say . . . just say for the sake of argument . . .'

'I don't think so,' she put in quickly, seeing what was coming.

'. . . that Charlie dropped the police, and waited and waited at the meeting place because Angela – if he *was* meeting Angela – didn't turn up.'

'Because she was dead.'

'And then all the life'd go out of it, and he'd maybe reckon he'd head for home, but it was rainin' by then, and maybe the car was washin' itself, but all the same he'd head for this back way in. But Charlie didn't know it so well as me. Hardly ever used it. It was dark and it was rainin', and maybe he bore just a bit too much to the right, and he wouldn't see the ramp till he was right on it, and because it was rainin' it'd be slimy so's it'd be no good using the brakes . . .'

'You're not to think that!'

'But if that's what happened, he could be down there, and when you come to think of it, that means I'd have killed him. Wouldn't that be a bloody laugh.' He illustrated with a harsh sound in his throat. 'It'd mean I killed him, not Angela, because I took off in her car.' He thumped the car's bonnet with his fist.

'That's just wild and stupid, Harry.'

'No wilder than your ideas.'

'It wasn't you who took her out of circulation.'

Virginia felt that something they had found was draining away. With his faith restored in his past friendships, he could now explore self-criticism to the full.

'I'm not having you blaming yourself,' she said angrily. 'If that happened . . . and I'm not accepting *that*, either . . . then the one to blame is the one who killed her.'

'Easy to say.' His shoulder was to her, his eyes on the motionless water.

'We haven't talked it through, Harry. If it was Angela he was going away with, then look what we've got.' She was trying desperately to distract him. 'She phoned the police. That would be a mistake, a throw-back to her instinct, and just the sort of thing she would do, if she was angry enough. She always lost all sense of reason when she lost her temper. But she also used the tenpence you gave her. Now . . . who would she call? Who . . . naturally? She'd been left by you in the lay-by. She should have been joining Charlie, somewhere. So she would try to contact him. At his home . . . his workshop. Their *private* means of contact.'

He jerked his head round, his jaw firm, its knobbles protruding. She couldn't look into his eyes. 'No!' he said forcefully.

'There'd be no other thing she could do. She might not have expected him to be *there*, but if the phone was answered she could leave a message.'

'Such as what?' he demanded.

'Something that could mean nothing to anybody else but him. If he calls, tell him the lay-by. Something like that. But she would be saying that to Cynthia.'

'Shut up, damn you.' Now his voice was loud enough to reach the buildings and rebound, probe the quarry, and resound. Damn you . . . you . . . you . . .

Virginia was beginning to realize that Harry's responses were in no way sophisticated. Especially when they involved emotions. She listened now to the echoes of his angry reaction, and knew she was treading a dangerous path. His joy at the revelation that Charlie might not, after all, have left him stranded, should have been a warning to her, not an encouragement. His affections and allegiances had been few. Heavens, Cynthia and Charlie could have been their sum total, and now she was forcing him into seeing that his confidence in Cynthia was to be undermined.

It was all she could do to go on with it, briskly because she had to demonstrate that the issue must be treated without passion. With Harry, everything had to be passionate. She was tossing a crackling firework from hand to hand.

'Cynthia of the stiletto heels, Harry,' she said. 'And what, getting that message, would she do? She'd go to the lay-by, that's what. She'd go to meet the woman she had had a suspicion existed, the woman who was causing such strange behaviour in Charlie.'

'Angela wouldn't have had this number,' he tried desperately, trying to split her ridiculous logic apart. 'He wouldn't have dared give it her.'

'Of course she'd have his number. But even if she hadn't . . .' Virginia put her arms on the hood of the car, mainly because her legs felt weak. She moistened her pale lips. Her mouth was dry. 'Even if she hadn't, there it'd be, facing her, in the phone booth. CB 259. A local number. It couldn't have meant anybody but him.

Oh Harry, it's all so logical.'

He took two paces back, keeping a good distance from her cool logic. 'That's all I get from you,' he said flatly, slapping his thighs. 'Logic and reason. Y'r all so damned cold and un ... unfeelin'. Like the rest of 'em. Oh, I've had some, don't you worry. Seen it in action. Some poor bleeder goes to the police station, half broken-down with worry 'cause somethin' terrible's happened, and all he gets back is what's y'r name, what's y'r address? As much feelin' as my ass. But I've got it reckoned out now.'

'What are you saying, Harry?' Oh God, she thought, and we came so close. I need him, need him to trust me. What can I say ... do ... think? 'Harry, this is ...'

'And what's Cynth to you? Tell me that. Nothin'. A picture you've cut out from a photograph, a shape, nothin' but a voice in a body. Y' don't know her. You talk about her killin' ...' He turned his head as though to spit, and changed his mind. 'She couldn't have done it. Never. In a fury, yeah, yeah. Could've. But not ten seconds later, when she'd cooled down. And it would've taken ten minutes to get to the lay-by. Words, yes. Nails and hair tearin' and screamin'. But not kill. Not Cynth.'

'All right, Harry.'

'It's not bloody well all right. Cynth! She'd give her right arm to help yerrout. Laugh with yer, joke with yer, an' kick all hell outa y'r ankle if y' pinched her bottom. Yeah, she had throwin' tempers, but kill ... no. She'd got mice, but she wouldn't put down traps. Rats came down from the embankment, and she'd throw 'em bread, and watch 'em haulin' it home. Kill? Not Cynth! Never! That's bloody crazy.'

She hadn't realized. They'd been closer than she'd thought. It should have been obvious. It was Harry who'd been proud of Cynthia, not Charlie. Charlie had taken his pride for granted, but to Harry it was a real and living thing. He'd beamed on Cynthia in his stupid pride, and gone no closer than a pinch of the bottom. Dear old-fashioned Harry with his unpossessive pride, because Charlie was his mate and Cynthia was his friend – his nearly-mate. She almost told him he was a fool, and that anybody was capable of killing, that Cynthia most of all was capable of it. But she didn't.

'Then we look deeper, Harry,' she said quietly, luringly.

'No we don't.' He flung out an arm in fury. 'Not you an' me. Because I've seen through you, Miss Bloody Virginia Brent. What is it – Inspector Brent? Woman Detective Inspector Soddin' Brent. Oh, I see it now. It's all bin a plot. An unsolved murder on the files. Wait till Harry Hodnutt comes out and he'll help. He must know somethin', so get close to him, con him, be friendly. Friendly! Hah! And that weasel Feltcher, what's he? Detective Constable? Get him to set it up, me have a word with Sergeant Tranter, all innocent like. An' next thing I knew, there's you, all clever and crafty, but y' didn't quite pull it off. Y' know why? 'Cause you're like all of 'em. Cold an' empty, like a bloody shell. I saw y' with Cynth, wanderin' round lookin' for clues, listenin' for slips o' the tongue, and if she's unhappy an' crying' 'cause Charlie's not come back, it's oh my dear I'm sure he intended to come back. Christ! An' with a paintbrush you'd nicked, there in y'r bag! You make me sick. I've had enough.'

'Get in the car, Harry.'

'Go to hell.'

'Get in the car, for God's sake, and drive, and let me think.'

'Drive it yourself.'

'You've had your say, so give me time to think what to reply.'

'More logic? No thanks. Just bugger off and let me be.'

She had lost him, and she knew it. All she could consider at the moment was how to get him back home. Home! Back to his damned barge. She walked round and climbed in behind the wheel. Started the engine.

'Harry, I'll drive you back to town.'

He stood, silently staring at her.

'I promise you. Not a word, and I'll drop you where you like.'

'I wouldn't want to soil the seats. What is it – a hired car for the job? What's the budget for the Harry Hodnutt case?'

She engaged reverse, backed out, and swung the nose round. She was now parked beside him.

'Get in the damned car,' she said, her voice tight.

He thumped the bonnet. 'On your way, Inspector.'

It was anger that jerked the car forward, kept it going until he was no longer a tiny figure in the rearview mirrow. But slower then, because of the tears. It was with a feeling of intense loss that she set oft for home.

7

Harry's first impression was of a blank emptiness. His abrupt and violent anger that Cynth should have come under suspicion had been a safety valve for his growing tension. Now he was drained, even of the encroaching uneasiness that had been haunting him.

Moodily, he kicked a stone around in a circle, coming back to where he'd been and with nothing decided. His blasted tongue! Better, perhaps, where a woman was concerned, than his fist, but with his tongue he was less expert. An argument was best settled with violence. So often, after violence, it was arms across shoulders and another pint all round, and it would be over. But after words a wound was opened that didn't easily heal.

Harry didn't work it out logically to that conclusion. He felt it. It had been in some way relaxing to take Virginia Brent at face value, but experience had nudged him, and logic – *her* damned logic – had warned him that she could not be what she claimed. And yet . . . he could not forget her delight when she'd shown him that Charlie, after all, might not have left him carrying the can. That had been real and genuine.

Hell, he thought, me an' my big mouth.

So now what did he do? Back to Cynth's? In spite of her initial welcome (discounting the shotgun) he could not be certain of another. Her situation had changed. Charlie was no longer there, between them. The safety was no longer there, to offer restraint to something that might not have been available or even valid without it.

This was something else that Harry felt rather than rationalized.

Besides, he knew that two miles limping over that hardcore would cripple his ankles, and by the time he'd walked back to the crossroads he had made up his mind. Turn right there, instead of left to Cynth's, and it would be five miles to Porchester, where he could get a bus to town. Then to the barge, and everything would be back to normal.

Well . . . almost.

He stopped in town for fish and chips, and a pint at the Mournful Parson, so that the light was going when he reached Hanger Lane, and completely gone on the wharf. But Harry knew his shadows and was sure-footed, knew and recognized the shadow-shape of his home, and realized that something was different about it. Somebody was sitting on the stern, which meant facing him.

Virginia? His steps quickened, firmed.

The figure stirred and lifted a head. A cigarette end was flicked, and sparked an arc into the canal.

'Harry, I bin waiting.'

It was Vic Fletcher. Because it was not Virginia, Harry was angry. His voice held danger. 'Get off my bleedin' property.'

Fletcher got to his feet. Harry had one foot on the deck. They were three feet apart.

'Language, Harry! Not so fast. I bin guardin' it for you.'

'You couldn't guard a kennel!'

Harry was able to detect that Fletcher smiled, could see his hand moving inside the breast of his anorak. There was no doubt that the hand, when it emerged, held a pistol.

'Guarding it with this.'

It was not a large pistol, as pistols went, and seemed to be a revolver. But Harry didn't need light to detect that it was real. It moved with an impression of weight, and Harry knew how difficult that would be to fake with a plastic toy. He'd done it.

'So what do I do?' he asked, his voice flat. 'Say ta very much before I sling you and the ironwork into the water?'

Fletcher laughed. He tried to produce delight, but there was a waver to it. In the dark, two conversing shadows could convey meanings only in sound. Fletcher came through as determined but scared. Slowly he lowered himself to his seat on the stern. Harry watched the stars appearing as Fletcher's head dropped below his own level.

There was no possibility that Fletcher would be invited inside. They both knew that. Harry stood with his back to the cabin, until he realized what a target his silhouette presented. He allowed himself to slip down, leaning back against the cabin wall and revealing huge expanses of lighter western sky.

'We've gotta talk, Harry.'

'I've got nothin' to say to you.'

'You've bin making a big fool of yerself. I thought I better warn you.'

Harry rubbed his face with his palms. It was true, he had. The rasping sound held its own warning. Harry knew the glib, apologetic voice that Fletcher used, as a barrier to aggression. It was the tone he'd employed when regretting that Harry would have to die. Harry was no longer impressed. He had to bear in mind that this could be Detective Constable Fletcher, still well into his act. Virginia would have had time to prime him and instruct him. But the pistol was confusing. Harry, like everyone who'd ever operated on the wrong side of the law, knew exactly the situations under which weapons were issued to police officers. He did not feel he met those requirements. Expectations of armed opposition, that was it. Since when had Harry gained that reputation? he wondered.

'Warn away,' he said, 'but make it quick. Two minutes, and you're in the drink.'

'That woman y're workin' with,' said Fletcher. 'You wanna be careful.'

'You know her?'

'Heard. An interfering bitch, that one. Get yer in trouble, that one will.'

The cabin wall creaked as Harry moved his shoulders. 'What did you hear?' His voice was gentle, the words carefully pronounced.

'She's got friends in the fuzz. Dad's some high up. She plays at it, Harry. Bored outa her pants, and plays coppers on her own. A detective marnkee, they call it.'

'Detective what?'

'French for frustrated.'

'Where'd y' pick that up, Fletcher?'

'You're ignorant, Harry. An ignorant slob . . .' Fletcher detected movement. The metallic click was clear in the night. Harry knew that sound – a revolver being cocked. 'Gently, Harry. Don't be more stupid than y' can help. I couldn't miss.'

Harry's voice grated. 'Say it, and sod off.'

'You're playing outa y'r league, Harry. It's known as slummin'. Gives 'em a kick to see how the poor, stupid oafs like you live. Don't let her make a fool outa you.'

'Had some, Fletcher? That it, is it?' The deep rumble of Harry's voice should have been a warning.

'Watch yerself...'

'Angela an' you, Fletcher. Slummin'. She couldn't get lower down in the gutters. I got no time for you, you an' your threats.' He produced a fair imitation of Fletcher's whine. 'Y' can see I gotta take the law in me own hands, Harry! Don't make me laugh! You wasn't her husband. A girl like that – she'd no more marry a creep like you...'

'Who said marry?'

'You did. Said she was your wife.'

Fletcher suddenly laughed, tossing it at Harry's hot anger like a spray of foam. 'Harry, Harry! You weird old-fashioned lad, you! That's for the religious nuts. Do you take this woman ... a loada crap. What's it to them? A girl an' a feller want to get together, so whose business is that except theirs?'

'A contract. Kind of a contract, Fletcher.'

'Who needs contracts? When they got yer into that warehouse job, where was yer contract? Did you get it on paper, Harry? Nah. Stuck a gun in yer hand and said they'd pick you up. Contract! This Angela an' me, we met in a pub, see, and that was it. We decided to shack up together, so we did. It's called a common-law wife. An' that's legal words. Common-law wife. Makes it legal, Harry. Six months we was together ... Angie an' me, an' you know somethin'? A bit more of her argie-bargin' and I might've made it to that registry place. Not her husband? Y' wanta test it out, Harry? All you gotta do is tell me you did her in at the lay-by. Won't go any further. Just that they'll dig yer outa the canal with a bullet in your big bloody thick head.'

It was not so much the sincerity of this speech that struck Harry, as the fact that in the dark he was no longer facing the Fletcher he knew. The voice held firmness and confidence. There was attack in it. Of course, Harry had to allow for the fact that Fletcher was holding in his hands two pounds of metal that had a reputation for inspiring self-confidence.

'I didn't kill her.'

'Y' got somebody else lined up for it?'

'No. But...'

'Then you see, Harry, I can give yer a bit more time ... not much, 'cause this thing gets heavy to carry around. A few days, mebbe. Then, Harry ... well, you do see what I gotta do?'

There was no sound as Fletcher's feet moved on the deck surface, as he was wearing joggers, but at one side of his head a star appeared, and two the other side disappeared. The old and familiar Fletcher voice had returned, the voice that had made it easy for Harry to accept that Angela would never have associated with such a person. But he'd met a harder and more commanding Fletcher, a man who knew what he wanted, and such a man could well attract a young woman with an eye to adventure and excitement, and with rejection of society's morals in her heart.

'Wait!' said Harry.

Fletcher continued to move, until he was standing on the wharf.

'Y' got somethin' to say?'

'Who did the bank job, Fletcher?'

'What bank job?'

'The day she died. The bank job. Y' know what I mean.' Harry got to his feet, stretching with his hands reaching high. 'Y'r a sharp lad, Vic . . .' He didn't realize he'd slipped back to Christian names. 'Nose t' the gutter, you'd sniff out anythin' smelly. And that job stank. Stank of somebody big behind it, who's laundered the money . . . and you'd know.'

'Come off it.' There was uneasiness in Fletcher's voice. He ought really to have walked away, but he hesitated. 'What y'rafter?'

'I want to meet him – the guy who set it up.'

'You do that and you've had it, Harry. Y' know how it is – nobody's left alive to tell. And you're mine, Harry.' The snigger was a soft comment.

'So you know?'

'I know nothin', I never said nothin'. Forget it, Harry, you're handlin' red-hot iron.'

'I only want to speak to him.'

Fletcher laughed and turned away. 'Stay alive, Harry, stay alive.'

Harry stood on the deck of his home. He made no move to go below to his quarters, but stood without moving for a long time. Thoughts always took a while to sort themselves out with Harry. He stood until the light completely faded away, so that Sergeant Tranter, in the sunken doorway that Virginia had favoured, could no longer detect whether he was still there.

Then Tranter left, but Harry remained almost motionless in the darkness for a full hour after that.

*   *   *

The house was three miles out of town, beyond the industrial development that had threatened to spread and envelop it, until the intervention of the recession. In anticipation of the expected invasion, the stately and weathered homes in that district, formerly treasured in their two acres of ground, had been allowed to deteriorate, until the weathering had progressed to the stage of dilapidation. But dilapidation was an inverted snobbery with their owners, a gesture, like jeans and casual shirts, that told the world you had money that was doing better things.

In the Victorian, solid house called The Chestnuts, ACC Oliver Brent failed to notice the trend, so that his home was in full repair, painted when necessary, gutters replaced, bathrooms refurbished, kitchen modernized. He was unaware of any social solecism, as he would have been unaware of the industrial encroachment, had it occurred. Brent was a self-contained man, introverted and dedicated. He lived only for his interests, on which he completely concentrated his attention to the total exclusion of all other matters. Three interests: law and order, his roses, and his daughter, Virginia.

After forty years of dedication to the police force, he believed he knew something about police work. On roses, he believed himself to be an expert. But thirty years of living with Virginia had taught him only one thing: that he didn't understand one aspect of her. Sympathize, yes, he could do that, which was a form of understanding, but this was a selfish sympathy because in so many ways she was a reflection of himself. Wasn't he just as independent? He had to admit it. But he hadn't thrown it at people as she did. Had he? That she could lock herself away in her thoughts and completely exclude him, he could understand. He'd been accused of it himself. But ... was it, from him, so hurtful? Had he so wilfully rejected all offers of assistance as she did? No wonder he was feared, if that were the case. Feared for his fierce dogmatism, he knew that. And yet, was that really no more than dedication to his duties?

Yet Virginia had no duties. She almost scorned her inherited role of housekeeper. Her mother had died at her birth, so that she had grown up as the natural lady of the house. And rejected it. She had insisted on a professional housekeeper, whom they still kept after fifteen years, and who could not, now, have been driven away with whips. Ada Harcourt loved Virginia as she did her father, though perhaps with less pain and anxiety.

He had begged Virginia to join the force. She was a natural for it. He had weaned her on tales of the police, stories of his cases, fables of the force. She was physically fit, with the brain for detail and patience that the force required. But she had scorned it. Oh, he knew what she balked at, though she never explained. She could never have accepted the discipline. Virginia was herself, unto herself, and in it she was alone, if not lonely.

But hadn't he, too, been completely selfish where his loves were involved?

Of the three, his greatest love was Virginia. Sometimes, seeing her quietly pacing the paths of the rose garden in the failing light, something would catch in his throat. Two of his beauties complementing each other. Sometimes, catching that light in her eyes when she saw through and beyond a problem, his pride nearly choked him. And when, in her moods of almost manic joy, she would throw her arms around him, for no other reason than that he was there, he could find himself unable to reply to her question: isn't it marvellous, daddy? Whatever it might be. She was sufficiently secretive to fail to mention that detail, assuming he was sharing it. As he was . . . sharing her joy if not her reason.

And now they rarely discussed his work, which she seemed to scorn since it had become mainly administrative.

She had returned home that evening too late for dinner, so that he'd dined alone, worried but not showing it. She had said she'd eaten out, but didn't seem to remember where or when. The Mercedes was covered with dust, and seemed depleted with effort. She had driven 180 miles, most of them fast, and her eyes held the blank, unfocused look of a person who has seen nothing but the road for a long while.

'Join me for coffee?' he said.

'Yes.' She stared at him blankly. 'Oh . . . yes.'

She led the way into the drawing room, the long, high room that overlooked the valley, with the hills beyond. Tara was at her heels. Brent observed the drooped tail and the misery in Tara's eyes, and knew from the dog more than he could observe from

69

Virginia's impassive face.

The sun had already set behind the hills, but there was still a glowing orange in the sky. He deliberately did not put on any lights, but crossed to his favourite chair by the tall windows and waited until Ada had been in with the tray. Virginia stood looking out at the view she had watched through thirty summers. Her back he saw was straight, held in her defiant stance. Tara appealed with his eyes.

'Father,' she said, 'I need your help.'

He raised his eyebrows. His pipe was taking a long time to prepare. When she called him father it meant they were speaking formally

'Delighted,' he murmured, not meaning he'd be delighted to comply, but delighted she'd asked.

'Can you get a team out to Porchester, and have a quarry dragged?'

The match burnt away to his fingers before he shook it out. 'I'd need a damn good reason.'

'I believe there's a car in there, probably with a man in it.'

'Believe? That's hardly strong enough. Where did you acquire this belief?'

She knew he was tossing her formality back. 'It was Harry's idea. It seems valid. The circumstances seem to fit the possibility.'

'It's not enough. A big job, that would be, and expensive.'

She made an impatient gesture.

'This Harry,' he said. 'Would this be the tough character you wanted to meet . . .'

'Yes.'

'The backstreet thug you thought might help you with Angela's . . .'

'Yes!' Now the monosyllable was crisp.

'Then I'm not sure I'd trust his mental processes.' He cocked his head on one side as he drew on his pipe. The glow from it was bright in the half light. 'More brawn than brains, probably.'

She turned to face him, and though he couldn't see it he sensed her grimace of impatience. 'He's a big man with a heavy brain. But when he stirs it into action it can work as fast as his body.'

'You've seen this?' he murmured. 'This fast action?'

'Daddy, I think he saved my life today.'

He paused, drawing on his pipe to inhale the shock. 'Then you must bring him here, and I'll thank him.'

'I can't do that.'

'You're ashamed of your father?'

Her tongue clicked. 'We had words.'

'Ah.'

'I as good as accused a friend of his of murder. Angela's murder.'

'Man friend or woman friend?'

'Woman.'

'Then that explains it.'

'Daddy, when you're in this mood . . . what d'you mean by that?'

'It would make it difficult for you to apologize.'

'I have . . . had no intention of apologizing.'

'I wouldn't expect it of you. It takes strength of character.'

She was so long in replying that he feared he'd alienated her. When she did finally speak she surprised him, her voice was so soft, so loaded with affection.

'I know you don't want me to go on with this, daddy, and I know I was late getting home, and you were worried. I drove and I drove. Leave it at that. But when you try to rattle me and force my hand, I know you're a little bit more than worried. You're trying to make me drop this, and it will not work. You know it and I know it. I will not apologize to Harry, because he's a stubborn idiot, and because my theory was valid. He'll see that . . .'

She stopped. He was chuckling. The pipe was bobbing up and down.

'Oh damn you, daddy, you're such a blasted fraud!'

'I have to be pretty crafty to keep up with you, my dear. This Harry person . . . you clearly admire him. No, let me finish, please. You won't be able to think straight until you've apologized . . .'

'But it was *him* . . .'

'All the more reason to apologize. You really must bring him for me to see.' He left it at that. He didn't want to say: to see the first person he'd ever known to unsettle her.

'There's another way to go at it, if you won't do the dragging of the quarry.'

'Take it that I'm reluctant.'

'That bank job. May the seventeenth, four years ago. And it's no good you saying which bank job, because I'm sure you're following this, through Paul. I want to know who did it, fixed it, planned it, master-minded it. Call it what you like.'

'Why?' He bit the word into the pipe stem.

'I want to speak to him.'

'Oh dear Lord!' he said. 'The answer, my dear, is no. A firm and categorical no.'

'Now daddy . . .'

'Not your little girl act, please. And anyway, if we knew, we'd have him inside.'

'You know that's not true. You know who it was. You always do, you or your supers and your inspectors and sergeants. You know, but can't touch him because there's no evidence. Don't deny it, because I know your job inside and out. There'll be a name somewhere in the file. All I want is that name.'

'Not under any circumstances. For you to see and speak to him . . .'

'So you *do* know.'

'Whatever him it might be – they're all the same. For you to meet him and expect to walk away again, I'd have to send you in with a couple of armoured cars and a team of marksmen. And how would *that* look in the Sunday papers?'

'Daddy . . .'

'No.'

'Then I'll have to ask Paul.'

'If he told you, I'd have him back in uniform walking the streets.'

'I'll get it out of him if I have to go to bed with him.'

'If you did that, my dear, he wouldn't have the breath left . . .'

They burst out laughing together, and he was well satisfied that he'd heard the last of that ridiculous idea.

But he hadn't.

Harry combed the town, exploring all the back street corners and the dives only he knew fully. He tried first the junk shops, which had once called themselves pawnbrokers, but no one admitted having handled the jewellery. He tried the fences, even the ones the police knew and had questioned, climbing concrete stairs in high-rise council flats, floating silently to penthouses in big-money blocks. No one had fenced the proceeds of the jewellery shop job.

He then switched to the money from the bank job, exploring cellars where poker games had to be waited through, but no one admitted unloading any of it on a straight flush. He explored sleazy clubs that were new enough to have been financed by questionable cash. All he got was thrown out. He mounted wooden stairs to harsh, hollow rooms where money was loaned on no security other than your lifeblood, progressed as far as the rear interview rooms of finance houses where rates were high but the loans were in straight cash, but no one admitted laundering over a hundred grand. Not even after persuasion. He trailed down alleys to itinerant jewellers, gave passwords to burly guards of semi-legal diamond merchants, but no one knew of cash being converted into gem stones. Nothing.

Then he looked for anyone who might have been involved in the bank job, had to fight his way out of Clancy's night spot, was invited into a pub yard gents, where Big Henry Brown showed him an open razor and lost an earlobe for his trouble, was kicked out of a gay bar by two ladies who might well have been female, and got nowhere.

Until he was joined at a table in the Mute Swan by Evan Williams, a police informer who obliged his friends by sometimes selling false information to the police, and therefore remained whole.

'What you drinkin', Evan?'

'Just a quick word, Harry.'

'I'll get 'em in.'

'Can't stop. The word's around you've bin asking questions.'

'I wonder how that got about.'

'Concernin' the bank job.'

'You know something?'

'I know you'd stay alive if you stop askin'.'

'I'll do that when I've got a name.'

'A tenner'll save your life, Harry.'

'How so?'

'Save you askin' any more.'

Harry had got a tenner. Ten pounds and forty-seven pence to be exact, to last him to next Tuesday, his Social Security pay-day. Still . . . might not see Tuesday, and die with it in his pocket. He slipped it under the table and felt it whipped away.

Evan Williams leaned forward and whispered an Irish name, which sounded strange in a Welsh accent.

She had Tara with her again when Sergeant Paul Tranter jogged to the park bench and sat panting beside her. Tara gave a low, soft growl, sensing the determined opposition Paul had brought with him. Or the sweat.

'I want a name, Paul.' She was in no mood for time-wasting chat.

'So I heard. Your father's been on the line.'

'Called you in? On the mat?'

'He doesn't call mere sergeants into his office.'

'Oh Paul, poor you.'

'And the answer's no.'

She lifted her chin, staring straight ahead. 'I thought I might tell him about the time you tricked him into going alone into that bar ... we laughed about it then, you and I. I wonder whether he'd laugh now.'

'You were only twelve!'

'Or that time when you both went to arrest Molly Durkins...'

Tranter had thought he was right out of sweat, but a fresh flood ran down his back. 'Whatever I say, I'm caught. So it's still no.'

She thought about that for a few moments, producing her brown cigarettes and her pistol lighter. She blew out smoke. 'Can you get me a gun licence, Paul?'

He coughed – or laughed – and choked into his fist. 'In no way.'

'I need a pistol like this.' She opened her palm and showed him the lighter. He got to his feet.

'I'll tell your father what it is you need. I'm in no doubt, myself, but I think he'll settle for putting you in protective custody.'

'Paul, you're forcing my hand. There's something I don't want to do ...'

'But you'll do it.' He forced his legs into a jog on the spot. 'You always did, always will.' He let in his mental clutch, and trotted away.

Tara looked up at her, the end of his tail twitching.

'This time,' she said, 'you can come with me.'

Together they went to apologize to Harry.

Hanger Lane and the wharf presented a different face in the daylight, a dirty, dilapidated and depressed face. She felt only sadness. Here, at one time, there must have been an unbroken
bustle of activity, of life and the pursuit of continuing existence.
But the world had turned its back on it, did not reach it with any
distant sound of traffic, not even a stench of fumes. The canal
presented a flat, undisturbed sheet of green, a lawn that could be
walked across. The decrepit barges seemed to grow from the
depths instead of sinking into them. There was no sound or
movement from Harry's.

Virginia had scorned any sort of disguise. She was in slacks
and shirt, with a grey blouson, her hair neat and her cheeks
flushed.

'Harry! Are you home?'

He came up on the deck with a wet undervest dripping from
his hand, stripped to the waist so that he revealed further scars
from past adventures.

'I came to tell you . . .'

'There's something I've gotta tell you . . .'

They spoke together and laughed at the same time. She cut
into it by saying: 'I was wrong about Cynthia. I wanted to say I'm
sorry, Harry.'

He made a gesture with his vest, spraying her with detergent
water, and jumped across to the wharf.

'It was all crazy, anyway. Angela . . . on her way t' meet
Charlie . . . the last place she'd phone would be his home.'

'Clever Harry.'

They looked at each other. He shrugged. Her lips quivered.
She said: 'Meet Tara. Tara, this is Harry.'

Harry crouched, glad of the chance not to look too deeply into
her eyes. These two knew each other at once for what they were,
recognized each other. Tara, who didn't know he bore a feminine
name, would flare into fury at the first threat to his mistress.
Offer friendship, and he was a sloppy mess of a dog. They knew
each other. Tara licked Harry's nose, so like a piece of steak.
Harry straightened.

'I know who master-minded the bank job,' he said.

'Good.' She was being very calm and sensible. 'So we'll go and see him.' Yet her heart raced.

'Not easy.'

'It's the only direction we can go now. Don't you see that, Harry? Charlie disappeared, and we'll have to find out where.'

'Nobody gets to see Sean O'Loughlin,' he assured her. 'I won't ask you aboard, it's chaos in there.'

'Laundry day, Harry?'

'Another ten minutes and I'd've been washing me jeans.' He glanced down at them.

She considered this phenomenon, a man with only one pair of pants. 'You can get to see him, Harry. You know everybody.'

'I know *him*. Met him in Pentonville, the one time they got anything on him, an' that was only wrongful diversion.'

'Conversion. Well, there you are. You met him inside. Old mates.'

'He was the only con nobody'd talk to. Little chap, nothing to him, an' nobody *dared* talk to him.'

'Scares you, does he?'

'Scares me,' he agreed. 'Look . . . can I meet you . . .'

'I'll wait.'

It was not as she had expected it to be, this reunion. She had imagined everything from a solemn and brusque handshake to a wild swoop into each other's arms. She could not know that for Harry their disagreement had ceased to exist. He had satisfied himself, by way of deep pondering, that his harsh thoughts about her professional position and her motivations had been false. This had been simple, because he'd wanted to persuade himself. But his almost savage desire – determination – to go on with it had been difficult to sort out. Somewhere in there was the awareness that he'd left Angela, whom he'd quietly liked, to be killed at the lay-by, so that he owed her the truth. Somewhere was a dogged loyalty to Virginia, in spite of the fact that she was not one of his own people, in his own world. But the most important was his eventual rejection of any impelling force inspired by Vic Fletcher's threats. He could not have gone on, he knew, if the main reason for continuing was fear.

So his welcome for Virginia was casual. They had not met for three days, because each had had work to do on it. His work, the persistent search for a name, he even felt to be on Virginia's instructions. He had an idea she would need this name. *They* would.

None of this could Virginia be expected to understand. There was simply in her a sense of relief, of a warm feeling that she was no longer alone. This was strange; she had coveted her independence. But in the past three days she had been desperately lonely. It had taken a determined emotional effort to consider continuing alone.

'I'll wait,' she repeated, because Harry was staring at her in embarrassment.

'I've gotta wash all me things,' he said at last. 'And wait for 'em to dry.'

'This is ridiculous,' she declared, standing with her feet apart. 'How can you *live* with only one outfit?'

'I didn't wanta dirty your seats.'

'I shall be,' she said flatly, 'in the bar at the Crown Hotel...'

'Posh.'

'At seven this evening. And seeing that you'll be clean and sweet-smelling, you'll be welcome there.'

'I couldn't...' He stopped.

'What?'

'Couldn't buy a tonic water at their prices.' He plunged on. 'I spent my last tenner getting that name.'

'You got it for ten pounds?'

He nodded.

'Then we go dutch on it, Harry. With my fiver I'll buy you a pint of bitter and a steak in the restaurant. No ... I'm not having any argument. And we'll discuss clothes for you.'

'I'm not letting you...'

'I'm warning you, Harry Hodnutt. Any more opposition, and I'm going to go on with this without you. Sean O'Loughlin, did you say?' She nodded, seeing she had him. 'I'm just not going to have you wasting hours of good time whenever you need a clean shirt. Whatever next!'

He watched her humbly as she whirled round and walked away. It occurred to him that the dog's rump moved in rhythm with hers.

At seven on the dot he presented himself at the bar of the Crown Hotel, the town's most respectable hotel, boasting two

77

and a half stars. He was wearing dark grey slacks which might have been tailored for him, a blue shirt, and an anorak that probably boasted a French name tag. No tie. A snow-white vest peeped above the V of the shirt.

'Whatever's happened?' She slid from the bar stool. 'Where did . . . ?'

'I looked for a pensioner my size and beat him up.'

'Seriously.'

'Toby Trent, the fence, owed me a favour, and I called it in. This is part of a warehouse job . . .'

'Harry!' she said warningly.

He shrugged. 'It's true.'

'Couldn't he find you a tie?'

'Half a dozen. But I couldn't do the knot. Never owned a tie before.'

'Lord, Harry, what you've missed.'

They drank, they went in to eat, and took long enough over the meal to make their plans.

'He owns a lake in Shropshire,' he said. 'Sean Lake, he calls it. Got a house on the island in the middle. We can't just knock on his door. We wouldn't even reach the island.'

'So how do we do it?'

'We ask. If he'll see us, then he sends a boat over. If not, we're out of luck, short of hiring a helicopter and going in with guns blazing.'

'Then we'd better think of a good excuse for seeing him.'

He looked past a chunk of steak at her, waving the fork. 'You still haven't got it, have you? I bin asking around. The word would get back to him. Evan Williams was *told* to give me the name. Otherwise he wouldn't have dared. A tenner? He wouldn't have opened his mouth for a thousand and a one-way ticket to Brazil. It means O'Loughlin wants to see *us*. It was what I was bankin' on when I started askin'.'

He bit on the steak and munched complacently. She eyed him with wonder.

'You're not stupid, are you Harry?'

'No ma'am. And I was born in this town. The slums're my home.'

'So what we do,' she said, refilling his glass with a Piesporter he didn't realize was absorbing the fiver, 'is keep him waiting. If he wants to see us, we don't rush it.'

'Not too long, though.'

'Just while we look into something else. I've been thinking. Don't frown, it's insulting. We know Angela had a tenpence coin for one phone call, and probably used it. The most obvious person she'd try to call would be Charlie Braine, because she was stranded. But Charlie's the last person who'd have killed her, if they were going away together. So perhaps it's entirely wrong to connect her one phone call with the person who killed her.'

Harry picked up his napkin, stared at it, and decided it was permissible to dab his lips with it. 'That leaves nobody, and we'd be back to a casual passer-by.'

'Not necessarily. There *was* one person who knew where she was, apart from you. Officer Graham, who was instructed to go and pick her up.'

'But that's just about as crazy. *He'd* be casual, the copper who just happened to be on duty in a car in that area.'

'So we go and check that.'

'But she wasn't raped. Nothing like that.'

'I know that. But Officer Graham is Woman Police Constable Freda Graham. So rape doesn't arise, does it? What're you having for afters?'

'What's tropical fruit sorbett?'

'It's sorbay, and you'll like it. I've got daddy to arrange for us to meet her. She's off-duty at ten.'

WPC Freda Graham had a neat and tidy second floor flat in a recently completed private ownership block. It stood in a squat U on the western outskirts of town, and had an air of quiet dignity. The centre of the U constituted parking space, and was plentifully scattered with cars in the young executive range.

She opened the door. They had watched her drive up in her own Volkswagen Golf, and given her time to change out of uniform. What she had changed into was lounging pyjamas with a wrap over them. Nothing about this outfit disguised her physical size, but whether she intended to deplete or accentuate it was uncertain. She had a plump, almost expressionless face, unless the flush was of anger. Her figure was full, her lips large, her stance aggressive. She was nervous and annoyed.

'Virginia Brent,' said Virginia.

'I suppose you'd better come in.' Freda Graham stood back,

79

her movements light for her size.

The door opened directly into her living room. It was furnished as though she'd ordered it for this visit, and seemed to stand where it had been placed, still waiting for organization. The room did not give an impression of comfort, though each individual item was comfortable. There was nothing to indicate an interest or occupation in Freda Graham's private life.

She gestured to a chair, and sat opposite to it on a two-seater settee that seemed to have been woven rather than built. Harry, ignored, slid round the wall and found an upright chair, sat, remembered he now possessed creases, and eased his slacks at the knees.

'I was told to expect you.' It was grudging. 'Are you anything to do with the old man . . . ?'

'ACC Brent is my father, and I'm sorry it was put to you like that.'

'I was told to answer questions.'

'Or like that.' Virginia smiled. Harry moved uneasily. The two women had nothing in common. They were already striking sparks. 'This has no connection with my father, and I wanted it to be informal. I'm interested in the death of Angela Reed.'

'Oh . . . that.' The unrevealing face set into a blank mask.

'I believe you were the officer who was sent to pick her up.'

'Stupid woman. She was told to stay there. Why can't they do as they're told?' It was what Freda Graham would expect of the public.

'Perhaps, to her, the word "there" would mean the lay-by. That was where she'd been left.'

'Yes.'

'You knew that?'

'No. I was told the location of the phone box.'

'So you went there, and she wasn't waiting, so you went away?'

'Of course not.'

When she seemed not to be about to go on, Virginia said gently: 'Then what did you do?'

'I cruised around, all the roads she could have taken – four directions, for your information – as far as she could be expected to have walked in the time.'

'Which was?'

80

'I beg your pardon?'

'How long between the time you received the call and when you arrived at the phone booth?'

Freda Graham stared at her blankly, got up, found a packet of cigarettes, and returned with one bobbing in her lips. She wore no make-up, but her lips were full and red.

'I don't like this. A police officer questioned by a civilian . . .'

'Surely that's not unusual. You must have answered questions such as: can you tell me the way to so-and-so?'

'That's different.'

'Because this is relating to your duties? But I'm only asking for facts, nothing that can betray official secrets. And you needn't reply if you feel under any pressure.'

Ash was flickered angrily towards an ashtray. 'For what good it'll do you . . . the call came at two thirty-seven, and it was a nine minutes' run to the phone box.'

'Thank you. Then she couldn't have walked far.'

'I didn't see her.'

'Perhaps she was dead by then.'

'I think not.' Freda's voice held contempt.

But Virginia's was as smooth as cream. 'She was found, in that road-grit bin, at four-forty . . .'

'By me.'

'And the doctor believed she'd been dead for only a short while before then.'

'No more than half an hour.'

'So she was alive for at least an hour and a half after her phone call.'

'I can work that out myself.'

'Yet you didn't catch a glimpse of her?'

'No.'

Freda was losing patience. The full lips were becoming thinner, the unplucked eyebrows creeping closer together.

'It didn't occur to you that she could've been hiding from you?'

'Not at that time. Later . . .' She shook her head, annoyed with herself for offering something.

'Later?'

'It seemed she could have been hiding.'

'Perhaps she regretted her 999 call.'

'She certainly must've phoned somebody else, who came

along and killed her.'

'That's what you thought happened?' Virginia waited, but there was no response. 'Afterwards,' she suggested.

Freda nodded, looking down, then up again in defiance. 'When it was too late.'

'Too late to save her?'

'I called in and reported and was told to return to my patrol. But by that time they'd got that Hodnutt creature . . .'

'Me,' said Harry proudly, glad to slip in his single word.

Her head came round sharply. 'What in God's name's this?'

'This is Harry Hodnutt. Shall we say I'm checking on his statement?'

'Say what you like. I'm going to ask you to leave.'

'Does his presence upset you? If so, I'm sure he'd wait outside.'

She struggled with her emotions for a moment, then stabbed them out beneath the end of her cigarette. 'Let him stay. He'll know the truth of this. He told them he'd left her in the lay-by, so they sent me back to have another look.'

'By which time it *was* too late.'

'Are you trying to get at me?'

'Sorry. By no means. Your actions were in no way reprehensible.'

'Well thank you for that, I'm sure. Who the hell're you to pass judgement?' Then she made an effort, and turned her bitterness in another direction. 'I got a reprimand for that. A big X on my record. Or I'd be a sergeant by now.'

'No commendation for finding her so cleverly – the second time round?'

'Ha!' Freda laughed flatly. On her face a laugh was ugly.

'In the grit bin? Inspiration, was that?'

'My eyes fell on it. Yellow. Standing there. I had a feeling.'

'No clue then? Nothing to point to it, lying by it or something?'

'Such as?'

'A tenpence coin, perhaps.'

'What the hell're you talking about?'

'Or perhaps a shoe?' At Freda's blank expression, Virginia went on: 'She didn't have any shoes on.'

'Didn't she? I never knew that.'

'You didn't notice?'

'You don't imagine I *looked*? One glance, and I dropped the lid.'

'So . . . no shoe lying around?'

'As though I'd have touched it if there had been! I was younger then, but not a damned amateur.'

'And that was aimed at me,' said Virginia, smiling.

'Right between the eyes,' Freda Graham agreed. 'And now . . .' Rising to her feet. 'I'll have to ask you to leave.'

Virginia nodded, stood and turned to Harry. 'Anything you want to ask, Harry?'

Harry stared at the outraged glare from Freda, and shook his head.

They left. The door was closed a little too close to their heels. They walked back to the car.

'An' a right waste of time that was,' said Harry.

'Oh, I don't know. Want to drive, Harry? No? Right.'

When she was pulling out onto the street he said: 'What did it get us?'

'A clearer picture, perhaps. Angela must have hung around for anything up to an hour and a half, obviously waiting for somebody. And hiding while she did the waiting.'

'The other side of that five-barred gate,' he suggested.

'Could be. She waited until somebody came, and that person killed her.'

'You're sayin' she managed to contact Charlie, and as soon as he could get there he came . . .'

'And hit her with his stiletto heel, Harry?'

'With *hers*?'

'Then what happened to the other, if he took the murder one away?'

'Search me.'

'It's beginning to worry me,' she admitted. 'Really worry me. Why would a man kill her with her own shoe, and then take away *both* of them?'

'You think it points to a woman? Using her own.'

'It would still mean that both of Angela's were taken away. It's just that I can't see why.'

83

9

The spell of fine weather was slinking towards the horizon when they headed into Shropshire. Ahead, the sky was uneasy, with heavy clouds bustling in from the west. The forecast had been for thundery showers.

It was ten o'clock the following morning. Once again she had picked him up in the town square, this time looking for a big, smartly dressed man. He had on another outfit: T-shirt with a leather jacket over it, new jeans that could have been designed for him, and soft tan leather shoes.

'Another change, Harry? Your fence must have been very grateful.'

'We shared a cell, and I kept the goons off him in the showers. He wanted to fit me out with an Italian suit, but y' got to draw the line somewhere. I insisted on British goods.'

'Smart, but casual,' she commented, held by the traffic lights at Trinity Street.

'Gotta impress O'Loughlin. Can't let him know I'm broke. Money impresses money. Where'd you get the Range Rover?'

'It's my father's. I looked for the lake on the map, and couldn't find it, but there were a lot of minor roads, so I played safe.'

They drove on in silence. Harry was wondering what she expected to get out of the coming visit, and whether she realized that only he would be expected by O'Loughlin. If they allowed her on the island, would she let Harry do the talking? O'Loughlin would be able to talk more easily with one of his own kind, even if Harry was only a minor, buckled cog in the machinery and O'Loughlin the main spring.

He wondered if she would brief him, but when she eventually spoke she was still thinking about Freda Graham.

'What did you think about our WPC Graham, Harry?'

'A tough character. Wouldn't take her long to clear a pub.'

'She didn't like you.'

'Because I was on the wrong side of the fence.'

'Not that, I think. She fancied me.'

'She what?' Harry twisted on the seat. 'She'd have had your eyes out . . .'

'No. She was aggressive because I wouldn't sweet-talk her. Don't you realize why I kept it so formal?' She glanced at him, her eyes bright. 'She scared me, Harry.'

'Scared?'

'You're such an innocent, that's your trouble.'

While Harry was considering this insult, she was hunting ahead for signposts. She said: 'You told me, aim for Craven Arms. That's it, up ahead. Where to now? I hope you know.'

'Roughly. Where's your map?'

They pulled in to the side of the road and consulted her three miles to the inch atlas. At that scale the lake, when he thought he'd found it, was tiny, and bore no name. Not even minor roads seemed to go near it, the only access appearing to be dotted lines.

'Left up here,' he said, 'and I'll guide you.'

They ran out of road with nothing but dark trees and tangled slopes ahead. It had been a long while since they had seen a sign of habitation. They were faced by a ride cut through woodland, a ride which soon forked, split again, crossed a ridge, plunged across a valley inhabited by a few sheep and a family of deer, negotiated a log bridge over a crisp, white stream, and eventually reached a crossing with one arm signposted: Sean Lake. The sign was a wooden slat nailed crookedly to a tree. It was small. Beneath it, much more prominent, was the sign: NO ADMITTANCE.

'Success,' said Harry. 'Carry on.'

They came down through the trees to a clearing on the edge of the water. The motionless lake was holding its breath in the hush before a storm, with crows calling warnings in the trees and wild geese paddling hurriedly beneath the overhanging branches.

It was not a large lake, but it would have required an experienced swimmer to reach the island in the centre of it. The island itself was thickly wooded, and the house was barely visible amongst the trees, being of log construction. They could see the runway down from it to the water, the jetty, and the two motor launches berthed at it, their paintwork bright in the half-light.

In front of them was another wooden jetty, with a post to one side of it, affixed to it a wooden construction like a nesting box. Harry said: 'Come on,' and led the way. His halting stride gave an impression of confidence, because he knew they were being observed, probably from a telescope on the house roof. He was also aware that they had reached this far only by the kind permission of the advance defences in the woodland they had just driven through. The very fact that they had reached the lake meant they were expected – at least, he was – so that when he opened the door in the front of the box and took out the phone he simply answered the snapped: 'Yes?' with the equally abrupt statement: 'Harry Hodnutt to see Sean O'Loughlin.'

'Wait,' said the voice. The phone clicked off.

'We wait,' said Harry.

Across the water, two tiny figures were seen walking down to the jetty and jumping into one of the motor boats. The engine fired with a throb of power. O'Loughlin, land-bound, would be satisfied with nothing less than a racing cruiser. Harry wondered how they'd got it there.

The cruiser putt-putted up to the jetty and nudged it gently. The two tiny figures turned out to be two very large and expressionless toughs in unnecessarily bulky parkas to hide the weaponry. There seemed no point in hiding it, thought Harry, but they'd have felt naked without their underarm reach for the dramatic snap draw. And useless.

They might have been twins, apart from their hair. The ginger one said to Harry: 'Hoist 'em.' Harry did so, and was patted all over. The bald one said to Virginia: 'You too, sister,' using the Bogart lisp.

Harry glanced at her. Her eyes had glazed. Slowly she raised her arms. Impersonally, impassionately, he patted her all over, reached for her shoulder bag and examined its contents, discovered her lighter, sneered at it, and tossed it into the lake. He stood back and nodded to his mate, who gestured towards the cruiser.

Harry led the way, in order not to study Virginia's expression. She was moving stiffly, with delicate precision. The boat took off in a splendid sweep and headed for the island.

During the time they were there they saw no one but those two, Red and Baldy, and Sean O'Loughlin himself. They were taken straight through the house, having no time to register anything but a general air of wealthy lack of taste. O'Loughlin seemed to own everything worth owning, and had packed it all into his headquarters. Out at the back he had a wooden veranda, on piles over the water, and here, apparently because he was in the open air, his only displayed possessions were a table and half a dozen chrome and moulded plastic chairs. Sean O'Loughlin, living the simple life, was dressed in a white silk and mohair suit, a pale blue silk shirt and a maroon silk cravat. He was sitting at the table, one leg negligently crossed over the other knee, and swinging a white Gucci shoe in lizard skin.

It was clear to Virginia that the reason he was sitting was that he was small. Small and mean and casually vicious, if those tiny, almost colourless eyes were anything to go by. A thin face, carved by time, which he clearly resented. Delicate hands, with slim fingers that twitched. He had a tic that flickered the corner of his mouth, so that a smile could easily become a sneer.

'Introduce me, Harry,' he said, his voice as thin as his face, as pale as his eyes, adopting a friendship that was clearly a trap.

'Virginia Brent,' said Harry. 'My friend.' Thus rejecting O'Loughlin's offer. The eyes narrowed fractionally.

'You've been asking around, Harry,' he said casually, looking out at the water.

Red had taken up a position with his back to the guard rail above the lake. Baldy was standing, legs spread, at Virginia's shoulder. She said: 'We would like to trace Charlie Braine.'

The eyes focused on her. 'Anybody ask you?'

'We would also,' she said, 'like to ask your advice about a bank job.'

'Harry?' said O'Loughlin, keeping his eyes on Virginia.

Harry, who had not been briefed, was unsure of Virginia's angle. She was no doubt playing it as it came. He said: 'We'd like to trace Charlie Braine, and also ask your advice about a bank job.'

O'Loughlin tapped a finger on the table surface. Red tensed. O'Loughlin smiled. Baldy took a pace back; the smile had come too close.

'Suppose we decide who's doing the talking. Harry, I know you're not too bright, so . . .' He inclined his head towards her, briefly revealing the edge of his toupee. 'The lady, perhaps? Why do you want to find Charlie Braine?'

'Because,' she said, 'he's missing. He's been missing for four years, from about the time that over a hundred grand in cash disappeared from the Mercantile Bank in Trinity Street.'

'You think they disappeared together?' he asked with distant interest.

'Possibly. The money hasn't stirred up any silt, so it's buried deep.'

'By that, I suppose you mean it hasn't shown?'

'That's what I meant.'

'Can't help you there, I'm afraid.'

'We didn't expect you to,' she assured him. 'We'd hardly come here and expect you to hand over a hundred and twenty thousand in cash, just for the asking. We're not interested in the money.'

His face wavered, then became set. Even the tic ceased to operate. Shock, she decided. 'You're not interested . . . I don't believe it.'

'We're interested in how it was done. The bank job. We thought you would know. When in doubt, consult a specialist, I always say.'

O'Loughlin laughed. At least, he spluttered, and so abruptly that it caught him by surprise and he had to whip up a hand to restrain his lower denture. He recovered. The tic went wild. 'By God, but you've got a nerve.'

Harry thought so, too. He had decided he could take Red, get him over the guard rail before he could draw, but he wasn't sure about Baldy and Virginia. She seemed relaxed, not poised for any violent action, even if there was any possible opposition she could offer to Baldy.

Inside, she was almost paralysed with fear, but the smile she managed seemed genuine from her side of it. This man admired nerve. The bank job, as she'd reconstructed it in her mind, had required nerve and audacity. She was risking everything on her assessment of O'Loughlin.

'I wouldn't venture to ask you whether that bank job was yours,' she said meekly.

'I should hope not.'

'Because I know you're too big for that. It was paltry. You might have planned it. Or you might have heard about it, and admired the technique. It's simply that I would like to hear how that job would have been planned by you – if you *had* planned it . . .'

'So that you can find Charlie Braine?' he cut in, his voice incisive. 'You think it would help you?'

'Exactly.' She seemed pleased at his lightning perception. 'I believe he was involved, in an obscure way.'

O'Loughlin was silent. His eyes wandered, and his two helpers stiffened as his gaze slid past. Virginia waited patiently, perfectly still, although the tension was shooting pains up her legs and her back. She knew only that O'Loughlin had virtually sent for Harry, even if he hadn't expected her. O'Loughlin wanted something. She waited to discover what.

'The risk would be yours,' O'Loughlin said at last. 'During any long discussion I might relax and slip up, and admit I organized it, in which event you couldn't be allowed to leave.'

'Nonsense!' she said, her contempt not entirely forced. 'An admission, here, to Harry and me – what would that mean? Nothing. Let's just assume it was your bank job, and get down to business. You talk or you don't talk. We can't stick red-hot needles under your nails. And you never – *never* – slip up. All we want to do is trace Charlie Braine.'

There was a taut ten seconds of silence. Baldy growled. O'Loughlin covered his mouth with pale fingers. 'Well now,' he said. 'There's a lot of assumptions there. Let me make one of my own. You want Charlie Braine because you think he's still got the money.' It was a statement.

She opened her mouth, decided to say nothing, and closed it.

'We both,' he said softly, 'want Charlie Braine. So perhaps . . . a little co-operation?'

She nodded, holding her breath. His smile was hideous as he went on. 'You've probably assumed I had the money and still have it. No, don't you shake your head at me. Nobody shakes their head at me. But you would assume wrongly. If I'd had the money originally, you believe it couldn't have been converted. Another wrong assumption. And you're assuming this very moment that I'm saying this to convince you it wasn't *my* bank job. Wrong again. Come here.' He crooked a finger. He pointed to a space opposite him.

Baldy snapped to attention and ran to one of the loose chairs, brought it over, and as Virginia slowly advanced to the table, slipped it beneath the bottom he'd so recently fondled.

She sat. O'Loughlin, close to, was even more repelling. She was wondering about his accent. Certainly not Irish – something mid-European.

With an air of benevolent patronage he slipped fingers into one of the pockets of his pristine waistcoat. She saw that he wore a fob watch with a gold chain. White gold. The fingers emerged.

'Your palm,' he demanded.

She extended it. Into it he dropped a diamond.

There had never been in her life a desire for jewellery, except in a most modest way. She had thought of large diamonds as being a useless ostentation. This one was blue. It caught from the dark sky a flash of lightning that dwelt in its interior, and captivated her. She drew in her breath. A lifetime of dogmatism flowed away.

'It's beautiful,' she whispered.

'It's worth a hundred grand.' For O'Loughlin, that was its beauty.

'You're telling me,' she asked, 'that *this* is the haul from the bank job?'

'All I'm telling you is its value. It could have come from the bank haul. There are ways of converting money, not necessarily in this country. At a loss, of course. But that . . .' He leaned forward and picked it from her palm, then dropped it again. He leaned closer. His breath smelled of violets. 'That,' he said, so softly that the word barely brushed her ears, 'will be yours, my dear, if you can find Charlie Braine and bring him and the money to me.'

The words 'my dear' on his lips sent a chill up her spine. She did not move her palm when he reached for the diamond again. He was fastidious in making sure their flesh did not make contact. In a second, as a blue flash, the diamond had found its way back into his waistcoat pocket.

She sat back in the chair, breathing quietly and deeply. This, she knew, had been the reason he had agreed to see them . . . to see Harry, in fact. But why should he believe that Harry could produce results, if he, with his organization, could not?

'What makes you think we can find him?' she asked.

'Harry has been out of circulation for four years. Harry knows his way around. He's got contacts I can't reach. My lot . . .' He gestured in contempt to Red and Baldy. 'They don't know anything but which end of a gun you grab hold of.'

'But Harry can't find him. He's tried.' Which wasn't exactly true. 'If there's something you know . . . that you'll tell us . . .

90

then maybe . . .'

'Tell me what you know already.' He wasn't prepared to concede more than he had to.

'If we find the money,' she said, 'why should I bring it to you? I could buy my own diamond. A better one.'

He seemed surprised at that. 'Because I'd send Carl and Llew to see you, to exercise their only ability.' His hand negligently indicated his two protectors.

'Then it's a deal.'

'Tell me,' he repeated, 'what you know already.'

She told him, every detail they had discovered already about the two crimes, or had worked out. She made no mention of Angela or Cynthia. She told him about the two-colour car, the fact that it had been washable paint, the way she believed it had been used as a decoy, driving up Trinity Street while the bank getaway car drove down it. O'Loughlin listened with attention, his face without expression. When she finished he at last took his eyes from her, staring down at his fingers on the table surface. Eventually he looked up.

'Do the police know all this?'

'No. Some Harry knew. Some we've found out. Some we worked out. We're not about to tell the police.'

'You said you weren't interested in the money. Then . . . why?'

'Harry's got a score to settle with Charlie Braine. I believe Braine killed a young woman called Angela Reed.'

O'Loughlin raised an eyebrow.

'In whom I have a close personal interest,' she said. There was a formality in her voice and an impatience in the movement of her shoulders, which rejected any further probing into the matter.

O'Loughlin frowned a complete lack of interest, but Harry found his mind involved again with the question: who, exactly, was Angela Reed? Virginia had not actually agreed that they were sisters. When he was functioning again, O'Loughlin was speaking, his voice a grating sound as he drew venom from somewhere inside himself.

'. . . tell you why I want the money,' he was saying. 'Suppose, for the sake of argument, that I had planned a bank job. Not *that* one, but another, a bigger one. In those circumstances, it might occur to me that a trial run at a smaller bank – such as the Mercan-

91

tile branch you mentioned – would be a good idea. Not risking any good men, of course, on such a paltry job, which could easily go wrong.'

She smoothed the way with flattery. 'I heard it was perfectly planned and wonderfully executed.'

He permitted himself a thin smile, inclining his head a couple of inches. 'In one way, that's why I find the outcome infuriating. Look at the basics. Four men on the bank operation, including the driver. Not my men, as I mentioned.'

'Of course not. As you said, we're only supposing all this.'

'You understand me perfectly. Four men . . . mid-range talent, paid a fixed sum directly from the back pocket, you might say. There was a reason for this. It was all in the timing.'

Beyond the trees lining the far bank, beyond the valley, there was a distant rumble of thunder. For a moment the sky lightened. Virginia glanced at Harry, who had his eyes fixed on her.

'You didn't mention . . .' she said quietly.

Harry got it in a flash. 'I remember now. Charlie kept glancing at his watch. Never saw him wearing a watch before.'

O'Loughlin, prompted by the talk of watches, glanced at his slim, gold Rolex, and frowned. He might have put in a request for a storm, and it was arriving too soon.

'As I said, all in the timing,' he went on. 'They were all supplied with chronometers, set to the second. You will understand why in a moment. There was another aspect to the job.'

'Charlie Braine and his two-coloured car?'

'That was his own idea. Clever, I thought. Yes. It would attract attention, though I wasn't sure it was what was needed. Not too much. But this was no more than a rehearsal for bigger things. It didn't really matter if it all went wrong. Ah! Didn't I tell you I might slip up? It *did* matter, as it turned out. Because it went wrong in the worst possible way.'

Behind his head the lightning almost split the clouds, sending them tossing. The crash was caught by the shoreline trees, and bounced around, rippling the surface of the lake.

'Braine,' he said, 'was *too* damned bright. His job was to pull the jeweller's job and attract the attention of the police. And get out of there at two-eleven exactly. The whole thing was based on time. Two-twelve to the traffic lights, forcing in to his left, and up the hill past the Mercantile . . .'

92

'Just as the others were coming down the hill with their take.' She nodded. So far, nothing new.

'But timed to the second,' he said, his face expressionless as he poised himself to reveal the genius that was facing her. 'To the second. You can see the point of paying them a fixed sum. The instruction was to leave the bank at exactly two-twelve. Without the fixed payment they would have been tempted to delay and get as much as they could. That was not the purpose of the exercise, but as it happened they struck lucky. Leaving at precisely two-twelve, they could be expected to be on a certain stretch of the road at the same time as Braine, within a couple of hundred yards. You know that street?' She nodded. 'Straight,' he reminded her. 'Fairly wide. They were both, the getaway car and Braine's car, to be in their outside lanes, Braine with his off-side rear window open.'

Again she glanced at Harry, whose face was abruptly stark white from a flash of lightning that seemed to hiss into the lake. He nodded. 'I remember that win . . .' The rest was lost in the crash of thunder.

'And they were to stop for the two or three seconds necessary to toss the take from one car to the other.'

But O'Loughlin was finding himself being hurried by the storm, its thunder robbing his. He frowned. His face stiffened with offence when a huge drop of rain splotted on the table near his hand.

'How very clever!' cried Virginia, her delight reinforced by O'Loughlin's discomfort. Would he hurry them inside? she wondered.

'I flatter myself . . .'

'Always supposing it *had* been you who'd planned it . . .'

His mouth was a hard, straight line. He had to agree. 'If it had, I would flatter myself that it was a superb plan.'

'But poor Charlie Braine – it left him on a kamikaze mission,' she pointed out.

'There had to be a certain reliance on the confusion this would cause,' he conceded. 'But the idea was that the police cars would chase after Braine initially. Then the news would come through about the bank job, which would take precedence over a bag of trinkets from a jeweller's, and most of the cars would be diverted to chasing the getaway car. If they caught it, there'd be no money in it. So maybe they'd return to chasing Braine. Maybe one or two cars were still after him. In any event, he got clear away with the money, and disappeared. An amateur, and he double-crossed me. Me!'

Heavy drops were smacking on the sawn pine surface of the veranda. One struck his forehead and trickled down his nose. His face was taking on colour, not entirely from the bitter memory, Virginia surmised. O'Loughlin refused to rise until she had left. She would probably top him by six inches or so, and his pride also refused to allow anybody to see him distracted from his purpose by a mere thunderstorm.

'One assumes,' she said, deliberately speaking slowly, 'that, had you yourself planned it, there would have been a fixed meeting place, where the take – even though paltry – would be handed over?'

He matched her measured tone, defiance mottling his cheeks. 'I have a farm, no matter where. These two goons were to be there waiting. There was even a powerful hosepipe waiting to wash-down the car. But Braine did not appear.'

She waited for a gap between the thunder crashes. She could now feel the weight of the rain on her head.

'You're certain of that?'

She looked round. Baldy was still standing where he'd been, legs apart, arms folded across his chest. Red, against the rail, seemed framed by the storm, and didn't like it, was pale, his eyes staring darkly against his skin, but he did not dare to move.

'Certain,' said O'Loughlin, having to shout the second syllable. 'I say jump and they jump. I say shoot each other, and they'd do it.'

'So you want Charlie Braine . . .'

'I want him *and* the money. How can I plan a job with confidence, and expect top-grade co-operation, until I have the money? *The* money, every single grubby note to the exact amount, to show, to convince people that nobody double-crosses Sean O'Loughlin. Especially a blasted amateur . . .'

He was speaking with such vehemence that for a moment he had completely forgotten the storm. His face glowed and flickered with the almost continuous lightning, the water poured down the runnels in his face, but his fury denied its presence.

'Your fault,' she said, 'through taking on an amateur. With a

94

pro, he'd have known you, and understood better. Charlie Braine wasn't scared enough.'

She got to her feet. She could now walk away with whatever dignity her clinging, soaked clothes permitted. But she hesitated.

'There's more?' he asked impatiently.

'Do me a favour,' she asked. 'Tell that bald clown over there to raise his arms. He threw my gun in the lake, so he owes me one.'

He stared at her as though she was mad, but she knew he would respond to the nerve of it, though her legs felt weak. He stared through the roar of the downpour, and the tic produced a smile. She had to read his lips. 'Another amateur, by God!' Then he stared at Baldy and snapped his fingers.

Harry tensed, and glanced at Red, who was so terrified by the storm that he was useless. Virginia saw Harry moving in, and gestured. Harry was still.

She walked over to Baldy and stood in front of him. Slowly, his eyes filmed with hatred, he raised his arms. She reached inside his parka to the shoulder holster and slipped out the automatic pistol he carried. It was beneath his right armpit, but she'd noticed, when he tossed away her lighter, that he was left-handed. Because of this, it came easily into her right hand, and as she withdrew it she flicked off the safety catch. It was a heavy weapon. She guessed it to be a .45. It was necessary, as it came free from the parka, that it should be for a moment pointing at Baldy's stomach. She lowered the angle a little, and looked up into his face.

It was grey and drawn. 'I hope it's loaded,' she said to him, but his bloodless lips did not move. Abruptly she lifted it to the sky and fired, the blast coming between their faces. She was appalled by the shock to her arm, and was nearly taken off her legs.

Baldy's eyes turned up. He swayed, but managed to stay on his feet. Still with her eyes on his, smiling slightly, she said: 'Harry, shall we go?' Then she turned and walked out of the rain into the long hall through the house, the gun hanging at her hip.

O'Loughlin snapped: 'The launch. Llew . . .'

Harry watched Red unclamp his hands from the rail and stumble after Virginia. He followed them, brushing past Baldy, who'd forgotten to lower his arms. She was already in the launch when he reached it, sitting in the stern with the pistol on her lap.

But Red was in no mood for trouble. All he wanted was to get across and back. He threw the boat through the welter of the storm, barely waiting for them to set foot on the jetty before he whirled away and became lost in the curtain of rain.

'You drive, Harry,' she said, but he didn't hear it for the roar in the trees. He knew what she meant, though, knew better than to lift her into the passenger's seat. It was no time for lifting. She was shivering beside him as he started the engine. She put her head back.

'For God's sake, drive, Harry.'

Which he did, pretending not to notice when she put her face in her hands with her shoulders shaking. It could have been rain, running from her hair and down her cheeks.

10

The storm had died by the time Harry found a roadside café. They picked their way round the pools in the parking area. The air was sweet and clean, the trees dripping.

He filled her with tea, and discovered that this and sandwiches was all the place could offer. He persuaded her to eat a cheese sandwich. At least she could smile. Weakly, as though testing it.

'I bet I look a mess.'

'Women only say that when they're sure they don't.'

'I'm still soaked to the skin. It's in my bones, Harry.'

'That's reaction. Why did you do that to Baldy?'

'My father wouldn't get me a licence for my own gun, and I felt I needed one.'

'The truth,' he said severely.

'You don't have to let them think they've got away with anything.'

'O'Loughlin will discard him. Baldy won't rest . . .'

'I've got his gun.'

'Which you won't use. It's too heavy for you, and it terrifies you.'

'Then you have it, Harry.'

'It terrifies me, too.'

She shrugged. Now that she was nearly back to normal she

could forget the past and look to the future. After a few moments she said: 'I'll have to get home for a bath and a change. But we can do a diversion and drop you . . .'

'I'll be okay.'

'But you're wet, too.'

'It didn't get through my jacket.'

'Then this,' she said, 'will be a good time for you to meet my father.'

'Heh now!'

'He told me to bring you to see him, and what daddy tells you, you do.'

Harry doubted that this was always true. 'I'm an ex-con . . .'

'For God's sake!' she snapped, then she snatched her bag from the table and marched out. The bag hung heavy in her hand.

When he got to the Range Rover she was behind the wheel. She told him she could find her way home from there and he could walk if he liked, so he sat meekly beside her and wondered how Angela Reed could have been her sister unless Virginia was married, and why, if Virginia *was* married, she called herself Brent. And wondered what her husband was like, and if he'd been unable to handle her and had run for the hills.

'We'll have to see Cynthia again, of course,' she said, and her snap of anger was also in the past. 'Unless *you* know where Charlie might have gone that day.'

'No idea. I don't see that this is going to get us any nearer the murderer of Angela Reed.' He stressed the surname, at the same time deliberately reminding her what was supposed to be the purpose of their collaboration.

She did not react. 'We're feeling around in the dark. There're things to be found out, and Cynthia might know something.'

'We can but try.' His voice was neutral and emotionless.

It was as well they had the Range Rover, as parts of the roads were flooded, and at one place a gentle ford had become a torrent. Harry became more and more uneasy as they neared the Brent residence. He felt distinctly at a disadvantage, having to meet an Assistant Chief Constable. Did he call him sir? Did he stand with the fixed attitude of neutral enmity that he'd learned to adopt with the screws in prison? Still, he reflected, it was early afternoon. The ACC would surely not be at home. But wasn't it true that the big boys in the police, like the big boys everywhere, spent very little time actually working?

He sobered at this thought, and recovered only when the old house, as she turned in at the drive entrance, failed to awe him. He had expected something more grand and showy, and in any event was distracted by the rose beds lining each side of the drive. Harry and roses had an affinity for each other.

'Can I get out here?' he said quickly.

'Are you going to turn and run, Harry?'

'I'll walk up. It'll give y' time to prepare him for the shock.'

She had the car at a halt. 'I wish there was some way to tell when you're joking.'

'Give *me* time, then,' he said, climbing down to the drive.

She grimaced at him, and drove on, parking beside her Mercedes.

Roses are best after rain, if given time to shake free of the weight of their petals. They smell stronger. They also look brighter under a lowering sky when the light is poor, seeming to have stored the last batch of sunlight for this eventuality. Harry strolled the drive, crossing back and forth as he recognized old friends. He could not have explained his delight in roses, which had caused no little derision amongst his fellow cons. The prison psychologist had murmured something about there not having been enough colour in Harry's life, not wishing to venture into the cliché of opposites attracting each other. Harry told nobody that it was their delicacy that fascinated him. He didn't want to be taken for a poofter, he told himself. But Harry had never understood any aspects of homosexuality.

Oliver Brent was waiting in the hall, mildly amused that he was being kept waiting. Virginia, not herself certain of the outcome of the meeting, hovered just behind his shoulder. They watched Harry through the open front door. Tara, sitting at her side, polished the parquet with his tail.

Harry mounted the steps into the porch, seeming only then to become aware of them.

'Harry,' she said, 'this is my father. Daddy – Harry Hodnutt.'

Brent offered his hand. Harry only just prevented himself from wiping his palm on the seat of his pants, then engulfed the small, neat hand in his paw.

He wondered how Brent had managed the height regulation. Pehaps he'd shrunk since then. He was two inches shorter than his daughter, stiffly erect to make the best of what he'd got. There couldn't have been more than ten stones of him, slim and crisp, with the pink and smooth and always clean appearance of a man who expects more of himself than of others. His hair had been chestnut, but was now almost fully grey, though plentiful and tidy. It did as it was told. His eyes matched the greyness, but they were the clear grey of the west sky on a fine morning, his eyebrows still chestnut. The moustache was clipped to precision, every hair regimented. His smile, on which he had to keep a firm rein at the office, had a boyish charm he had never outgrown.

'I hear I have to thank you for saving my daughter's life,' he said, his hand light on Harry's shoulder and piloting him through the wax-perfumed panelled hall towards the room at the rear.

'Hardly that. She wouldn't have fired the thing,' Harry protested, caught off balance because he hadn't thought he'd done anything extraordinary.

'She *did* fire it,' Virginia said.

'I upset her.'

'That's true.'

Harry had never entered such a magnificent room before. The ceiling was so high that he could barely make out that the plaster was moulded. He wondered whether the chandelier lit up at night, and decided that paintings were a pleasant change from pin-ups. The soft carpeting made him wonder whether he should have wiped his feet, the upright chairs seemed too delicate even to look at, and the easy chairs were covered in such light, silky-looking material that he wouldn't dare to relax in one.

'I noticed you're interested in roses,' said Brent, walking over to the tall windows. 'More of them out here.'

The rear garden was terraced, had sunken walkways, a distant formal pool, and raised flowerbeds confined by miniature walls. Roses flared and flamed everywhere, climbed over pergolas, spread over mounds, flaunted themselves in bowers.

'Past their best, I'm afraid.'

'Not really,' said Harry, recovering his breath. 'The second flush . . . I hope you can keep up with the dead-heading.'

'It's quite a job.'

'Noticed a trace of magnesium shortage along the drive,' Harry observed.

'Shortage? But I use Tonks formula.'

'Ah!' said Harry. 'There y'are then. In the spring, do you get the new buds leaning over at an angle? Not drooping, growing like that?'

Brent stared at him in surprise. 'Well yes.'

'Magnesium shortage.' Harry nodded. 'Epsom salts. A good dose of Epsom, nothin' like it.'

Virginia was watching them with amusement. She was aware of the weight of the pistol in her shoulder bag, worried whether to surrender it to her father and have to endure explaining its presence.

'If you two will excuse me,' she put in, 'I want to take a shower, and change.'

'Oh yes, yes,' said Brent, not attending. 'To be sure.' Then he stood back, his policeman's eyes surveying Harry critically. 'Your clothes are wet.'

'Nearly dry now.'

'I can lend you a dressing gown . . .'

'No . . . no. I'm all right,' said Harry, appalled. 'I only called in. Ought to be off . . .'

'Nonsense. I'm not having it. You'll come with me . . .' He paused. 'Have you had lunch?'

'A sandwich.' Even going dutch, it had emptied his pocket.

'We eat at seven-thirty. You can use my bathroom, and I'll find you my longest dressing gown. Probably hardly come below your knees, but no matter. Ada will dry and press your slacks and do whatever's necessary with the rest. Is that jacket real leather?'

'Yes.' Harry prayed he wouldn't ask where it'd come from.

'Then she'll have to be careful. Afterwards, we'll have a drink and a few of her tiddly-bits to keep your strength up till dinner, and we can have a good long chat. Was that magnesium or manganese?'

'Magnesium. The indications for manganese are different.'

Harry felt himself trapped. He couldn't see how he was going to return to the luxury of his private barge unless Virginia agreed to drive him. But Brent, when set on a purpose, was not to be denied, as many a Chief Super had discovered. Harry was led up a staircase that swooped round one side of the hall and along a corridor, mildly protesting.

Virginia, stepping from her shower, heard them walk past her door.

100

'Where did you learn about roses?'

'Inside. You get masses of time to read. I was in charge of the Governor's garden, but he didn't think much of roses.'

'Passed the time for you, though.'

'It just fled.'

'I'll remember that. Encouraging words for our customers.'

The voices faded. She hid the pistol beneath her underwear in the bottom drawer of her dressing table, first making sure that the safety catch was on.

Later, she managed not to laugh at Harry, barefoot and with half a yard of muscular legs protruding from beneath the hem of her father's maroon dressing gown, delicately sipping sherry and trying not to wince. Tara was showing an interest in his hairy shins. She was intrigued by his strange dignity when Ada draped his dried clothes over his arm, Ada already awed by the size of the clothes she had dried and pressed, now over-awed by the man who was to wear them, terrified when Harry tried his smile on her.

'If I can use your bedroom again, sir,' said Harry in a stiff voice, having rehearsed the words in his mind, the sir at the end slipping out before he could trap it.

'Where else, my dear chap? Not here, certainly.'

After dinner (Harry a fraction behind because he had to watch which cutlery came when) Brent mentioned that he could use a chap like Harry around the garden. Harry's heart sank. They were devouring him. His life was to be taken up, shaken around, and replaced in tidy, compact patterns. His independence was to be stolen. His sense of dignity was to be assaulted. A crust was to be tossed, and he, ex-con as he was and therefore a no-hoper, was to be grateful.

'I'm not one for the country,' said Harry, and though he tried not to seem brash, he noticed that they glanced quickly at each other. The subject was dropped.

Even later, coffee and brandy having been disposed of, it was suggested that Harry should stay the night.

'Must get back to my place,' he said. 'If you don't mind,' he added. 'Somebody might move in,' he explained in apology.

'I'm a little tired . . . ' Virginia began.

'Don't worry. I'll walk down to The Cross, and get a bus.'

She lifted her chin. 'I'll drive you, Harry, if you insist on leaving. We mustn't forget you haven't even got your bus fare left.'

Brent, glancing from one to the other, raised his eyebrows, and said nothing.

She drove him into town in the Mercedes. He insisted she should drop him in the square.

'You're a stubborn man, Harry Hodnutt,' she said, as she drove down the hill from the house.

'I can walk from there. You can't take this car into Hanger Lane.'

'You know I didn't mean that.' She was impatient, not understanding him. 'What's the harm in taking a job when it's offered? A room over the garages . . . '

'Your father's a fine man,' he said with apparent irrelevance.

'I'm glad you realize it. The offer was made in all sincerity.'

'I know that.'

'A job you would have enjoyed, too.'

He mumbled something. 'Pardon,' she said. 'Speak up, Harry.'

'When this thing's done.' There was a trace of anger in his voice. 'When I know where I stand.'

She parked in the square, which was quiet at that time, and sat back. 'Explain that, please.'

He almost shouted: when I know who you are, and what you're after. He said carefully: 'You might eventually decide that I killed Angela after all, and then how could you kill me, in your father's rose garden?'

'She was still alive when you were arrested,' she said, her teeth barely separating.

'And nobody thought of that?'

'You could just have raced straight from the lay-by into the police trap,' she qualified.

'Ah.' But he was satisfied he'd distracted her from his true concern.

'I shall,' she told him, 'pick you up here at ten tomorrow morning.'

'For a briefing?'

'We have matters to discuss with Cynthia. *I* have matters to discuss. If you're not here, I'll assume you've lost interest.'

He climbed out of the car, said goodnight, to which she didn't answer, then raised his arm in salute in case she was watching

102

him in the rearview mirror.

Then he walked home to Hanger Lane and his barge. It occurred to him that he would like to be in ACC Brent's garden during the following spring. Would love to. But he shrugged aside the thought as a weakness. They were offering him a hand-out. Poor old Harry!

Having worked up a grand mood of opposition to change, Harry, who was unused to alcohol in glasses of less than a pint, and had therefore taken too much, wandered morosely down Hanger Lane. It was so dark that he failed to notice the figure in the doorway. But he paused, lifting his head and sniffing. Apart from the rank odour of the canal itself, there was something different. An acrid smell. And ahead on the wharf, at that moment not directly in his angle of vision, there was a red glow.

He broke into a stuttering run, burst clattering on to the wharf, and saw that his home was on fire. The run became a gallop, but steps behind him faltered his purpose.

A voice called out: 'I wouldn't, Harry. The gas cylinder . . . '

The cylinder exploded to make the point. Harry watched the roof of his cabin lift, releasing a fountain of flame, and then the blast and the heat hit him and almost had him off his feet. He could almost hear his eyebrows frizzle, and ducked his head behind his arm. The flames roared for a further minute, then they sank into the water with a sullen hiss. The surface boiled and throbbed, until there was silence.

Vic Fletcher was at his elbow. 'Good job you weren't two minutes earlier, Harry,' he said.

'Was *that* you?'

'Don't be a fool. As though I would.'

'A fine guard you are.'

'Only just got here, Harry.'

Harry stared at the spot where his barge had rested. Three good outfits had gone down with it, but hardly anything else of value. He looked round. Behind him the lane was empty and silent. In all directions the craggy outlines of derelict buildings jutted against the sky. Silence. In this district an explosion would attract no more reaction than a head ducked lower and an ear afflicted with deafness.

They both stared at the canal. Its surface had ceased to surge.

'Got anywhere to stay the night?' Fletcher asked.

103

Harry stared at his feet. 'No.'

'Better come to my pad, then.'

Harry stared at the shadowy face. 'Yours?'

'Why not? Only got a chair, but it's softer'n cobbles.'

'And have you slit my throat in the night?'

'Nah!' His shadow moved in rejection. 'When the times comes, I'd want y' to *know*, Harry.'

'The time could be now.'

Fletcher laughed softly. 'You givin' in? No more suspects to check on?'

Harry said: 'Right. I'll take yerrup on it. Lead on, I'm at your heels.'

'Not shoulder, Harry?'

Harry gave the canal one last glance. 'You're callin' the tunes, you lead.'

But nevertheless, by the time they'd weaved their way between the old warehouses and come to a road with a streetlamp, they were shoulder to shoulder, Harry stumping along stolidly, Fletcher moving with loose-limbed and effortless stride.

Baldy? wondered Harry. Had he struck so soon? Or, in spite of his denial, Vic Fletcher himself? But, if Vic Fletcher, why? Surely he hadn't forced an opportunity to offer friendship.

They were now in an area where at least there was movement, if furtive. Two pubs, close to closing, were beginning the routine chucking-out. A fish and chip shop was open late for the staggerers on their way past. ('You hungry, Harry?' 'Lord, no.') They walked on. A street where prostitutes glanced, moved, resettled at their lack of response. A street with moving traffic, with hurrying pedestrians, and finally a side street of ancient and forgotten dignity. Three yards of front garden to each, with stairs plunging to basements, mullioned windows with crumbling stonework, tiny porches with doors still boasting one or two of their original stained-glass panes. Every house was converted to flats. Ground floor cost the earth, second floor only a hemisphere. Vic Fletcher had a basement.

'This is it,' he said, opening the door into a damp passageway. 'Livin' room here, bedroom next, kitchen opposite. Class, this is, Harry. Good address. Cars parked nose to nose in the street.'

The cars, Harry had noted, were mainly wrecks, drifting away as rusty water down the drains. He didn't know how to class Fletcher's pad. The only thing he could say for the place was that there might not have been water just below the floorboards. Fletcher ushered him into the living room, reaching past him for the light switch, and it was at once evident why he had brought Harry there, and might even have started the fire to bring it about.

A woman had been there, that was certain. The curtains at the high-placed window were chintz, certainly not of Fletcher's choice. The shelf over the fireplace, its throat stuffed with newspaper, was lined with ornaments of a quality that did not suggest Fletcher. Two framed pictures on the wall indicated careful selection, a row of hard-backed books in a low, two-shelved bookcase bore titles that would be way out of Fletcher's world, which probably ceased at comics. The chair that Harry was probably intended to sleep in was soft and well-padded, and nearly new. There was an order about the room. There were vases that had clearly been used for their intended purpose and had boasted flowers. Not recently, perhaps. The rest of the room remained untouched, carefully swept round and dusted, but preserved. Carefully? Lovingly. A woman had made this room, and that woman had been Angela.

Harry crossed to the framed photograph above the dormant fireplace. He remembered her at once, though the dancing hair was motionless. Those large, innocent and mocking eyes, the wide mouth and chin, the laugh. Oh yes, Harry wouldn't easily forget those. He was surprised to find that, although he'd thought there was a resemblance, nothing in her face now reminded him of Virginia.

Angela was laughing in the arms of Vic Fletcher. The picture gave the impression of having been taken on a seaside promenade. Both were laughing at the camera, she with her head against his chest and both arms round him, he standing with one arm round her shoulders, his head tilted so that his cheek rested on her hair.

Harry knew that photographs could be faked, but surely not to this perfection.

Hanging from Fletcher's free shoulder, his thumb hooked in the strap, was Angela's shoulder bag. Except that it was the same bag that Harry had last seen hanging from Virginia's shoulder. It had then been carrying a .45 automatic pistol.

11

'What's y'r game, Fletcher?'

Fletcher walked past him and fell heavily into the easy chair. 'In my own place, it's Vic.'

'All right. What's y'r game, Vic?'

'Wanted you to see that. Recognize her?'

'It's Angela.'

'Bet she wasn't laughin' when you killed her, Harry.'

Harry walked round the room. 'Why can't y' cut out the crap?' he demanded. 'You know I didn't do it.' He jerked open a drawer in the sideboard that stood against the rear wall. 'Where's that gun?'

'You're not scared, Harry? Shook yer a bit, though, ain't it? But you wasn't believin' what I said, so I thought you'd better see for yerself.'

'So now I've seen. You lived here with her. For six months . . . '

'It took that long to get it like this. A right rat-hole it was, before she came here.'

'Cost a bit to do up, I bet.'

'Sure did.'

'Her money?'

'And mine.'

'So she'd got money? You knew that?'

'Sit down, Harry, for God's sake. The gun ain't anywhere in this room. There's a chair over there. Not comfy, but it'll save me twistin' me bleeding neck.'

Harry sat. His mind was charging around like a bouncing ball, thudding from the insides of his skull. Hadn't Virginia said (or given him the impression) that she had cleared-out Angela's place? Otherwise she wouldn't have known about the missing pink shoes with the stiletto heels. But surely Virginia hadn't been here? Not here . . .

'You got any of her stuff here?' he asked. 'Her personal stuff.'

'Think I'd throw it away?'

'Mind if I take a look?'

Fletcher was watching him with amusement, enjoying the

panic in Harry's mind, even if nothing showed through the battered mask of Harry's face. He waved an arm negligently. 'Help yourself.'

'Later,' said Harry, further questions he wanted to ask jostling in his mind for precedence. 'Did she keep her old place on? The place she was in before . . .'

'Know what you mean,' cut in Fletcher, only a flicker in his eyes betraying any annoyance. 'Don't know, do I? It was nothin' to do with me.'

'But she could afford to?'

'Could 'ave, I suppose. I'll make a pot of tea . . .'

'Later,' said Harry, having detected Fletcher's unease. 'You knew she'd got some money, then?'

'I told yer. Sure I did.'

'So you knew she was slummin', gettin' a thrill from livin' with the dregs?'

Fletcher looked pained. 'Harry! You're my guest. So don't be insultin'.'

'But you knew. Look at you. Hardly a maiden's dream. Where'd the excitement be, the romance, the thrill . . .'

'Listen feller, you're way outa line. You ain't been inside all y'r life, but you certainly ain't done much livin' outside. It's a different world. What y' think the thrill was? In the other room, in the double bed. That's what it was.'

'Oh Christ . . . the great lover.'

'It ain't all soft words and perfume behind the ears, Harry.'

'Reckon not,' said Harry, who didn't know how to pronounce soft words, and who sometimes wondered behind whose ears the perfume went these days. 'You knew about her car?' he asked.

'She parked it on the street outside.'

Harry tried to rattle him. 'So you were happy enough to live on her money?'

It didn't work. Fletcher put back his head and laughed, though through it his eyes didn't leave Harry, and they were cold. 'Man, you don't know nowt from nowt,' he said. 'I earn money, Harry. Time to time, I earn it. Not often. But it's good when it comes.'

'Doin' what?'

'I'm an entryprenoor, Harry.'

'A what?'

'I arrange things. I know people and what they want, and know how I can help 'em get it.'

'You're a crook then. Same as me.'

'Give over, Harry. You never bin more'n small time. I move in circles.'

'Sean O'Loughlin sized circles?'

At the name, Fletcher blinked. 'Not that big.'

'Charlie Braine sized circles?'

'I knew Charlie.'

'*Knew* him? So you know he's dead?'

'Knew him before. What d'you think? Sure . . . he's gotta be dead.'

'O'Loughlin doesn't think so.'

'He'd know better'n me,' Fletcher said equably.

'But you did know Charlie Braine?'

'Did one or two tricks f'r him. Before your time, Harry. Log books, sort of. Small time stuff.'

'So you'd know Cynth?'

'Met her. Hardly spoke, though. What *is* this. What's all the questions? You ain't the police, an' you're doin' it lousy.'

Harry stirred. The chair was hard, the cross-stave wedging against his kidneys. 'You brought me here, so you must've expected questions.'

'I'll make that tea.'

'Can I see that gun o' yours?'

'Scared it ain't real, an' you might be wettin' your pants over a toy?' Fletcher leaned back and gave it thought, then as he leaned forward, the movement masking his hand, he was suddenly holding the pistol. For a second he grinned, the muzzle aimed at Harry's left eye, then he tossed it in his palm and offered Harry the butt.

Harry found himself holding two pounds of beautifully engineered steel, every loving ounce of it having been put together with the sole purpose of projecting a bullet rapidly and taking a life. It was a six-shot revolver, along the side of the barrel the impressed information: LAWMAN MK 111, beneath it the description: .357 MAGNUM.

Harry knew nothing about guns, and didn't want to. His examination was cursory. He saw only that the visible portions of the cylinder showed the noses of four cartridges.

'Where'd you get this?'

'Had it for years. I told you, I arrange things. This character wanted t' get outa the country quick. I knew a guy . . . forged passports . . . I fixed it up. That gun was part of the payment.'

'Did Angela know about these deals o' yours?'

He laughed. 'Lordy, no. I gave her what she wanted, an' she was happy. The clubs and the pubs an' the smoke, an' a few stories about things that fall off lorries. She thought it was just great.'

No she didn't thought Harry. Angela would have thought it was paltry stuff, so that Charlie, who'd been intending to rob a jeweller's and finish up with a bank haul as a bonus and vanish under the nose of the boss-man, Sean O'Loughlin, was the tall white knight with the glamour that caught her breath. It was ironical, he decided (though he thought of it as being a laugh), that Vic Fletcher, if he'd been honest about his true criminal activities, could have counted on Angela's admiration and love for ever. Well, her admiration, anyway. She had been a volatile young woman. In Harry's language: skittish.

He handed it back. 'You didn't get any clue she was into something?'

'What was she into?' asked Fletcher, disposing of it inside his clothing. 'Getting hi-jacked by you, and killed at a lay-by?'

'You know it wasn't like that. It don't look like it was somethin' casual. She *was* into somethin', and it got her killed. Didn't she give y' one hint? That mornin' . . . did she just drive off?'

'How'd I know that? I was outa town, sitting by a phone all day an' waiting for a call.'

'And did it come?'

'I got a call – yes – but not the right one.'

'Bad luck.'

'Bad luck when I got home and found she was gone.'

'No farewell note?'

'Nothin'.'

'And she left her stuff?'

'All of it. So she wasn't into somethin', was she? I'll make that tea.'

This time Harry was clear out of questions, so he nodded, levering himself to his feet. 'I'll take that lookaround . . . '

'Please yourself.'

109

Harry was left alone in the sitting room. Whatever personal possessions Angela had left in there he'd already seen. A quick dig through drawers uncovered nothing but domestic equipment. He followed Fletcher into the passageway, in which Angela's personality had not ventured, heard him rattling away in the kitchen, so helped himself to a handful of bedroom doorknob.

Her presence in here was less marked, although the wardrobe and dressing table were hardly what Fletcher would have bought for himself. The bedclothes, though, had been changed any number of times since Angela's death. The bedspread need not have been her choice. The bedsprings might well have rebounded to a large number of subsequent adventures.

There were no women's toilet articles on the dressing table, but in its drawers he discovered dusting powder and creams, tissues and powder puffs, hand creams and nail varnish, mascara and eye-shadow. Possibly hers. He tried the wardrobe. Half of the clothes inside were carefully segregated from the other half. On one side, his. On the other three dresses, two pairs of slacks and a pair of jeans, and a trouser suit on a man's hanger. To his inexpert eye they seemed to be about her size. He recalled her as not much taller than five feet. On the floor of the wardrobe were sitting, side by side with Fletcher's spare joggers and pointed shoes, her sandals, her low-heeled walking shoes, and a pair of shoes with stiletto heels. They were blue. He parted her clothes and discovered her pale blue two-piece costume.

Angela had not meant to go away . . . or perhaps she had. She had not been the type of person to worry about discarding a few clothes, but the sort who'd place bets on two horses in a two horse race. There had been for her a thrilling impetuosity about Charlie Braine's scheme, something madly wild that would catch her adventurous spirit and set it alight. But the practical corner of her mind would have told her that it could all so easily go wrong, and in case Charlie failed to turn up at their arranged meeting place, she had left her retreat open and could return here to Vic Fletcher's.

So much for the passionate love affair this flat had witnessed. To Angela it had been an exciting adventure into new pastures. She hadn't really grown up. Hadn't been given the chance to grow up. But to Fletcher it had been the love of his life, something on which he still brooded. But he'd said it himself: the passion had been expended in that double bed. Perhaps he hadn't grown up, either, and never would now, if he cherished to himself a memory so immature.

For a moment Harry felt the temptation to tell him all they'd discovered, and explain what that meant regarding her intentions. *That* would chop him down to size, might even get him off Harry's back. But Harry hadn't a vicious brain-cell in his head, and in any event he no longer felt in any danger from Fletcher. He picked up the shoes with the stiletto heels and took them out into the passage, as Fletcher edged his way from the kitchen with a tray in his hands. The tea things were set on an embroidered traycloth. Perhaps Angela had taught him that.

'These hers?' said Harry.

'They're not mine.'

'I thought . . . possibly another woman.'

Fletcher snarled with such fury that Harry almost dived for the gun while Fletcher had both hands busy. Then he recovered.

'You're a bloody clown, Harry. Watch it. You'll go too far one of these days.'

Harry grinned, and held the door open for him. Fletcher marched into the sitting room.

'What was she wearin' that day?' Harry asked to his back.

Fletcher replied without turning. He had it off pat. 'Pleated grey skirt, maroon cardy over a pink blouse, grey shoes.'

It in no way agreed with what Harry remembered her wearing. 'Not pink shoes? Stilettos, like these?'

'She din't have any pink stilettos.'

So Angela had so far rejected one life for the more splendid one Charlie presented that she'd returned to her own place and changed into a different outfit. It was something else he decided not to tell Fletcher. After all, he wanted to sleep that night, not keep waking to check his throat was intact.

Yet he did sleep, and soundly, his mind undisturbed by thoughts of where he might be sleeping the next night, or where his next meal was coming from. He had a simple philosophy . . . something would turn up.

The next something would be Virginia at ten o'clock, and this was his first thought when he awoke, to find Fletcher bending over him with a cup of tea.

'This is great,' said Harry. 'I owe y', Vic.'

'What you owe me is some action. You're gettin' nowhere. Breakfast in a few minutes.'

They ate from plates on their laps. Harry, chewing, was wondering how Angela had met Charlie. Fletcher himself had to be the connection.

'I suppose it was you what introduced 'em,' he mumbled.

'Eh?' said Fletcher, not having access to Harry's thoughts.

'Charlie and Angela.'

'Can't remember doin' that. I wouldn't, would I? Y' know what Charlie was like.'

'No,' said Harry, who'd known him only in the single setting, his spraying shed.

'Anything in skirts.'

'Mostly they're in jeans.'

'Just a sayin', Harry.' He eyed Harry with interest. 'You're telling me they knew each other?'

Harry shrugged. 'I'll do y'r washing up.'

'I'll do it. Mustn't hold you up. What did y' mean by Angela an' Charlie . . .'

'I oughta rush. Got an appointment at ten.'

And Harry managed to get away without giving an answer.

He was waiting in the square at ten, but she was late. The phone had caught her in the hall on her way out.

'It's Paul, Virginia. Is your father there?'

'He left early. Try his office.' She had detected urgency in Sergeant Tranter's voice. 'What is it?'

'Harry's barge got blown up last night.' A pause. 'Virginia?'

'How is . . . was he there? Paul, is he all right?'

'If it was timed to catch him at home, they got it wrong. It went up just before he got there.'

She released a long breath, giddy with having held it. 'You said "they". Who, Paul? Do you know?'

Paul Tranter was in a dilemma, and having to think fast. His information was that Virginia had been venturing where no sane policeman stepped, but he'd hoped to be speaking to her father, who would be able to exert more authority with her. Perhaps. At the same time, he didn't want to alarm her. He cleared his throat.

'I heard our Harry's been asking around. The word is out that he could have annoyed a gentleman called O'Loughlin. If so, he's lucky to have lost no more than his barge.'

'It was all he'd got. Has it *all* gone?'

'There was nothing but a smell of singed canal this morning,' he said cheerfully, not wanting to make it seem too dramatic. 'I thought . . . if you're seeing him in the near future . . .'

'Who? Harry? I could well be. Is there a message, Paul?'

'Only that I'd like to have a word with him. And soon.'

'I'll tell him that.'

She hung up. The conversation had wasted only three minutes, which she could easily have made up. But she did not hurry. There were a number of matters to consider, one of them being that Harry was now in a situation where he might listen to reason, and her father had already phoned three rose-growing friends to enquire about magnesium deficiency, and to no good effect. So Virginia had asked Ada to air the rooms over the garage, just in case.

Harry had been waiting for five minutes. It had given him time to decide that destroying the barge had not been Fletcher's idea, as Fletcher seemed quite confident that he needed no more subtle encouragement than his Lawman Mk 111. So Baldy was the obvious suspect, and it need not have been intended as a warning. He might well have believed Harry to be in residence at the time. From this conclusion it was easy to progress to the next step. The death of Harry could have been intended as a warning to Virginia, adding flavour to her eventual death with a sprinkling of terrified anticipation. In that event, Harry decided, he would have to be near her as much as possible. Consequently there had come a time when pride had to be put aside. He could be closest to her by going to work for her father.

Each decided to allow the other to introduce the subject.

He climbed into the Mercedes. 'You're late.'

'So I am. You could've used the time for a shave.'

He looked decrepit, having slept away all Ada's careful ironing and pressing.

'My barge got burnt-out last night,' he explained.

'Vandals?' she asked casually.

'Must've been. So I spent the night with Vic Fletcher.'

'That,' she said, overtaking a 39 bus, 'must have been interesting. I hope you grabbed the chance and gathered plenty of useful information.'

113

He told her, as fully as he could remember. 'So it's certain he *was* living with her,' he finished. 'Though it doesn't seem to've been as serious for her as it was for him.'

'That sounds like Angie. I can see why you didn't have time to get a shave.'

'He hadn't got a razor. He's trying to grow a beard, so he threw it away. On the principle of throwing away your lighter when you want to give up smoking.'

'If you'll remember, it wasn't me who threw it away.'

'You swapped it for a pistol,' he remembered. 'Fair exchange. Where are we going?'

'To see Cynthia. You know that.'

She glanced sideways in time to see his nod, and to detect the single line of his frown.

'Have you got it with you?' he asked. When she didn't reply, he added: 'Baldy's pistol.'

'It's in my bag. I daren't leave it for Ada to find.'

'You'd better let me have it.'

'But you're scared of guns, Harry.' She chased a Lotus for half a mile, then gave it up. 'The bag's on the back seat.'

He reached behind him and lifted it on to his lap. The gun constituted most of the weight but only a small amount of the quantity. He took it out and slid it into his side pocket. 'By heaven, you do carry around a load of stuff.'

'A girl has to be prepared.'

'It's *her* bag, isn't it? Angela's.'

'How d'you know that?' The car did a little kink, although the road was straight.

'It was in the photo I told you about.'

'I gave it to her for her birthday. I carry it to remind me what I'm supposed to be trying to do.' She paused. 'The lighter was hers.'

'The bag was on the back seat of her car, I suppose?'

'Yes.' She took a breath. Harry was carefully steering the conversation away from Cynthia. She said: 'You've upset my father, Harry.' And damn it, so was she.

'I thought we got on fairly well.' His voice was distant.

'You've got him really worried about his roses.' Which gave her a neat lead-in to the subject of Harry moving in to help.

'No need. He'll find I'm right. Remind him – Epsom salts. A

114

handful round each rose. Why're we going to see Cynth?'

'Because she might be able to tell us *some* place Charlie might have gone that day.' Damn him, he'd done it again. 'Are you sure you're safe with that gun?'

'No. I know I'm not. But I know a feller, he'll tell me what to do.'

'If you'll take my advice, you'll sell it to him.'

'I can't do that. It's yours. It was you took it from . . .'

'Then sell it to him on commission,' she said with a shade of impatience. 'Ten per cent for you.'

'Oh yes. Thanks. I could use it.'

'What you need is steady work, Harry.' Got to it at last.

'Don't we all?'

'And what does *that* mean?' she demanded. 'If you're referring to me . . . If you think I ought to be earning my keep instead of playing private detective . . .'

He didn't know how this had come about. 'I didn't mean you. Why're we stopping here? Haven't we seen enough of this damned lay-by?'

'There would have been no need to stop, Harry,' she said distinctly, carefully drawing on the handbrake with not one grate from its ratchet, 'if you hadn't wasted time talking about anything but what really matters. You don't want to go to Cynthia's again, do you? Shall I tell you something? Neither do I. But I know it's necessary. You . . . all you think about . . . oh, Harry, I wanted all this settled between us before we got there.'

He was sitting with his face set, staring straight ahead, shocked by her sudden outburst and not understanding, not knowing what to say. He realized that her thinking on this business had probably progressed much further than his own, but he could only wait and hear what she meant. He waited, but she didn't enlighten him. She had reached back for her bag and was fumbling inside for her cigarettes and lighter. It was an ordinary one now, ordinary to her, but all the same, gold.

'Get what settled?' he was forced to say.

'You and Cynthia,' she said sharply, more angrily than she'd intended.

'There's nothing to worry about there.'

'Isn't there? There have been hints, Harry. You . . . admire her. You can't hide it. Damn it all, you nearly devoured each other.'

115

'Why don't you say it?' He couldn't look at her.

'You've got to realize, Harry, that all I can go on is what people tell me: I have to assume I'm hearing the truth.'

'Have I told you a lie?'

'Ask yourself! How the hell can I know that?'

'I thought . . . '

'Your thinking is biased, Harry. You can't get round that.'

'Because of Cynth? We were only friends.'

'But good friends. Good enough, perhaps, for you to lie for her.'

'What about? I don't understand. I don't remember any lies.'

'If you thought, at the time it happened, that Cynthia had killed Angela, I believe you'd lie. And after all, who had the best motive? Angela was going off with Cynthia's husband. And the killing . . . Harry, it was done with the stiletto heel of a woman's shoe. That was the forensic evidence. The wound was exactly the right shape. They spoke about a thin skull, all medical language. But a woman could have done it. With her own shoe . . . '

At last he turned to her. 'I don't know why you're sayin' this. Y' said yourself . . . that shoe business was all complicated, and didn't prove anything, anyway.'

'I said it was perhaps important. But Harry . . . don't look like that.' She was finding she was beginning to read his expressions. 'I've got to know. Be sure. The shoe business (as you call it) is complicated *only* if you're telling the truth about them.'

'I don't get it.' His voice sounded strange. 'I never did understand women. Never will.'

He jerked open the door and was ten yards away before she could run to his side and catch his arm, half shaking it in impatience with his anger, half hanging on to it in order to turn him to face her. He stopped, looking down at her. God, she thought, he's a stranger.

'Harry, please listen to me. If we assume Angela had her shoes, then it means nothing. By that, I mean it doesn't *point* anywhere. Anybody could've killed her with one of them, and taken them both away, for some obscure reason. But if she *didn't* have them . . . '

'How would she get to the phone and back . . . '

'I can cover that. Later. Listen, please. *If* we can assume she didn't have her shoes, then it means she was killed by a woman, because men don't normally come equipped with them.'

'A woman? You mean Cynth? Why don't you say so! Be honest.'

She bit her lip. 'Cynthia, then.'

'I told y',' he said, his voice clipped. 'Angela shouted after me for her shoes. I didn't want 'em under my feet. So I chucked 'em.'

'What if she didn't see you do that?'

'Would *you* miss it, if you'd yelled fer me to chuck 'em out?'

'Perhaps you'd already gone out of sight. You turned . . .'

'Left.'

'You see? You could have been out of her sight.'

'So that'd make it all right, huh? Harry makes a mistake, that's just the ticket. Makes it fine. But tellin' a lie . . .'

'I meant . . .'

'I threw 'em out. She saw it.'

'You're quite determined to cover for Cynthia, aren't you?'

'I'm not covering. Tellin' you the facts.'

'This could've occurred to you. If you thought Cynthia had done it, you could well have invented the shoes. Can't you see . . . it clouds the issue.'

He stared into the distance. 'Angela couldn't 'ave walked to the phone without 'em.'

'But what say,' she told him with tense triumph, sensing a hint of withdrawal, 'Cynthia did *not* stay at home, haunting the phone? What say she suspected something funny was going on and got worried, and toured the district in her little car . . . and came across Angela here, marooned and with no shoes, drove her to the phone box, suspected something, took her home – all sympathetic – for a cup of tea, got some of the story out of her, then drove her back here? And killed her here with one of her own stiletto heels. Eh, Harry? What d'you think?'

He stared at her in wonder. 'Oh, that's just great. Got it all worked out. Just like the police . . . decide who's done it then twist and turn and juggle every bleedin' fact to make it fit. No mistakin' who you got it all from . . .'

'That's a rotten thing to say.'

'Why worry, if you're gonna assume I'm always lyin'?'

'Not lying, Harry. Mistaken.'

He wiped his hand over his face. 'And that's what y're takin' to Cynth?'

117

'With your help. If you will.'

'Oh, I wouldn't miss this. But if you expect me to lie to her and tell her that there were no shoes in the car . . . that's out.'

She looked up into his face for a moment, then she turned away angrily. He couldn't know that it was with herself she was angry. Not another word, she told herself. Not one.

'Oh, I wouldn't expect you to lie to Cynthia,' she threw over her shoulder.

He very nearly said: if that's your attitude, but choked it back in time. He couldn't afford to let her out of his sight. When he fell into the car beside her, no other words occurred to him, nothing showed on his face.

Silent, they drove away.

12

This time they approached Charlie Braine's place by the more conventional method of turning right at the crossroads and driving for two miles. It was a minor road. The village of Harley Green was so negligible that they drove through without noticing it. A farm separated the scattering of village from the smallholding Charlie had converted.

The original five-barred gate was still hanging on its pins, but was now permanently open. It invited them into a yard with a surface of pounded earth. The bungalow sat back to the left, looking neglected behind a screen of blackberry bramble that had gone wild, and to the immediate left there was a crumbling hen house, which Harry remembered Cynth had used for that purpose. But the hens had become pets, and the venture had died of affection. Farther back and on the right was the spraying shed, looking like a young hangar, with its blank front and curved roof of corrugated iron.

As they approached, a thrush-egg blue Police car pulled out of the yard. Virginia drew right over, one wheel up the bank, for it to get through. Its driver had clearly not even seen them.

She coasted the Mercedes into the yard and parked it beside Cynthia's hatchback.

'Did you see who was driving that car?' she asked.

'Looked like Freda Graham.'

'I wonder what's up.'

The bungalow's front door was wide open. They approached it cautiously. Harry tapped gently, with his weight of fist rocking it.

Cynthia's voice came chokingly from the rear. 'Get away from me, damn you.'

The words were so similar to their previous welcome that it seemed a fair assumption they'd been intended for the same person.

'It's Harry, Cynth,' called out Harry tentatively, but Virginia had detected the underlay in Cynthia's voice and pushed him aside impatiently.

He followed her along the passageway to the kitchen at the rear. Virginia had stopped in the doorway, and Harry stared over her shoulder.

Cynthia was sitting at the table with an empty mug cupped in her palms, seeking comfort from its departed warmth. She turned at their entrance, lifting her distraught face to them. For a moment her puffed eyes, her slack cheeks and loose mouth, her tears, were still those of the recent encounter. Harry was shocked. She seemed so desperate and old.

He would have gone forward, her name forming on his lips, but Virginia's suspicions restrained him. She glanced quickly at him over her shoulder then went at once to Cynthia, swinging a chair with one hand as she went, sat beside her, put a hand on Cynthia's wrist, and said: 'What's this? Trouble with the police?'

Cynthia stared at the mug. Harry walked past them to look out of the window. From here, Cynth could have watched Harry's arrival with every one of the stolen cars, bumping down from the hardcore of the old railway track. She must have known exactly what Charlie had been doing. She was probably still existing from the proceeds of that caper. Behind him there was a murmur of voices. He turned. Cynth had pushed the mug away from her and was sitting back.

'I thought she'd come back.' She put her fingers through her hair distractedly.

'What've you been doing?' Virginia asked gently. 'A motoring offence? Speeding?'

119

'She wasn't on duty,' Cynthia mumbled.

'She was in uniform. She was in an official car.'

'Heading back to the station to sign out. She called in. She's always doing that.' Cynthia gave a twist to her lips, which might have been a smile. Harry looked away. The flat, unemotional voice went on. 'I'll kill her one of these days.'

Virginia glanced quickly at Harry, warning him. She already had an idea what was facing them. 'It must be lonely for you here.'

'I get by.'

'She'd be an old friend, maybe, calling in for a chat?'

Cynthia swirled her hair, her head coming up and awareness entering her eyes. 'What's it to you?'

'What is it to *you* rather?' Virginia said softly, praying for Harry to keep out of it.

'I can live without it.' Cynthia shrugged away her distress. Furtively she explored with a finger for tears remaining on her cheeks, to which colour was now returning. 'What d'you want here, anyway?' The abrupt aggression was feeble.

And Harry, knowing Cynth, recognized how much this sudden attack, rising from distress, had cost her, and could suffer it no longer.

'Come t' see you're all right, Cynth. I mean . . . how're you managing? There can't be much . . . '

Cynthia looked at him with burning eyes. 'We're not all looking for handouts, Harry. So keep your big nose out of my affairs, if you don't mind.'

Virginia cut in quickly. 'He was only being kind, Cynthia. Harry's been worried about you.'

'Then he's taken a long while to show it. Four months he's been out.'

'I'm here now,' he pointed out.

'Sticking that nose in . . . '

'We're trying to help you.'

'Oh great! That's just fine. Help me how, if I might ask?'

Virginia had found Harry impervious to eye signals. She turned a shoulder to him, and he stared out of the window in disgust.

'We thought it might help if we could find out what happened to Charlie that day.' But Cynthia shook her head. 'We've already got a good idea why he didn't return here afterwards . . . '

'After what?' Cynthia bent her head, looking sideways, only one eye visible and that shrouded by her hair. It created an impression of evil.

'After the jewellery shop robbery, Cynthia. You know that. You know why he drove away from here in a two-coloured car. And after the bank robbery . . . '

'He'd got nothing to do with that.'

'I believe he had.'

'Who cares what you believe?'

'I believe he didn't come back here because he was afraid to. It would've been the first place they'd look for him.' She made a quick gesture of restraint to Harry. 'By they, I mean the team that did the bank robbery. All the evidence we're getting points to the fact that Charlie got hold of the bank robbery money, so he'd head for somewhere secret, where he could wash the paint off his car and disappear. What we don't know is where he went.'

Slowly Cynthia levered herself to her feet as though all the energy had been drained from her. She stood back from the table, her face expressionless. Her attitude bore the signs of a householder about to order out unwelcome visitors.

'And?' she snapped.

'And I rather hoped you'd know such a place.'

'If I did . . . why should I tell you?'

'I'm not the police.'

'What's that got . . . '

'If you tell me, I might be able to find out why Charlie didn't come home. You naturally refuse to tell the police. That's why Freda Graham keeps calling, isn't it? You're on her circuit. She comes, on instructions, to wear you down. Bit by bit.'

And Cynthia, her mouth distorting, threw back her head and laughed, a choked parody of a laugh, so hollow and bitter that Harry took a pace forward. And stopped. It had ended as abruptly as it had begun, on a whimper, an indrawing of breath.

Virginia sat unmoved, though one hand drew the shoulder bag closer to her slowly, as though she was about to jump up and run from the room. She waited until Cynthia was silent, then the fingers relaxed.

It was an effort to stare into the withdrawn eyes and unstable face and keep all emotion from her voice.

'But I was forgetting, Cynthia. You didn't really expect Charlie to return here. You said it yourself. He didn't say: see you. Silly of me, I forgot. But you knew there was something going on in the background. Another woman. And you weren't going to wait around here doing nothing about it. So you got into your little car and went out looking.'

'I told you . . .'

'I remember what you told me. But I don't believe you'd wait here so . . . so meekly. You went out and you discovered a young woman abandoned at a lay-by. Only two miles from here.'

'What in God's name are you talking about!'

'And you found out *she* was the one your husband was supposed to be meeting.'

'I told you I was here!' Cynthia shouted.

'Oh yes. You told us that. Waiting here in case Charlie phoned. Or somebody else did. It's just not acceptable.'

'I waited in that bloody yard out there!' Cynthia flung out her arm.

'Yes. You said. Two phones to listen out for. But I don't believe you did that. It's much more logical that you'd go out in the car . . .'

'All afternoon I was out there.'

'What were you wearing?'

'What?'

'To wait in the yard, you must have worn something.'

Cynthia's lips twiched. 'Jeans and something, I expect. My raincoat. It looked like rain . . .'

'It *did* rain,' put in Harry. 'Later.'

'And your stilettos?' Virginia knew it was ridiculous, but it had to be said.

'I was wearing my wellies.'

It was Harry who laughed, but he covered it with a cough.

Virginia did not look at him. 'But all the same, the police must believe you went out. You would be the obvious suspect.'

'And why?' Cynthia's chin jerked in defiance. 'Why me?'

'Because the young woman who died was the one your husband intended to go away with.'

Cynthia thrust herself away from the sink and finished up with both hands on the table, her face a foot from Virginia's, her hair damp with sweat. 'That's a lie! That's just a rotten lie!'

122

'It's true, Cynthia. Why else d'you think Freda Graham is sent round here to keep pressing you?'

'She isn't sent, you stupid creature.'

'No?'

'It's nothing official.'

'Ah! I see. You're telling me you *did* drive to the lay-by. Freda Graham saw you, and comes here for money . . .'

'You crazy bitch!' Cynthia shouted into her face, spittle flying. 'It's because of Freda that Charlie went away.' Then her face crumpled, and the rest came out as a whimper. 'Because of Freda he left me.'

She fumbled blindly for a chair. Harry pounced forward, and with one hand whipped the one she had used over the table and banged it down behind her. His other hand, on her shoulder, eased her on to it.

Virginia looked up at him. She pursed her lips and shook her head. Cynthia put her elbows on the table and her head in her hands. Her shoulders were motionless but her fingers moved in her hair.

Virginia said softly: 'Harry told me. He didn't know, but it was there. The first time he met you, it was at a disco. You'd gone there with a woman friend. He brought you home, and Charlie didn't seem concerned that a man was with you. Perhaps if it'd been a woman he'd have been worried. That was Freda you'd gone with, wasn't it? And that was three years before Charlie disappeared. Time for the affair to have progressed, Cynthia.'

Slowly Cynthia's head was lifted from her hands. Her eyes were calm, but the life had gone from them. It seemed that she was relieved to share it, though her voice was dull when she spoke.

'It wasn't an affair.' Not a denial. A statement.

'Then what was it?'

'She'd have liked it to be an affair. She called it that. She was proud. She told me that Charlie was no good for me. That she . . . that he couldn't do the things she could . . . that my life had been empty before she came . . . that she loved me and would cherish me, like he couldn't.'

Virginia was aware that Harry was shaking with the effort to remain silent. She did not glance away from Cynthia.

'And could she?' she asked, very gently and with infinite understanding.

'She won't leave me alone.'

'Could she provide more for you than Charlie did?'

'No.'

'But she tried?'

'Drop it,' Cynthia whispered. 'I told her I never wanted to see her again.' She put thumb and fingers to her brow and squeezed.

'When did you tell her that?'

'When Charlie . . . w-went.'

'But she's persisted?'

'Won't leave me alone!' The last word came out almost hysterically.

'After four years?'

'She's obsessed.'

'She must feel very strongly about you.'

Cynthia's lips twisted in disgust, but she said nothing.

'But not you for her?'

'I hate her. It was all a mistake. A mistake. I didn't realize . . . '

'Then why didn't you go away?'

Cynthia looked startled. 'But Charlie might come back.'

Virginia bit her lip. It was difficult to go on, but at any moment Harry was going to burst in with God knew what nonsense, so that she didn't even dare to pause for breath.

'So it's come to the point where you're ready to shoot her?'

'I'll do that.' Cynthia nodded. 'If I have to.'

'She's a stubborn woman. Obviously. Though of course, if she had something she could use as a lever, some knowledge . . . ' She paused. Cynthia's eyes had flickered. 'Perhaps she *did* see you at the lay-by . . . '

'I told you I was here!' Cynthia's voice broke.

'Or something else.'

This time there was no reaction. Cynthia simply drew in her lips and stared fury at Virginia, until there seemed nothing to do but to slap her palms on the table with an air of finality.

'Perhaps I'd better go and ask her, then.'

Still there was no reaction, simply a dull acceptance.

'Though perhaps,' said Virginia, 'you'll phone her and warn her.'

Cynthia gave a short bark of cynical laugher. 'If you were taking her a dose of poison, I wouldn't warn her.'

124

'I'm not sure poison would touch her. Coming, Harry?'

At last she looked at him. Harry was standing as though in shock, one hand hovering towards Cynthia and his eyes blurred with pain.

'Harry!' she said softly.

He blundered after her to the car. She backed up and took it out on to the road. 'Don't say anything, Harry.'

'I don't know anything to say.'

'These things happen. Two women. Two men . . . '

'In prison . . . yes . . . I know.'

'But in prison, is there love?'

'Love!' he said in disgust.

'For it to have lasted so long . . . oh Harry, please! I can feel you quivering there. When we get to Freda's, you've got to let me handle it. You'd rush in like a bull, and I can't have that. Promise you'll behave.'

'*Me* behave? Good Christ!'

She glanced sideways with gentle affection. Freda had hurt Cynthia. That was about all he understood, and he was in a mood to pick Freda Graham to pieces and toss her out of the window. It would not occur to him (he wouldn't understand if she explained) that perhaps Cynthia had hurt Freda.

'It's a woman's work.'

'I never get a chance to say a word,' he complained, but all the same he settled his shoulders into the seat back. He wouldn't have known what word to use.

13

Her own car was in the parking area. That seemed to confirm that she had, as Cynthia had said, been on her way to sign off. But when she opened the door she was still in uniform, less the hat. Virginia thought she had possibly expected this visit, and needed the authoritative support of the uniform. She said: 'Oh, it's you,' and backed away from the door.

'Cynthia said you might be home.'

'So it *was* you. I thought I knew the car.'

Freda's face seemed puffy. It was normally plump, as though there was no solid skull inside, so the indications had to be sought for. She was moving stiffly, every muscle tight with opposition. No offer of seats was made, and she was too restless herself to sit. Virginia deliberately lowered herself into an easy chair.

'How . . . how was she?' Freda asked at last, Virginia appearing to be waiting for her lead. The angry gesture of Freda's hand, whipping hair from her eyes, was intended to convey indifference.

'Upset,' Virginia said, one eye on Harry as he moved restlessly. 'As you'd expect. As she always is, I suppose.'

Freda seemed to make up her mind. One hand flapped at her breast pocket. Another second and her notebook would appear. 'I let you come in here because I want to get something settled. Something you'd better get clear, then I needn't set eyes on you again. It's this, and just you damned well take note. I had to answer you before. I was told to, and God knows what influence you've got. But I'm not . . . I am *not* . . . having you sticking your nose into my private life. Do you get that? Do you understand, or shall I say it again?'

'I understand perfectly. But you make it difficult. I'm permitted to speak about your official duties, but not your private affairs. The snag is, where does one end and the other begin?'

Virginia was polite about it, and was surprised at the flush of anger she provoked. 'I warned you . . .'

'No, Freda. I'm doing the warning. You've allowed your private life to slip into your duties, that's what makes you vulnerable.'

'Get out of here!' But there was no spirit in it.

'As Cynthia has been vulnerable,' said Virginia calmly.

The dark blue skirt swirled, the regulation shoes stamped into the carpet. Freda headed for the door.

'Cynthia hates you, you know,' Virginia went on. 'Really hates.'

'That's not true.' On an indrawn breath. 'She's unsettled and confused.' But she released the doorknob.

'Then she's been like that for four years. Since Charlie went. Since your affair with her drove him away.'

'You don't know what you're talking about.'

126

'Oh yes, I do. Only too well. It might have been wonderful at the time, but for Cynthia it was an interlude, call it an experiment, and then it was over. Over, Freda. Finished. Done.'

'You're not to say that,' she whispered.

'But surely Cynthia's been saying exactly that for a long, long while. And you wouldn't listen.'

'She'll come round. If she'll only talk it out! I can explain . . . '

Harry moved. Virginia gestured – a command to Harry with one hand, a reproving one for Freda with the other.

'She doesn't want to see you again.' It was said with sadness.

'After all I've done for her!' It was a muted wail. Freda stared at her palms, willing herself not to cover her face.

'And that's where your official duties overlapped with your private . . . affairs.'

Virginia gave her time. Freda was looking round distractedly. Virginia wished she would sit. On her feet, the bulky policewoman looked as though she could be dangerous, and Harry wouldn't need much provocation to become active. It was words Virginia wanted, not violence.

'Why don't you sit down?' she asked quietly.

Freda allowed her knees to give way. The seat she'd chosen, and which just happened to be there, was a dining room chair, allowing her to sit primly with her knees together, and gather herself into one perched, defensive mechanism.

'I don't know what you mean,' she said stolidly, staring at the wall opposite.

'I believe the official overlapped the private when you saw something that day–the day Angela died. Perhaps it was Cynthia, in her car, in the area. You didn't report it. You drove away, not wishing to observe any more, and later . . . '

'This is complete nonsense.'

'You saw Cynthia close to the lay-by . . . '

'I saw nothing and nobody.' The response was not energetic. Freda was gaining confidence, and Virginia realized she was on the wrong tack.

'After all you'd done for her. That was what you said.'

'All the love!' Freda shouted. 'All the understanding, the emotional support!'

Harry groaned softly.

'But if you didn't see her there – if you didn't have some reason to believe she killed that young woman – then what else did you suppress from your superiors?'

Freda's face was disintegrating. Her eyes were puffed with suppressed tears, her mouth moving with protest, with anger . . .

'She hates you now, Freda,' said Virginia in a flat, unemotional voice. 'If *you* don't, she'll tell me. I think we'd better try that, Harry.' She glanced over her shoulder to Harry, who looked as though he'd try anything to get out of there.

'No!' Freda threw out the word.

'She's been rejecting you for four years,' Virginia said with confidence. 'The way she spoke, she must have told you herself that she hated you. So you must have had something you could pressure her with, something she would not like to be known, something you could wave in her face and keep saying, over and over, this is what I've done for you, Cynthia. This is what I've done . . . risked my career doing . . . and all because I love you and can't let you go . . .'

'Shut up!' she screamed.

'Then what was it, Freda?'

At last she clamped her hands to her face, and now the uniform did nothing for her, except to accentuate the contrast between its stolid authority and her quivering collapse. Virginia waited. She glanced at Harry and nodded towards the door. Harry crossed quickly and stood with his back to it. It gave him something to do.

Freda choked a few words into her cupped hands.

'I didn't hear that.'

The red, collapsed face was raised. 'I phoned her,' said Freda.

'You phoned her when? And from where?'

'I was . . .' Freda lifted her chin and sniffed heavily. The voice was throaty. 'I was on patrol in Porchester. I got a message to drive to the phone box by the lay-by and pick up a young woman. Instead, I went to a phone in Porchester and called Cynthia.'

It was said in a colourless monotone. Harry's shoulders went back against the door. 'And told her what?' Virginia asked crisply.

'That Charlie's fancy piece was stranded at the lay-by.'

'And why did you do that?'

Freda stared at her with contempt. 'So that she could see for herself.'

128

'I see.' She did not see, but assumed it would all emerge. 'Then you drove there yourself?'

'Yes.'

'And saw what?'

'Nothing.'

'You're telling us all this, after a great deal of reluctance, and now you say you saw nothing?'

'I'd ... sort of ... delayed. To give Cynthia time to have it out with Charlie's fancy piece.'

'To give her time ...'

'And I saw nothing.'

'You're telling me you gave her time to *kill* Angela, and when you saw nothing you assumed she'd done just that?'

'No, no! Oh, let me say it. Why do you keep putting words into my mouth?'

'Say it, then. Start with how you knew this was Charlie Braine's fancy piece, as you called her.'

Freda licked her lips, looked round wildly until she spotted her packet of cigarettes, swooped a hand for it, and fumbled one out.

'I'd been listening on the car radio. All the messages coming in, about the jeweller's and the bank robbery, and of course I knew that was Charlie ... oh, don't you raise your fancy eyebrows at me ... I knew all about Charlie and what he was doing in that shed of his. But my source of information made it impossible to reveal ...'

She stopped, apparently aware that she'd fallen into a misplaced formality.

'You knew from Cynthia?'

'There was talk.'

'Of course.'

Freda was now anxious to have it said, so that they would leave. 'I knew about Charlie, and I knew about his young woman.'

'And how would you know that?'

'If you'll let me *say*!'

'Sorry.'

Freda lit her cigarette with a match. She held it like a man, between first finger and thumb, and flicked the match across the room, throwing up her chin as she drew in the smoke.

'I knew about them because they used the lay-by for their meetings. Nothing new to me. Courting couples there every night. But I knew Charlie. I took the number of her car. I had Records dig it out for me. Her name and address. I knew everything about her – messing about with Charlie while she was living with another feller! Disgusting.'

'You told Cynthia about it?'

'Certainly. She didn't believe me.'

'Your duties took you into town then?'

'What?' She drew in smoke, and expelled it with encapsulated words. 'Oh, I see. In my spare time. I traced her to that stinking basement they were living in.'

Virginia nodded. Freda had worked hard at it.

'So . . . ' Freda cocked an eyebrow, awaiting another interruption, then went on. 'So I knew, listening to the car radio, that Charlie was involved. That stupid two-coloured car! And when they gave me the number of the car that somebody . . . ' She jerked her cigarette towards Harry. ' . . . that oaf over there had taken, I knew who was waiting there in that lay-by. So I phoned Cynthia.'

'And gave her time to get at her and kill her?'

'So that she could see for herself! She hadn't believed me,' explained Freda with heavy condescension.

'And that was what you had to offer her?' asked Virginia. 'To prove how much she meant to you. A phone call you'd kept secret, just for her, when you wouldn't have been able to reveal it to your superiors anyway.' Virginia was contemptuous.

The smoke must have affected Freda's throat. 'I *thought* she'd killed her,' she admitted hoarsely.

'Oh, I see. That was a better offer. I can see that. Cynthia, I know you killed Angela Reed, but I'm risking my career to keep it secret. So why can't you be nicer to me . . . as it was before . . . '

'It was not *like* that.'

'Perhaps I missed something.'

'I really thought she'd killed her. She's wild enough. I'd phoned . . . I only wanted her to *see* . . . to see how she couldn't trust Charlie. I swear. And it was *my* phone call that did it. I thought she'd killed her, and we . . . we sort of shared it. It brought us closer.'

'But you're lying, aren't you?'

'I don't . . . I can't . . . why won't you believe me?'

130

'Because you're in the force, Freda. You'd know. After a few days, the news would filter through. You'd know that Angela Reed didn't die for an hour – more than that – after Cynthia would have reached the lay-by. Even if she'd gone there...'

'But I didn't know *then*!' Freda screamed, in fury at Virginia's lack of understanding.

'You didn't know, at the time you found Angela's body in the grit bin, that she'd died very shortly before?'

'Yes! For Christ's sake, yes!'

'But I don't see how that affects what you told Cynthia later – later the same day I assume. What...oh, I think I see.' She was drawing out the words, trying to clarify for herself a wayward thought. 'When you found the body, you thought Cynthia was responsible. At *that* time you thought she was. So that affected your actions...your thoughts... Something happened! You did something to protect her...oh, dear Lord!'

Freda saw the realization burst on Virginia's face, and was on her feet. 'I've had enough of this!'

'Harry,' said Virginia deliberately, 'have you been following this?'

'I dunno.' Harry levered his shoulders from the door.

'I want you to search the flat.'

'You will not!' Freda shouted.

'Whaffor?' asked Harry.

'If you'd been following it, you should know. Just search it, Harry. You'll know, I'm sure.'

'I'm not having that great clown pawing through my things!'

'Start with the bedroom, Harry.'

Harry, completely lost, reluctant to leave the two women alone together, hesitated. Virginia said firmly: 'Harry!'

He left. Freda's hand slapped down on the phone. 'I'll have a car here in two minutes.'

'Yes, you do that. I'll have quite a few official misdemeanours to outline. Better, perhaps, to get them into a copper's notebook while I can remember all of them.'

Freda sat back on the chair. Her face was now pale, like punched putty. She fumbled for another cigarette, drawing on it angrily. Virginia reached out her own brown ones, and smoked slowly, quietly, considering the outcome she expected – and feared. Inside, she was shaking.

131

Two heads jerked round as Harry entered. He looked baffled and worried, his frown like a knife wound across his forehead. 'In the wardrobe,' he said gruffly.

He was carrying a single pink shoe with a stiletto heel. Virginia held out her hand. He seemed pleased to be rid of it.

'So . . .' said Virginia. 'Didn't I tell you the shoes mattered?'

'What's it all about?' Harry muttered.

'Perhaps Freda can tell us.'

Freda tossed her head. It was a gesture designed to avert her eyes.

'Well, perhaps I can guess.' Virginia peered into the shoe. 'Yes, it's the correct size. Certainly Angela's shoe, her left one. Now let me guess. Freda phoned Cynthia, then hung back to give her time to see for herself, as she insists. But when Freda eventually got to the scene there was no sign of Angela, not by the phone box, not at the lay-by, and Freda began to believe that Cynthia had taken it a little further than just seeing for herself.'

'Hmph!' said Freda.

'So she reported in, and was told to return to her beat, but later, when Angela still hadn't been heard of, she was told to take another look. It was then that she discovered Angela's body in the bin, and there was every indication that she'd been attacked with one of her own shoes. A woman, assaulted, always has one weapon. She whips off her shoe. It's a good weapon if it has a stiletto heel. But if that shoe is taken from her and used against her . . . a different story altogether.'

'Why don't you get on with it?' demanded Freda angrily.

Because Virginia was feeling her way into the mind of a woman tortured by the rejection of her lover. She had to ease her way into it.

'The murderer had taken away the murder shoe. But Angela was still, at that time, wearing the other shoe – her left one. Now . . . Freda has said she believed, *at that time*, that Cynthia had done it. But already she had something to offer to Cynthia to prove her devotion.'

'That?' asked Harry, pointing at the shoe.

'Now don't be foolish, Harry. What she had to offer was the fact that she was intending to keep silent about her phone call to Cynthia. No more than that. See how I love you, Cynthia darling. My career on the line. I know you did it, but I'm with you all the way.'

'Oh God, you bitch!' said Freda.

'Trying to get the feel of the part, dear.'

'I didn't think it out like that.'

'Clearly you didn't, if you took the shoe.'

'All I thought was that she'd done it.' Freda's face was red with passion.

'But you did take the shoe. For heaven's sake, why?'

Freda made a dismissive gesture. For one second a tiny smile of pride had flickered across her face, of superiority. Panic or not, she'd known what she was doing. 'It seemed obvious.'

'The obvious thing to do? You intrigue me, Freda. Perhaps it was the *only* thing you could think to do? Confusing the issue, was that it?'

'You're so clever, work it out for yourself.'

'I can see you would have to do *something*. You couldn't have the CID coming along and sorting it out in no time at all. But . . . that! Didn't you see – can't you see now – that if you'd left the shoe, the evidence could have pointed to a man or a woman. Take it away, and it looked more like a woman's crime. But you *do* see. I can tell you do. Don't tell me . . . ' She tapped her teeth with her thumb nail. 'By heaven, I get it! You could go to Cynthia, tell her you'd faked the evidence, not just keeping quiet about your phone call, but actually taking something away . . . '

'Oh, clever.' Freda lifted her chin in contempt.

'Another detail to present to Cynthia. I'm protecting you, dear. Stuck my neck out for you, sweetheart, made myself an accessory.'

Freda was stubbornly silent, staring at the far wall. No protest, no approval for the theory.

'Surely not,' said Virginia. 'Did you actually suggest it'd be thrilling, if you both ended up in the same cell?'

She had taken it deliberately to the point of ridicule, trying to spark a reaction, but there was still no response. Freda was complacent. She could not, Virginia decided, have been very bright.

'Not very sensible, was it?' she suggested gently, and the hint of compassion drew Freda's head round, her eyes now blazing. 'No matter.' Virginia waved it away. 'You took the shoe to confuse the issue. Later you'd visit Cynthia to tell her what you'd done to protect her. And there she'd be, flatly denying she'd

133

killed Angela.'

'Pitiful!' But Freda did not say whose efforts were pitiful, Virginia's or Cynthia's in denial.

'Throwing your precious gift back in your face. But three days or so later you'd have heard about the medical evidence and the timing involved. Then it seemed impossible Cynthia could have done it. But did you take her *that* gift! I suspect not.'

Freda tossed her head. It was a feeble appeal for sympathy. 'If you'd heard what she said . . . '

'But by that time, or not very much later, it would have filtered through to you from the CID that Angela's lack of shoes had been considered, and that she'd been assumed to have driven without them. So they were working on the assumption that she'd been killed by a woman, using one of her own shoes.'

Harry spoke, his voice a deep and dangerous growl. 'I see now. I begin to see.'

Virginia said nothing. Her eyes were fixed on Freda. Her voice took on an edge, an acidity. Something was bitter in her throat.

'And that was when it changed. No more gifts – they were simply rejected by Cynthia, anyway. Now it was the threat. No more pretence that you believed she had done it. Now you could tell her you believed what she had told you . . . but would anybody else? With Cynthia's motive, what chance would she have? With you, Freda, revealing the truth about the phone call to her, what chance then? Oh, no mention of the medical proof of her innocence. Keep that secret. But plenty of mention of the shoes. Oh yes, the *lack* of shoes. With *that*, the case against Cynthia would be clinched. But if you're nice to me, Cynthia, as it was in the old days . . . and believe me, Cynthia, you'll soon see it's the only way to live . . . if you're nice to me Cynthia, one day I'll bring you a really terrific present. I'll bring you the proof that you *didn't* do it. I'll bring you Angela's other shoe.'

'Now I see,' said Harry, but he said it with a baffled frown.

Virginia got to her feet, surprised to find she could barely stand without swaying. 'So I'll save you the trouble and take it myself. For God's sake, Harry, let's get out of here.'

Freda was on her feet. 'Nobody'll believe this twaddle.'

'A psychiatrist might.'

Virginia bit her lip. As an exit line it might have gone well on the stage, but she was aware that it'd been flip and gratuitous, when she'd tried so hard to be subjective and unemotional.

Freda threw her cigarette at her. Like her authority it had no weight, and fluttered down to the carpet, where the regulation shoe stamped a full stop to the scene.

Harry was silent. He had said he understood. This was not true. There was something in the reasoning he couldn't quite accept.

'You take it, Harry,' said Virginia, thrusting the shoe at him. 'Stick it inside your jacket. A present for your Cynthia.'

It made an awkward bulge. That, with the heavy pistol in a side pocket, along with thoughts of the coming meeting, made Harry distinctly uncomfortable.

14

The front door was still open, but there was no response when Harry tapped his lightest and called her name.

'She's not in.'

He looked round. Virginia waited, staring beyond the house and watching the movement in the shrubbery up by the railway hard-core.

'Cynth!' Harry bellowed.

The side door in the spraying shed swung open. 'I'm in here.'

'Got somethin' for you.'

Harry marched ahead across the dusty surface of the yard. The mud from the previous day had hardened. Virginia was content to allow him to take charge. This was Harry's scene.

Whatever Cynthia had been doing in the shed was not evident. Perhaps nothing. Perhaps communing with Charlie's ghost. She waited for them, standing back against the bench in a defensive posture. The light was again poor, as before consisting of daylight from the gap in the main doors and the open side door. It would have needed only a flip of the switch. Virginia located the switch beside the door she'd just entered, but she did not touch it. Her eyes were becoming accustomed to the gloom.

Harry was making a performance out of it, advancing with a prancing parody of a stately dance.

'It's y'r birthday, Cynth!' he cried. 'Got a pressie for you.'

Then, with a cross-draw that Baldy would have admired, he whipped out the shoe from its hiding place and offered it to her.

She stared at it, lying in his great palm, but made no move.

'It's for you.'

Then her face was lifted and her eyes contained understanding. 'You've been to Freda's?'

He nodded vigorously. 'An' we persuaded her to part with this.'

She took it from him with both hands and looked down at it, then clasped it to her and laughed, though there were tears in it, and said: 'You great idiot, Harry.' And leaned forward and kissed him on the corner of his grinning mouth.

Then she threw back her head and laughed fully. 'Bet she was furious.'

'Didn't seem happy,' Harry agreed. 'Four years she's kept it, four years usin' it to frighten you. Cynth, you can tell her to go take a jump. You can tell her . . .'

Cynthia turned away and placed the shoe on the bench. She spoke away from him. 'I don't think I'll burn it.' She whirled to face him, her eyes alive, her face, now that she'd completely accepted it, dancing with delight and mischief. 'You know what I'm going to do with it, Harry? I'll have it mounted and put in a glass case, and I'll fix it to the wall over the fireplace. Like a stuffed stag's head in those posh places, so's when she comes she can see it there, and *know* . . .'

'When she comes?' he asked. 'You mean Freda?' He was shaking his head.

She reached forward and caught his wrist. Her eyes were now dreamy, her smile, if he hadn't known this was Cynth, complacent.

'She'll come. In two days, perhaps three, she'll come creeping round, tap on the door and put her head round. It's me, Cynthia. Then there'll be the apologies and the protestations. I'll understand, Cynthia, if you never want to see me again. I can hear it in her voice. And I'll be all grand and forgiving, then there'll be tears and laughter, and . . . and . . . Harry, you *are* a dear, to have understood . . .'

'Am I?'

'Because it'll be *there*, Harry, staring at her, and she'll know I've got it now. And all her silly threats . . . how furious that made me, Harry, Freda believing she could threaten me! But now it'll be me, and she can lump it. And d'you know something? She'll like it. Love it. Lap it up. Oh, I know my Freda! Harry, don't look at me like that. Did you think she was hard and callous and strong? Oh no. Not Freda. She could be so . . . so tender and gentle. Like a big, purring neutered tom cat with his claws in and tapping gently at a ball of wool. God . . . so tender . . .'

She turned back to the bench. The tears could no longer be withheld.

'As long as you're pleased, Cynth.' Harry didn't know what he was saying. Anything would fill the gap.

Virginia's voice cut in, calm and practical. 'But we'd expect a little co-operation, Cynthia.'

Cynthia turned with her face fixed in a hard smile, tears salting it. 'Not a present, then? You expect payment.'

'Only information. Charlie went somewhere in his car. Nobody's seen him since. Where could he have gone? Simple enough. It wouldn't hurt you to say . . . if you know somewhere.'

The smile, with the barest flicker of change, became cynical. 'You work hard for it, no mistaking that. I suppose you're entitled to something, though. There was a petrol station. Charlie bought it years ago, when they built that stupid industrial estate place. Said it'd be a gold mine when all the factories opened. But they didn't open, did they? Two or three tried it, and fizzled out. So Charlie had that place – some grand scheme of selling his own cars or something. Got it all rigged out, repair bay, shop, car wash, petrol pump tanks and the bases for the pumps. But it never got as far as petrol pumps. Never sold a gallon or saw a customer. Go and look at it if it'll make you happy. It's derelict.'

'And its location?'

'The corner of Fourteenth Avenue and C Street.'

Harry was looking from one to the other. Was this what they'd come for? He had come in order to witness Cynth's joy at her release from Freda's domination. Get her off her back, he'd put it to himself. He didn't understand what was happening.

'But the shoe . . .' he murmured.

'Harry, Harry!' Cynthia cried. 'It means nothing. This silly shoe!' She turned, picked it from the bench, and threw it away from her. It clanged against a distant empty paint can. 'As though it meant a thing! *She* thought it did. Poor Freda, she never

137

had much on top ... and wonders why she hasn't made sergeant! All it meant ... all her taking it away from that bin meant ... was that the murder looked like a woman had done it. Looked like! It didn't mean that it *was*. It was still anybody's murder, man or woman. As though I'd be scared of a silly shoe! She couldn't take it to her Inspector and say: look what I took from the body. It was the *not* producing it that mattered. So ... what's changed? Now it's *me* not producing it. Harry, I'm happy. Can't you see you've made me happy? Don't pug at me like that.'

'I was,' he said with dignity, 'working it out. You're telling me that now *you* can produce it and say: there you are, that means it doesn't have to be a woman?'

Her shrug was as large as she could make it. It expressed her despair that he'd ever understand anything. 'If you like, Harry.'

'If things got bad, you mean, and they actually accused you?'

'If you *like*.'

'Because you think that's likely?'

Harry was driving on stubbornly, with his head down between his shoulders and his eyes unhappy, because he had to hear it and from Cynth herself. Her eyes snapped. He would normally have ducked for cover.

'You can just cut that out!'

'Well ... I dunno.' His hand came up and rubbed his chin, rasping away. 'Are y' tellin' me ... you ain't sayin' you did do it, Cynth?'

'No!' she shouted. 'No, no and no. How many d'you want?'

'But Freda phoned you ... that day. You said nobody phoned.'

'All-bloody-right. So I told you a lie.'

'An' now you're sayin' you didn't drive there?'

'I'm saying nothing. Not another word.'

'You mean you didn't? Didn' go there and see Charlie's fancy piece ...'

'Of course I went there!' she shouted. 'Now you know. So what?'

Harry didn't know what. He knew only that this was his Cynth, only she wasn't his Cynth at all. He was losing something, was watching it drain away. And he couldn't prevent himself from giving the plug another jerk.

'But you didn't dash off straightaway?'

She nodded agreement, impatiently. 'I'm not gonna dance to

anybody's tune.'

'You wouldn't do that, Cynth. Never. You'd wait a bit . . . but you'd go, all the same.'

He'd meant that as a compliment, but she took it as a sneer.

'I waited until I was good and damn well ready. Then I went.'

'Waited long?' He could hardly get the words out.

'D'you think I timed it?'

'But you went there . . . and saw somethin'?'

'I saw nothing. I did nothing. I came back here. Now bugger off, Harry. And don't come back.'

She might just as well have slapped his face, though that would have hurt her too. She realized it, put a hand to her mouth, but he was already turning away.

It was Virginia who rounded it off for him. 'If you saw nothing and did nothing, Cynthia, it was a waste of time bringing you the shoe.'

Then she stood aside for Harry to fumble past her, and closed the side door behind them.

They were a mile along the lane before she spoke. 'You did that well, Harry.'

'Sarcasm,' he said, 'I can do without.'

'No. Really. It was splendidly calculated.'

He jerked round in the seat, straining the seat belt to full stretch. 'Calculated? You think I worked it out?'

'Getting her to think she owed us something – and we got the address of the petrol station. Then pressing her until she lost her temper – and we got the information that she did drive to the lay-by after all.'

'Is that how *you* do it? You work it out in a pattern, and steer it . . . Damn it, that's indecent.'

She laughed. 'Harry, I'll let you into a secret. I just talk, and see where it leads me. But honestly, you did do well. I'll treat you to lunch.' Knowing he was broke.

'Take it from my ten per cent of the money I might get for this damned gun in my pocket.'

'We'll have to start an accounting system, Harry. Who owes who what.'

'You've got a mind like a . . . what-d'you-call-'em . . . a computer.'

'Thank you, Harry. I'll take that as a compliment. Where to?

139

Back to town or on to Porchester?'

'Porchester. I know a little place. Then the industrial estate'll be on your way home.'

'So it will.'

'And I'm sure you won't be able to digest your evening meal until we've had a look at Charlie's petrol station.'

'You're reading my mind.'

'That'll be the time.'

Harry's little place was better than she had expected, and they enjoyed a respectable cheese soufflé. They had a licence, but Harry refused wine. 'You'll have me dozing off.'

Then they went to explore the industrial estate.

The experience was depressing. This was the encroachment that Oliver Brent's neighbours had feared, but it had never bloomed, had never even flaunted more than a few minor buds. The council, bravely facing a hinted depression and ignoring the warnings of closing factories in the region as mere evidence of outdated practices, had requisitioned large expanses of what had been farmland. The excuse had been that farming, too, was declining in that area. They had cleared the site and constructed a lattice of roadways, and between them had thrown up single-storey factory buildings. In practice, they hadn't finished either the roads or the buildings. Three-quarters of the way through, it was realized that only three of the early constructions had been rented. Industrialists, large or small, were not flocking in and competing for choice lots. The project had failed, and was abandoned.

They drove now along rutted, half-tarmacked roads between row after row of uniform block constructions, some small, some extensive, all grey, and all with every window smashed. The parking lots had never felt a wheel. The flat roofs had never echoed to anything louder than the tinkle of glass. Nothing moved. The plots between were now high with weeds, the signs sagging drunkenly amongst them. To let: 2000 square feet. To let: 200,000 square feet.

The sad folly waited, the winds restless around it. It watched the progress of the Mercedes with blank indifference.

To let: one petrol station.

Charlie had chosen a choice site, a corner plot so that he could lure two streams of traffic. The forecourt was large, encumbered

140

now by six slabs of concrete, destined for pumps, with threaded bolts jutting from them, these bent over and rusted. The shop Cynthia had mentioned was a half-circular kiosk, now a complete wreck, shards of glass still scattered around it. The service bay was one of the standard block constructions – the mini model – though in this case with up-and-over roller-blind doors. Both were up-and-open, revealing a concrete floor scattered with beer cans and chip bags and blown, dead weeds.

They parked on the forecourt. Charlie had chosen his corner with discretion. Their route into the desolation had been from the rear, so that they had now reached the main entrance to the complex, which was visible only a hundred yards away by its large sign raised high in welcome across the wide roadway. The planners had had visions of grandeur, and had named their north–south streets by numbers and their east–west ones by letters. Had they been standing at the welcoming side of the sign, Virginia and Harry could just have read its crumbling information: MANHATTAN INDUSTRIAL ESTATE.

Harry said: 'Can't see why Charlie would drive here.'

'The car wash, obviously. Where else would he be able to drive secretly and check he wasn't being followed, and be able to convert a two-colour car into a black one?'

'Yes,' said Harry. 'Sure. That building at the side? Would that be it?'

They looked at it. What must have been the car wash was a brick erection built on the side of the service bay. It looked solid and unvandalized, as its steel roller-blind door was down, and obviously locked. Charlie had allowed for the fact that the premises would have had to be left very vulnerable at night.

'Let's look round the back,' she suggested. There was a hint of eagerness in her voice.

They walked through the service bay. It had a rear, wooden door, now hanging from one hinge.

The back of the car wash bay looked the same as the front, solid. This steel door was also locked. When in operation, presumably, both doors would have been left open.

'Nothing here,' said Harry.

Virginia stood looking at it. The lock was close to the concrete surface, operating a deadlock into a steel channel. The lower edge of the door showed indentations where the vandals had

141

tried and failed. The finger grip was clogged solid with dirt.

'Harry,' she said, 'there's a tap dripping. I can hear it.'

He had walked on a few yards, looking round him with boredom. 'They forgot to disconnect,' he told her.

'I think we ought to have the door up.'

He came and stood beside her. 'To turn off a tap?'

'Can you break it open?'

He gestured to the bottom edge of the door. 'There's been enough people trying. Why worry for a drip?'

'You could do it. There're tools in the back of the car.'

He looked at her doubtfully, pulled at his lower lip, then went to see what was inside the Merc's boot. Probably, he thought, the tool-kit would consist of a set of feeler gauges and an instruction book in German. He was surprised. He could have stripped the engine with that lot. There was even a crowbar with a point at one end, which would probably lock into the socket of the wheel-nut wrench and provide sufficient leverage. It was almost with triumph that he marched through to the rear again.

'I suppose you know this is breaking and entering.'

'I shall plead ignorance,' she assured him.

'No defence in law,' he said, from his vast experience.

The tongue of the crowbar just wedged itself beneath the bottom edge of the door. The socket of the wrench just failed to slip from the pointed end. He bore down on it, and the lock went with a crack.

'Just to turn off a flamin' tap,' he said.

He cleared the handgrip with the point of the crowbar, got his fingers in, and heaved.

Four years of confined damp from the leak in the car wash sprays had rusted the inside of the door. It did not roll up with a satisfying rumble. It creaked up an inch, so that he could spread his feet, get both hands under the bottom edge, and put the muscles of his back to it. The door groaned to its full lift.

The blue nylon roller brushes dripped mournfully on a black, rusting Escort XR3, its rear to them, its glass smeared and steamed in the confinement. Harry stood, his hands still raised. Behind him, Virginia said in a strange, tight voice: 'Stay where you are, Harry.'

He didn't do so. He stepped back. 'So he did get here,' he said.

'But Angela didn't manage it.'

They stood and stared at it. With the intake of fresh air, the condensation on the outside of the glass was clearing, but inside the car there was another condensation, a finer one, like a thin, grey curtain. This had accumulated over a period of four years, as the car was closed all round.

But it was now possible to see the interior, gradually emerging to become the shapes of the two front seats and their headrests, and the shape of something in the driver's seat. Not Charlie, thought Harry, his brain sighing with relief. Charlie had been bulkier than that. The impression was of a shrivelled form, held there by its seatbelt. But not Charlie! Good Christ, thought Harry, his brain clutching on to it, it can't be Charlie!

But he knew it had to be.

Virginia cleared her throat. 'Can you stay here, Harry?' Her voice was thin.

He wasn't sure about that. He wanted to turn and run. 'Yes.'

'I'll drive to a call box. Don't touch anything.'

He choked. 'No.'

'Be as quick as I can.'

He turned his head. 'I left the boot open.'

'I'll shut it.'

Then he was alone.

He heard the clump of the boot lid closing and the car driving away, heading for the main entrance, and then all he had to do was listen to the water drip, and locate its splash on the roof of the car. The voice behind him nearly took the top out of his head.

'What y' got here then, Harry?'

He turned to face Vic Fletcher, standing there with his hands on his hips and trying to hold a weak grin, but with his face pale.

'For Gossake! Where the hell did you come from, blast you?'

'Been followin' you. I was that patch o' dust on the horizon.'

'Keep y'r distance, Fletcher. I'm warnin' you.'

Fletcher put up his hand in protest. 'Take it easy, mate.' He craned his neck, trying to see past Harry's bulk. 'What y' got . . . heh, that's Charlie's Escort. Well – clever you. Ain't that just dandy!'

'If you've got any sense you'll get outa here. She's gone to get the police.'

Fletcher pursed his lips in a silent whistle. 'Police, eh? That's tricky. That sure is a turn-up for the book. You an' the coppers!

I'm off. Take y' with me, if you like.'

'You ain't funny any more,' Harry told him.

'Knew you'd get to it some day,' Fletcher said, expressing pride in Harry's ability. 'Y' crafty devil. This is what you was after, all the while. I knew it. All that money from the bank job! You'll get ten per cent o' that, I reckon. Nice goin', Harry.'

'Don't be so damn simple. As though there'd be any money here. Whoever did this will've taken it all.'

Fletcher cocked his head. 'Did this? Did what, Harry?' His eyes opened wide. 'Heh! You ain't tellin' me Charlie's in there ... Whew-hew! Well now.'

'I'm not tellin' you anything. Bugger off, Fletcher, an' I can pretend you ain't been here.'

Fletcher shook his head sadly. 'An' there was me, gonna offer you another night at my place.' He brightened. 'Never mind. You'll have a roof over y'r head – at the local nick.' He raised himself on his toes, grinned again, and made a gesture with one hand. 'Be seein' you.'

Harry watched him go. He was left alone with his thoughts. There wouldn't be any money in the car, would there? Nah! Charlie had tried a double-cross on O'Loughlin, but O'Loughlin had been too clever for him. He'd known about this place, and had had a couple of his men waiting for Charlie. So the money *had* reached O'Loughlin after all. He'd simply been trying a bluff, almost telling Virginia the truth when he flashed his blue diamond under her nose. But admitting nothing. Just laughing to himself.

No, he decided, there couldn't possibly be any money in the car. He got no further with his ponderous thoughts, because the Mercedes appeared, followed closely by two police cars.

It was too late to turn and run.

15

They sat in the Mercedes with the hood down. Lowering it and tucking it away had been something that absorbed time, and they both needed air. Now they merely sat, saying nothing. It was seven-thirty and they'd been there for four hours.

Virginia's father was somewhere amongst the group at the rear of the premises. His presence was not necessary, but he'd been sent for because Virginia was involved. A detective-superintendent was in charge, supported by an inspector and two sergeants and the teams from the town's crime squad. Paul Tranter was one of the sergeants.

It was he who walked through the service bay and out to the front to speak to them. He had been instructed what to say and how to say it, so that his approach was formal. He put one hand on the driver's door and stared at it. After one glance at his expression, Virginia turned her face to the windscreen again.

'You can both go home now,' he said. 'Any questions will be asked in the morning. We'll see about that.' The implication was that Oliver Brent would see to it.

Virginia spoke in a lifeless voice. 'It's Charlie Braine?'

'Almost certainly. The press have been informed, so you'd be advised to get moving.'

'Almost certainly?' she asked, knowing it could be nobody else.

'Contents of pockets – a tinge of colour to the hair.'

'You haven't sent for Cynthia?'

He did not say that there would have been nothing for her to identify. 'She's being informed. They're sending a policewoman.'

Virginia breathed out through her teeth. There had been a fear that she would have been asked to see Cynthia, a ridiculous fear because now it was all in the hands of the police. She reached forward for the ignition key in its lock. He said quietly:

'You haven't asked how he died.'

She raised one shoulder. 'By violence, it's not hard to guess.'

'A bullet through the brain. From behind.'

She glanced at him sharply. 'The back of his head? He didn't carry a passenger on that trip, so it's unlikely he was shot in the car.'

'The indications are that he wasn't. Manhandled into the seat after death.'

'So he had time to wash the car.' Strangely, she was pleased that he'd made it that far, and had seen the culmination of his plan.

Paul Tranter gave a grimace, something close to humour.

'You'd have thought he was intending to re-spray it, too.'

'What does that mean, Paul?' She tapped the back of his hand. 'There'd have been no need for that. He only had to wash it clean.'

'There are eight gallon spray-paint cans in the boot.'

'Eight?'

'With no paint in them. Cleaned out, and full of bank notes. We haven't checked, but I wouldn't be surprised if they add up to around a hundred and twenty thousand pounds.'

And that, thought Harry, was a right laugh. He couldn't wait to tell Fletcher that he'd guessed right, after all.

So Charlie, thought Virginia, took time out on the way here to switch the money from the bags to the empty cans he'd supplied himself with. Clever Charlie. What a pity . . .

'There was a white plastic bag,' Tranter said in a neutral voice. 'The proceeds of the jewellery shop robbery were in it, and a pistol.'

'Fired?' she asked quickly.

He shook his head. 'Not even loaded. By heaven! Two goons, one with an empty pistol and one with a toy. Makes you want to cry.'

Harry said: 'A policewoman? Where from?'

'Harry, we were talking about money.' Virginia was grave.

'The policewoman who's gone to tell Cynthia,' Harry explained.

'County,' Tranter told him.

'About that money, Paul. I'd keep it secret if you can manage it. The fact that it's there with him in the car, I mean.'

'Why?'

'Oh . . . I don't know. But people are interested in it. If it's thought he *didn't* have it . . . Oh, I don't know.' She shook her head, annoyed with herself for not being able to clarify the thought.

'Which policewoman?' Harry asked.

'How do I know?' Tranter said acidly. 'Not my region. Whoever's patrolling the Porchester district I'd expect.'

Virginia and Harry glanced at each other. 'Oh Lord,' said Harry. 'Perhaps for the best,' said Virginia.

She reached forward and switched on the engine. 'We'll be off, Paul. Thank you. Tell my father we'll be at home.'

As they drove off the forecourt she said tersely: 'Which way's the quickest, Harry?'

'Back the way we came. But ... Virginia ... it'll be a sea of tears and ... and ...'

'We'd better check. Who knows, with your Cynthia?'

'She is not,' he said flatly, 'my Cynthia.'

She drove fast. The wind ruffled her hair and the increased noise made it difficult to speak. Harry sat quietly, trying to work out how Charlie's death affected the situation. O'Loughlin could well have been responsible, but how could his men have failed to find the money? They'd have torn the car apart before they'd be prepared to return empty-handed to their boss.

A few spots of rain pattered on the screen. She switched the wipers to intermittent. Harry felt their impact on his forehead. The sky was heavy ahead. He felt that his brain was inert, and the cold air round his face did nothing to provoke it into movement.

The blue police car was parked in the yard, and they drew in behind it. 'Better put the hood up,' said Harry, 'or we'll be sitting in water.'

'You do that, then,' she replied, not looking at him as she climbed out of the car. She walked ahead. The headrests were masking the interior of the police car, and the light sky on the horizon was reflected in the rear screen, clouds racing across the glass. She paused beside the car.

'Harry,' she said quietly.

She was standing at the driver's door with one hand on the handle, but hadn't opened it. Her tone alerted him. He strode to her side quickly.

Freda Graham was sitting behind the wheel, her hands clasped to it as though about to drive away, though the engine was dead. She was staring directly forward, the checkered cap firm on her hair, her eyes beneath the peak sightless. Her face was set, like hardened wax. She had not noticed their arrival. Harry detached Virginia's fingers from the handle and opened the door himself. A dash of rain swept his shoulders, and drops fell on Freda's knees. She did not move.

'Freda!' said Virginia sharply.

There was not the slightest response. Virginia thought that if Freda did not blink soon she would scream. Harry touched the fingers gripping the wheel. They were cold, and he couldn't detach them. For one second he thought she could be dead, but

147

there was a steady, though too slow, rise and fall of the bosom beneath the uniform jacket.

Virginia's eyes roved wildly. The front door of the bungalow was open, as they'd seen it before, but so too was the side door to the spraying shed.

'Harry, quickly.'

Leaving the car door swinging, they ran to the side door.

During their previous visit, Virginia had not noticed Cynthia's shotgun. Perhaps it had been lying on the rear bench. The shoe, which Cynthia must have rescued from where she had thrown it, now stood on the bench, at the position Cynthia had been standing. Perhaps she had been standing there, having just replaced the shoe. It was directly beneath the shoe that she was now lying, face down. The shotgun lay at her side.

Thoughts crowded Virginia's mind as she went forward tentatively, but over-riding them her conscious mind still operated.

'The switch is by the door, Harry.'

He pressed it, and Charlie's overhead lights, now dimmed by accumulated dust, snapped on. In the semi-gloom they seemed to be brilliant. He hurried to her side, not wanting her to approach Cynthia alone.

The back of her head was smashed in, the obvious conclusion being that it resulted from a single discharge of the shotgun. This was at once dismissed, as it was the butt of the shotgun that had clearly been used. Matted blood was on it.

Harry's first feeling was of relief. She had known nothing – it had been from behind. The second was of a hot pride, that this had not been suicide, and that it had been necessary to sneak up from behind in order to destroy his Cynth.

The rain was thundering on the iron roof. Virginia drew back. 'The telephone, Harry.' Harry moved towards the side door. 'Try the one on the bench.' She gestured. He wondered why she didn't do it herself. He didn't know she was close to collapse, so close that only intense concentration kept her on her feet.

The phone set was black, overlaid with a thick patina of grey dust and vagrant spray from a hundred cars. It was not possible to read the numbers on the dial, but he didn't need that for 999. He was surprised to get a dialling tone. He asked for police, and at a second thought for an ambulance. When he replaced the handset, Virginia was clinging to the open doorway.

148

'Your car,' he said. 'Come on.'

But she rejected the touch of his hand on her arm. The lashing rain seemed to revive her, and have her panting for air to her starved lungs. They ran for the Mercedes.

Harry paused at the police car. Freda had not moved, but she was now making whimpering noises, and tears ran from her chin. The right side of her uniform skirt was soaked black. Harry closed the door and hurried on.

Virginia was standing staring at the wet leather seats, the car door open and taking her weight.

'Damn you, Harry,' she screamed. 'You didn't put the hood up.'

She collapsed on to the seat and buried her face in her hands. Harry stared at her heaving shoulders, then set about erecting the hood over her. He slid in beside her, reached back for her bag, found cigarettes and lighter, lit one for her though he didn't smoke, parted her hands, and when she glanced at him popped it between her lips. For a few moments it hung there, then she drew on it, coughed, shuddered, and sat back with her head against the rest.

She finished the cigarette before she spoke, with meek gravity. 'Thank you, Harry.'

He nodded, but she didn't see. He got out of the car because the first of the police cars had arrived, containing a policeman and a policewoman, in uniform.

'In there,' said Harry, indicating the shed. 'I sent for an ambulance.'

'The word came through she was dead.'

'For your mate.' Harry jerked his thumb.

The policewoman went over to the car door, opened it, and spoke to Freda. Getting no response, she went round and got in beside her. Harry saw her take Freda's cap from her head, then her fingers from the wheel and clasp the hand in hers. He couldn't see whether they spoke together.

Other cars began to arrive. Harry prowled the yard restlessly, now so wet that he hesitated to enter Virginia's car again. These were the county police, but once they'd had a word with Harry, ('We just drove here from the industrial estate.') and when the officer in charge had sat beside Virginia for ten minutes in her car and it had become evident that the two crimes were linked, radios were used and the team from the town force drove over.

One of these was Oliver Brent. Both teams were under his jurisdiction. Another was Paul Tranter, who avoided Harry's eyes. After a while Brent came out from the shed and gestured to Harry, leading him over to the Mercedes, where they stood beside the open driver's window. Brent's face was expressionless but his eyes were ice-cold. Rain dripped from the brim of his tweed hat.

'As it's clear that you two did no more than drive here and discover this, you're not being detained. You will drive home, Virginia, both of you, get yourselves dry and warm and some food inside you, and wait. I shall be a long while here, but we have to talk. Tonight. Understand?'

Virginia nodded. For a moment his fingers touched her shoulder. 'It's been a bad day, my dear.' Only then did a hint of warmth enter his voice.

Harry walked round and slid into the passenger's seat with a squishing sound. She backed into the lane, edging round the clusters of cars and vans.

'You're all right?' he asked.

'I can drive.'

But she'd driven a hundred yards before she put on the lights, seeming surprised that it was dark. The wipers were still on intermittent, a wipe every five seconds. Half a mile later she switched to normal wipe.

Ada fussed and worried, and Harry found himself once more in the same dressing gown, his clothes commandeered before he thought to remove the pistol from the pocket of his leather jacket. Then there was soup and a hot plate of something strengthening, on a serviette on their laps, all informal. And finally, Ada marching in with a tray on which rested a bottle of brandy and glasses, along with Baldy's pistol.

'And what,' she demanded, 'may I ask, is this?'

Virginia sighed. 'Put it on the table over there, Ada please. My father will take charge of it.'

Ada nervously did so, raised her chin, and walked out with quivering dignity.

'There goes my ten per cent of possibly three hundred quid,' said Harry lugubriously, hoping Virginia would take it as a joke.

Her eyes danced at him. She handed him a balloon glass with a tiny pool of brandy swimming in the bottom.

150

'Harry, you *are* an idiot. You and I, together, have found the bank haul and the jewellery haul. In due course we shall receive a just reward, probably ten per cent of something like a hundred and twenty-seven thousand pounds. That's over six thousand for you, and you're worrying about thirty pounds.'

Harry, to whom £6000 was a sum you heard about but never actually handled, puckered his lips and said: 'In due course. Could be months.' It was difficult to accept the possibility.

'But *then*, Harry, you'll be independent. You can go your own way.' She cocked her head at him. 'You won't need to find work...'

'No.' He wondered why so large a glass held such a small amount. 'You've got it wrong. Then I'll be independent, and I can afford to take that job your father mentioned.'

She hesitated, wondering whether she would ever understand him. 'Yes,' she murmured. 'Of course.'

Then they waited. She put a tape of Bach on her hi-fi, through which he dozed. She watched his face in repose. It was strange that the character his battered features normally concealed was now more clearly revealed.

Oliver Brent arrived at two o'clock. They were both asleep, but instantly alert. For a moment he stood in the doorway, and if he smiled it brought the barest flush of colour to his strained, grey face. He seemed smaller inside his clothes.

'You stayed up,' he said in grave approval, and walked past the table on which the pistol lay. He seemed not to notice it, but headed straight for the easy chair Virginia had placed for him.

'I see you've been at my brandy. Virginia, I'd appreciate...'

'I'll get a clean glass.' She was on her feet at once.

The movement of his hand was weary. 'It doesn't matter. Whichever glass doesn't smell of lipstick.'

'I'm not wearing...'

'I know that. It was a pleasantry, my dear, indicating that I'm not too annoyed with you. But make it a large one. By the time you've told me what's been going on, I may well need it.'

All this, Harry realized, was a setting of the mood between them. Each had to know how matters stood. There was a mutual trust that had to be treasured. There was a hint that honesty all round was imperative.

Harry sat back and let it happen.

151

'How is Freda?' she asked.

'Tell me where the firearm came from.'

She handed him the glass. 'I'm concerned about Freda.'

He sniffed at his brandy. 'At this moment she's in hospital. My latest news is that she's not spoken.'

'Catatonic.' She nodded. 'The experts call it catatonic.'

'Do they? The pistol, my dear.'

She sat opposite him, leaning forward, and related the O'Loughlin episode as though drawing him into the excitement of it. Apart from the fact that his lips tightened, he seemed not to be affected. When she'd finished with O'Loughlin he said: 'I trust you appreciate the danger you were in.'

'Harry was with me.' Thus she dismissed the danger.

'Even so . . .'

'And Cynthia?'

He sighed. 'Dead, of course. You must have realized. One blow from the gunstock.'

'Freda found her. No wonder she's in shock.'

'You know something there, too?'

She told him what they had discovered about their relationship, and the way the shoe had been used.

'We saw the shoe,' he told her.

'Angela's.'

'I realized that.' He sighed. 'Miss Graham will not, I should imagine, be long in the force.' He sipped the brandy and raised his nose from inside the glass. 'If not worse. Now tell me how you came to locate the petrol station, and the body of Charles Braine.'

'Harry used the business of the shoe to pressure Cynthia into telling us *somewhere* he might have gone.'

Harry stirred. 'It wasn't quite like that.'

Neither of them took the slightest notice of him. Although their dialogue seemed idle and undramatic, they were locked in a conflict that had been going on since her teens. Oliver Brent had always encouraged her into a spirit of independence. Having no wife to advise him, he'd not understood how dangerous this might be. Since she'd reached the age of twenty he'd been trying to undo the result of his efforts, but, being basically a kind man, he'd not had the necessary ammunition. Now they competed in methods that allowed each to emerge unscathed from their clashes, and happy that neither had inflicted distress. Sometimes, for Brent, it was difficult.

'But surely,' he said now, 'you didn't expect Charles Braine still to be there?' Sometimes, by trying too hard, he heard his voice emerging with a ridiculous formality.

She smiled at him. 'Of course not, father.' She too could be formal. 'Nor did we expect to find the money intact, and the gun and the jewellery.'

'The gun was empty,' he said. 'Unloaded.'

'I know.'

'Who told you that?' he asked sharply.

'Paul Tranter.'

'I'll skin him.'

'You'll do nothing of the sort.'

He smiled thinly. 'And that's *all* the trouble you've got yourself into?'

'Every bit. Tell me how things stand.'

He blinked. 'It's all official . . .'

'Oh . . . come on. I know my thinking on it, but I'd like to hear whether you agree.'

'*I* agree? With you? Well . . .' Then he laughed. Harry smiled. She said: 'Let's have it, daddy.'

Brent got up to pour himself another measure of brandy. With his back to her he permitted himself another grimace. He was not a very good liar, and although what he was about to say was not going to be a direct lie, there was to be a certain amount of evasion in it. The moment his eyes fell on the pistol, he'd realized he had to put an end to Virginia's activities. If orders wouldn't do that, and he knew they would not, then guile it had to be. Guile he detested, partly because he was a basically straightforward man, but also because it required too much mental effort. Besides, she usually saw through him.

He sat down again, leaned back in the chair, and crossed an elegant ankle over his other knee.

'I'll have to talk myself into it, because what you've told me is fresh evidence. Freda Graham hasn't said a word. I left orders for them to phone if she did, as I believe she's under sedation. But now, taking into consideration the emotional involvement between her and Cynthia Braine, and the possibility that Angela was therefore linked with it, we'll have to give fresh thought to the original murder. The difficulty at that time was that nobody but Harry knew Angela was stranded at the lay-by, so that only the casual motorist driving past seemed a possible alternative suspect. But the actual crime didn't have the elements of such a set-up. You'll have thought of all this, my dear?'

'We discussed that, Harry and I.'

'Then you'll have considered the fact that there was one other person who knew she was there, Freda Graham, though she was there as a policewoman. Suspicion never even drifted in her direction.'

'And surely not now,' Virginia suggested quietly.

'You think not?'

'Angela was the one person she'd want to keep alive. Angela was taking Charlie out of Cynthia's life, and leaving Freda a clear field.'

'Hmm!' he said. 'I get your point.' He thought about it, and whilst doing so reached sideways for a silver box with a cedar lining, and helped himself to a cigar. 'Harry? No? Good man. May I borrow your lighter, my dear?'

By the time he had it going to his satisfaction he'd worked out what he was going to say.

'Of course, I'll have to have a word with the psychologists about this. But it seems to me, from what you've said, that she *hasn't* had such a clear field of it, even with Charles out of the way. This ... business with Cynthia ... I understand it was going on before Charles left her ...' He was hesitant.

'Most certainly. It was *why* he left her.'

'But since then it's fallen on hard times. Yes. Perhaps Freda realized that could happen. A clandestine affair, even a normal one between a man and a woman, can be exciting. The very unattainableness ... is there such a word? Anyway, you can see what I mean. Perhaps Freda would realize their affair would collapse when Charles wasn't there as a kind of safety barrier.'

Harry, who had thought of Charlie, perhaps not consciously, in that way, said: 'Oh yes.'

Virginia tossed him a frown. 'Freda said she wanted Cynthia to *see* the woman Charlie was going away with.'

'She said that recently. Four years after the event. There's been time for a full defensive mechanism to have been erected.'

'Yet she *did* phone Cynthia. Cynthia confirmed that.'

'And told you she saw nothing. Which would be the case if she

154

delayed long enough, and if Angela was dead and hidden by then.'

Virginia pouted, then shrugged. To Harry it was clear that Brent was no mere figurehead in the scheme of things, as he'd always thought was the case with top men in the police.

Brent waited politely for any comment, received none, and continued. He was now well into his verbal stride.

'Freda knew what was going on from her personal knowledge and from what she'd heard on the car radio about the two crimes. On the trip to the lay-by she worked out what she would do. Her reasoning would be that her affair with Cynthia stood a better chance with Cynthia's husband back at home, and conducted clandestinely, than with him out of the way with Angela. This seems to have been borne out by subsequent events. So she seized the chance to get rid of Angela by killing her with the heel of Angela's own shoe. Freda's strong enough for that. She took away both shoes, the right one because it was the murder weapon, the left one for a very practical reason. As you yourself worked out, my dear, and so cleverly . . .'

'Father!' she said sharply.

He grinned at her. She hated condescension. 'I meant that. As you worked out, the complete lack of shoes indicated a woman murderer, but more specifically a woman who must at the time have been wearing stiletto heels. So this also protected one other person, a woman too, who would certainly not be wearing stiletto heels. A woman police officer in uniform. Freda was practical, you see. Self-defence. It would only be later, when the affair with Cynthia seemed to be running into heavy weather, that she would realize the shoe might be used for persuasion.'

'Sheer blackmail.'

'Not, I think, so direct as that. But it was used in such a way. Freda Graham must have a tortuous mind.' He frowned over that for a moment.

Virgina pushed him on. 'And Cynthia's death?'

'Well . . . you know yourself how emotionally charged the situation had become. I rather feel that Cynthia was still clinging to the possibility that her husband would return to her. Heavens, the poor woman was in a completely confused state of mind over the situation with Freda. She *wanted* Freda's affection, but not in so . . . heavy and wholesale a manner as Freda presented it. She

155

might well have taken refuge in it, if she could have been the dominant figure. But if Charles Braine returned . . . then it could all go back to its light and playful and secret bit of fun . . .' He grimaced, finding himself unable to find the correct words. 'And be safe. Yes. Be safe. How would she feel, then, if Freda arrived with the news that Charles had been found dead? Freda, telling her that, and waiting to take charge . . . no, I think Cynthia would reject her outright. I think Cynthia, in those circumstances, would turn her back on her.'

He was silent. Harry stirred in his chair. Virginia bit her lip.

'So who killed Charlie Braine?' she asked at last.

'Who else but O'Loughlin? Not personally, of course, but through his minions.'

Harry, who had never heard that word actually used, was sparked into activity. 'He said he didn't.'

'As he would.'

'Nah! It was the way he said it. What he wanted was the money.'

'He'd want that, of course.'

Harry shook his head. 'None of his men would miss the paint cans.'

'All the same, O'Loughlin's the obvious bet.'

Virginia shot a glance of approval in Harry's direction. 'He offered me a diamond to find the money for him.'

Brent pouted. 'Paste. Worthless. He was seizing the chance to establish an alibi.'

'An alibi, father, is legal proof that you were elsewhere at a specific time, and of *course* he was elsewhere.'

'I know very well the definition of alibi. A bluff, then. A cover.' But the irritation in his voice indicated that at last they had reached a point on which he was uncertain. Virginia nodded. She knew. He saw that she knew.

'It's getting late,' he said.

'Perhaps Freda will be fit to make a statement in the morning,' Virginia suggested. 'And deny it all.'

'Perhaps you two will be fit to make statements.' He heaved himself to his feet. 'And perhaps you'll show Harry the guest room. Good night to you both.'

They watched him leave, Virginia with a frown of concern.

'The poor dear's exhausted.'

156

'Yes,' Harry agreed. He wasn't feeling too grand himself.

'Or he wouldn't have tried to fool me with all that nonsense. He knows I can see right through him. Did *you* believe it, Harry?'

He pulled an earlobe. 'Not altogether.'

'Not about Angela's death?'

'It wasn't convincing.' He scratched his chin.

'And Cynthia's?'

'I can't see her turning her back on Freda, not from what she told us.'

'And Charlie's?'

'I'm not sure o' that. Could just be, I suppose.'

'My own thinking exactly. Come on, I'll show you the guest room.'

16

Harry had never known anybody who kept special accommodation ready for guests, except at the prisons. This room was different. She had told him that he had his own bathroom, and to come down to breakfast when he was ready. As it was after three by that time, that promised to be late.

Having no pyjamas, he slipped between the sheets in his Y-fronts. Never before had he encountered the luxury of that first intimate contact with fine, cool cotton sheets. It occurred to him that his pants were probably less clean than the sheets, so he got out of bed, shed them, and climbed in again to enjoy once more the initial contact. He then decided that *he* was less clean than the sheets, so he ran himself a hot bath, soaked himself in scented water, dried himself on a large, soft towel, and once more slid between those wonderful sheets. His last thought was that he would never be able to get out of them again.

'Sleep well?' she said.

'What day is it?'

She laughed. Her father had left her a note: The station at 11.0. They were already late.

'I made the bed,' he told her.

'You didn't need to do that.'

157

'They taught us that in prison.'

She looked down at her cornflakes. 'Yes. I suppose they would.'

They both realized, at the same moment, that they were awkward with each other. No more was said until Ada brought his clothes and Virginia reminded him they had an appointment to make statements for the authorities.

In the car, he said: 'I suppose this is the end of it.'

'Not if you come to work for my father.'

'I didn't mean that. The case. *Our* case.'

'But I thought we agreed . . . surely you agreed with me, Harry . . . that Freda couldn't have killed Angela.'

'Of course she didn't. *That* wasn't what I meant.'

'Then what?' She lifted her chin and pouted.

'When you look like that . . . there's a word for it.'

'Patient?' She glanced at him. 'I know what you mean. You're thinking they'll put a stop to us.'

'You knew all the while.'

'Just wondering if you did,' she said, turning into the yard of the police station. 'And you know as well as I do that we can't back off now.'

'Your father obviously expects us to stop.'

'He needn't know.'

'Will he be here?'

'I've just parked in his reserved space. No, he'll be at headquarters.'

'What doesn't he need to know?' he asked suspiciously.

'That we're going to have to see O'Loughlin again.'

She locked the car door. 'Can't trust this lot.' They looked at each other across the hood. 'Ohoh!' he said. 'And why have we got to see *him* again?'

'You must have realized, Harry. If O'Loughlin's men weren't responsible for Charlie's death, then it must have been linked with the Freda-Cynthia-Angela-Charlie set-up. That's all we've got left. So we need to be certain about O'Loughlin. That was why I asked Paul to see if they could keep the money secret.'

'Clever. Quick thinking.'

'No it wasn't. I just had a feeling. It's taken me all night to work out what that feeling meant.'

They walked into the police station shoulder to shoulder.

158

It absorbed a lot of precious time. They were met by Sergeant Paul Tranter, in the suit she'd seen him wearing often, but in a cloak of officialdom she had not. They were two witnesses who had been so unfortunate as to discover two murders in one day. They were not his god-daughter and Harry Hodnutt, with whom, in different circumstances, he might make idle conversation.

'You will go into that room, Miss Brent, and the sergeant will take a statement. Mr Hodnutt, you will go into that one to make yours. Afterwards, the statements will be typed and you'll be asked to read them before signing. If you do not wish to read them, they will be read out to you and you will make such a statement at the end before signing. Is that understood?'

'Miss Brent,' thought Virginia. Chopping me down to size.

'Mister Hodnutt,' thought Harry. I really am going up in the world.

They made their statements, and were allowed to wait in the canteen while these were minutely checked by the inspector for discrepancies, before they were sent for typing. The inspector gloomily thought that they could well have managed with one statement, so closely did they agree.

Eventually they were released, but not before Sergeant Tranter had given them an official warning that they'd better keep their noses out of police affairs from that moment on.

'Yes, Paul,' she agreed, and, at his frown, 'yes, Sergeant.'

'Better get some lunch,' she said, as they went to the car.

'About money . . .'

'I'm not going to start arguing with you on that again. Until you've got your own, it'll be on me.'

'You'll be driving me to crime again,' he complained.

'What we're going to do this afternoon probably is crime. Shall we stop for lunch on the way? I like to get a few miles beneath my wheels.'

'You're paying the piper.'

They stopped in Kidderminster for lunch. Her mind wasn't on it, and Harry, realizing that her brain was otherwise engaged, was silent. Shortly afterwards they drew in and topped up the tank, and Virginia insisted on checking her tyre pressures. Harry said nothing.

'You take the wheel, Harry, and see how she handles.'

He glanced at her, but was still silent.

159

During three years with Charlie Braine he had driven almost everything on wheels, and, the success of his endeavours sometimes depending on a fast journey of evasion, knew all there was to know about handling. This car felt as though the four wheels were at his fingertips. He could place it with confidence, rely on his reflexes and find it eager to comply, and sit back and simply let it go.

'She's a beauty,' he said, easing back to eighty.

She breathed out slowly. 'Where did you learn to drive like that?'

'Guess.' He was now down to sixty. The rearview mirror was clear of police cars. 'Are you going to tell me what we're trying to do?'

'It's fairly logical. We went to see O'Loughlin. He wanted to see us, or we wouldn't have got near, and what he wanted to put over was that he'd planned that bank job – without actually admitting it – but that he'd lost both Charlie and the money. He talked a lot about his professional standing, and needing the money in his hands in order to prove that nobody got away with anything where Sean O'Loughlin was concerned. You with me?'

'If anything, ahead.'

'Good. Now ... he offered me a diamond if I could produce the money, and produce Charlie as a bonus. He said that stone was worth nearly as much as the bank haul, on the surface to tell me that it wasn't the *value* of the haul he was worried about, but the actual stuff, to rustle under the noses of his contacts. That could have been a bluff, or it could have been the truth. What I want to know is which.'

He turned the car into the mountain rides. The surface now was not as firm as they'd encountered with the Range Rover, but the Mercedes, with its wide tyre treads, handled it well. Harry barely slowed.

'Now you've lost me,' he admitted.

'What we want to know is whether his men, on his orders, killed Charlie, but for some reason failed to find the money. That's *all* we want to know. He'll have heard that we found Charlie's body. It's been on the news and in the papers. But he doesn't know the money's been found.'

'Your quick thinking.'

'I told you. It was a feeling. If we can make him believe we still

160

have ideas about finding that money, I think I can persuade him into giving enough information about what actually happened that day to clear the air on Charlie's death. If he didn't have anything to do with *that*, then we can forget him.'

'But will he forget us?'

She tapped his shoulder. He'd forgotten how sharp her knuckles were. 'Why d'you think I checked the tyre pressures, Harry? Why have I taken the opportunity to see how well you can drive? If things work out as I hope, he'll put somebody onto following us, and I'll be happier if you can drop them.'

He was continually being surprised by her naïvety. The way he put it to himself: fools rushing in. And yet she was by no means a fool. He tried to understand her attitude, and decided that it arose from the fact that she lived in another world. Crooks, to her, were merely the people her father's minions (he loved that word) put behind bars. They were not real people. O'Loughlin was not real to her, he was a puppet who played at being a big, tough captain of crime, supported by a cast of extras who allowed her to take their guns away from them. Heavens, he thought, to her he might not, himself, seem real.

With an abrupt shock he realized that the difficulty could well be that Harry *was* real to her, the only genuine villain she'd actually come to know. And she'd found him, he was embarrassed to admit, simplicity to handle and about as tough as stale elastic. Good Lord, he thought, she's taking us there on the assumption they're all as harmless as me. Startled, he burst out:

'We might never have a chance to drive fast and drop anybody. What if he's not interested in the money, and now that Charlie's been found dead...'

'But he'll be ever so pleased we found him,' she said eagerly.

'Oh sure. Sure he will. Particularly if it was him who had him killed.'

She was silent. He drove on, and took the turning to Sean Lake.

'I suppose it's too late to turn back and give it some more thought?' she said quietly.

It was the first time she'd hinted at a lack of confidence. He said: 'We're already past his early-warning guards. Better keep going. We'll sort 'em out.'

If he'd glanced sideways he'd have seen her smile a small, secret smile.

The lake looked depressing. Although there had been no rain that day, the sky hung dark and thick over the water. The surrounding trees seemed still to be bowed by the weight of the past rain, and the water itself was sluggish and dense. The jetty waited, its plank surface black and slippy underfoot. Across on the island, indistinct in the poor light, the log-faced mansion appeared to be deserted. The two power boats lay close to their landing stage, huddled against it for comfort.

Harry took the phone from its box. It was slimy in his hand. 'Yes?'

'Virginia Brent and Harry Hodnutt to see Sean O'Loughlin.'

'Wait.'

Harry did so, not certain whether that meant wait there for the boat, or wait with the phone to his ear. He hadn't heard it click off. To his surprise, O'Loughlin himself came on.

'Now what?' It was a snarl, and there was phlegm in it.

'Things to discuss.'

'I know what things. I hear the news, you damned fool. He's dead, ain't he?'

To Harry, who'd been listening with the phone away from his ear so that Virginia could hear, this was their answer. O'Loughlin was savage because Charlie was dead, which meant that he was disappointed he couldn't bring that about himself. Which meant he hadn't been responsible for it.

Virginia touched his elbow. 'Let me.' He handed her the phone.

'Don't you want your money?' she asked calmly.

'You mean you've got it?'

'Not with me. Be your age O'Loughlin. I'm not going to discuss this over the phone, so do we come over or not?'

There was a pause, then he snapped: 'Wait there.'

She hung up the phone, shut the door of its little hut, and told Harry: 'You don't want to let them shout you down.'

Harry sighed. His shoulders sagged. Across the water two figures were climbing into the ocean-going racer that yearned for the sea.

Red was one of the two. He stepped on to the jetty with his handgun in full view, clasped in his right fist. His companion was a weazel with a sneer and no obvious weapon. To Harry he was the more dangerous. A knife man, Harry decided, a man who enjoyed his work. So Baldy was no longer on the strength.

'We're not armed,' said Harry, 'and if you think you're goin' to check, forget it.' He had noticed a tenseness about Red, a nervousness.

But Red's companion leered and said: 'Stand aside, bigmouth.'

Harry moved in front of him, and smiled. 'Relax,' he said. 'Reach for your blade and I'll break your arm.'

'Okay, Lou,' said Red huskily. 'As he said, relax. Let the boss sort it out.'

Lou took it badly, backing off, the leer retreating to become nothing more suggestive than his normal sneer.

They sat in the stern, silent, as Lou watched them every second. From time to time his tongue moistened his lips. Red put the boat against the landing stage where he wanted it without a bump, and gestured with his pistol. He followed them, once more, through the house.

For a moment Virginia couldn't understand why, on such a dull and cool day, they should again be met on the terrace outside. Then she did. It was, in effect, a wooden platform suspended on piles above the water, and, as it overlooked an inlet, it was equally true that it was overlooked by the surrounding growth of trees. They would be in clear view from both sides, so that hidden marksmen could pick them off at a signal from O'Loughlin, and yet themselves be out of hearing. Red, she saw, was the only one who was to be present, and he only as a token gesture, a distraction from where the danger really lay.

O'Loughlin was at the same table. He was wearing a blue suit and black shoes. His eyes were expressionless, his fingers restless on the table surface. There was a chair already placed opposite to him. He made no invitation, but she walked across and sat down.

'We've not been searched,' she told him. 'I didn't find it pleasant last time. But I give you my word . . .'

He laughed flatly. 'Your word?'

'You're getting nothing else.'

'My dear young woman, I can raise a finger and you'd both be stark naked in one minute flat. Let's get on with it, for God's sake.'

She glanced at Harry, and nodded towards the rail. It placed Harry in the greatest peril, because he was right out in the open,

Red having remained well back. But she did not believe the peril was valid. O'Loughlin wanted to talk. Harry leaned against the rail, glanced down at the water, then he was all attention. He smiled at Red, who gave no indication that it reached him.

'You know about Charlie?' she asked.

'He's dead.'

'You don't seem pleased. Isn't that what you wanted?'

'Don't play around with me. Of course I wanted him dead, but I wanted to do it myself.'

'There was a bullet in the back of his head.'

'Why've you come here? Get on with it.'

'You're going somewhere?' She waited for a reply, but all that happened was that his lips tightened. 'All right. He was shot. That seems like your men's work. No money. Perhaps that was their work too.'

He leaned forward. His voice was brittle. 'We've had this. Not one of my men would dare, and I knew where every one of them was that day. To the inch. To the second.'

'So there's something missing,' she said, nodding her satisfaction.

'The money's missing, you stupid . . .'

'Something missing out of your story, too. A link.'

'Story! Are you doubting my word?' He fingered the knot of his tie, daring it to be out of alignment.

'Your memory . . . perhaps. You say you still want the money – well, I've got an idea, but I'd need more information from you.'

'You've had all you're getting.'

'This is a waste of time,' she told him impatiently. 'I could well find the money, but why the hell should I hand it over to you?'

'Otherwise, you'd die.'

'You wouldn't know I had it. Let's stop bandying words. What's in it for me? For us?'

'The blue diamond.'

She made a gesture of contempt. 'My information is that it's paste.'

'If I tell you . . .' His fury was more disturbing because of his effort at control.

'Let's see it again.' She put out her left palm.

His eyes held hers. 'What do you want to know?'

'First of all – if it's real.'

164

'I have an assessor's valuation . . .'

'On the one it was copied from.'

'By heaven, I'm glad I never married.' His lips twitched. It could have been a joke.

'Perhaps, if you had, she wouldn't have let you make the mistake.'

'Mistake! What mistake?'

'The one that resulted in you losing the money. Which I might yet manage to recover for you. For me, if that diamond's fake.'

But indeed, he'd loved the word-play. Surrounded as he was by men whose accomplishments did not include conversation, he was a starved man, shrivelling on a diet of mundane inanities. He laughed. What was the odd diamond here and there? He reached into his top pocket, extracted a folded blue lawn handkerchief, and produced the diamond from it. He placed it in her left palm with grave care.

She stared at it. She picked it up between finger and thumb on her right hand, and held it up to the light.

'It seems very dull.'

'There's poor light,' he offered.

'All the same . . .'

Then she tossed it with apparent contempt towards the lake. Her crisp: 'Harry!' led it by only a fraction of a second, but she'd admired his reactions at the wheel of the Mercedes. She admired them now. Like an annoying fly passing his head, he snatched it from the air, and held it in his palm over the water. Then he changed his mind, placed it carefully on the curved upper surface of the log rail, and held it down with a huge forefinger.

'Gotcha!' he said.

O'Loughlin sat with both arms resting on the table surface. Colour mounted to his cheeks, and receded, being unwelcome. The tic flickered. His lips were grey.

'You will never know,' he whispered, 'how close you came to death.'

She smiled. It cost her a year of her life.

He raised both hands beneath her nose, forefingers to thumbs. 'Snap my left fingers, and you would die. My right, and he would.'

'And lose your stone?'

'But if . . .' Life returned to his eyes. '*If* that stone is paste, as

165

you claim, then I'd be willing to lose it.'

'So ... as we're still alive, that means you were telling the truth about it?'

'Perhaps.'

'So we'll use it as insurance, and hope you'll go on telling the truth.'

Behind Harry, a fish raised its head, disliked what it saw, and disappeared with a plop. O'Loughlin's head came round. Harry felt the sweat between his shoulder blades, but managed a thin, reassuring smile, bottom lip only, and raised his eyebrows. O'Loughlin cleared his throat, and Red relaxed.

'Nobody pressures me, my dear,' O'Loughlin said at last. He sounded sorry she'd gone so far.

'I needed something as a persuader.'

'But you see ... with every word you say you persuade me more and more that I'd enjoy watching you die. There could come a point where it would be worth the loss of a genuine stone.'

'Then I'll keep it short.'

'I'd advise that.'

She sat back. 'Let's get on to the bank job, which we both know was yours. You fixed it with Charlie to do the jeweller's, as a diversion, and to drive away in a garish car to draw off the police. Clever. You added to that by timing it so that the bags of cash could be thrown from the getaway car into Charlie's Escort. Still clever, though it was getting a little fancy.'

He leaned forward, taking her into his murky confidence. 'I was worried about that. Simple is best. But it was only a trial run. Lose the cash, lose a few men ...' He shrugged.

'But not so casual a loss when Charlie out-thought you? When that happened, you lost more than money.'

'I never guessed he'd be so damned stupid.'

'And *there's* the missing link I spoke about. You missed something out.'

'I did not.'

'You can't tell me you'd allow one man, amateur or not, scared of you or not, to drive away, alone, with the complete haul. You'd have that covered. Especially you, because you never miss a detail. But you haven't mentioned ...'

'Oh ...!' He waved it away with elegant fingers. 'I didn't think

166

you'd want to know. Of course I covered it. A man to tail him. It should've been easy, with all those police cars chasing Charlie. But the idiot lost him.'

'Did he, though? *Did* he lose him?'

'He reported back that he'd lost him.'

'And you believed that?'

'I believed it.'

'I thought we were onto the truth game,' she snapped.

'His name was Kieron,' he said gently. 'Kieron O'Loughlin. My son. My best driver. If he said he lost him . . .'

'You said "was".'

'He died.'

'I'm sorry.'

'I don't like to talk about it.'

'I said I'm sorry.'

'But to you . . .' His voice was acid. 'To you, I will. He died at Le Mans. Two years ago. Driving a car I'd financed for him.'

She hesitated a moment for thought. Her next line was obvious. His vicious eyes challenged her to use it. She plunged.

'Which perhaps he'd have preferred to finance himself?'

'What?'

'If my guess is right, and he *didn't* lose Charlie.'

Harry listened to the dismal drip of water from the trees into the lake. It was a cold drip. He wondered if he'd be past feeling its chill by the time his body broke its surface.

O'Loughlin's face gathered itself. It had been crumbling, but now it returned to a grim mask. 'Explain!' he rasped.

The chair creaked as she shifted her weight. 'Charlie Braine was more clever than he was given credit for. He had plans. He was going to disappear with your money. This money was last seen in canvas bags, being thrown into the back of his Escort. We know now that he intended to wash his car at the petrol station car wash, where he was discovered yesterday. By that time there were no canvas bags and no money. Just imagine how he was fixed. He had the police after him. He'd have expected that, and planned for it. Until he reached that car wash he was conspicuous. He'd want to drive to it when he knew he was in the clear, and when he hadn't obviously got canvas bags of money in the back.'

'Keep it short.'

'Trying to,' she assured him. 'I'm trying to tell you that he'd need somewhere to hide, somewhere he could switch the money into something less obvious. I happen to know that there are about ten empty one gallon paint cans missing from his spraying shed. The shed is as he left it, except for those. It's obvious he'd cleaned them out in order to hide the money inside. He'd go to his hiding place and switch the money to the cans, and wait until the hunt had died down. But what if your . . . your son *hadn't* lost him? What if he saw his own chance to finance a racing sports car? What if he forced Charlie Braine into loading the cans into his own car . . . ?'

'It wasn't his own car.' O'Loughlin seemed to recognize that this was a feeble point, and explained weakly: 'He'd stolen it for the day.'

'Better still. He could afford to dump it. I know a place where Charlie could have driven to hide. At the same place, a car could be hidden for years, with the money safely sealed in their cans. I know such a place. The recovery would be difficult. But I can do it. Your son might well have discovered that he couldn't. *That* is what I've come to tell you. And now that you've convinced me the stone is genuine, I'll accept it on delivery.'

'The actual bank notes?'

'Sealed in their cans.'

'I could force you to take me there . . . hold Harry as security . . .'

'And not be able to recover the car,' she assured him, not even blinking. 'I can do it. I . . . you know who I am. You know who my father is. I can get him to do anything. The old fool, he trusts me. I will tell him it's a friend's car, or Harry's car, some such story, and he'll use police resources to recover it for me. And why should they think to look inside a few paint cans? Why?'

Then she smiled and sat back. After a moment O'Loughlin also smiled and sat back.

'And I am another old fool who trusts you.'

But the smile had been evil.

17

'It stuck to m' finger,' said Harry.

'Keep your eyes on the road.'

'When I lifted my finger it wasn't there. The diamond wasn't. I thought it'd gone in the water.'

'Not too fast, Harry.'

'My back crawled.'

He was glad to get clear of the trees and feel tarmac beneath the wheels again. 'Why not too fast?'

'We're being followed.'

'Of course we are. What'd you expect? Watch me drop him.'

'You will do no such thing,' she said steadily, drawing away at half an inch of brown cigarette. 'You drive and I'll watch. If he's good, we'll only get the odd glimpse or two.'

'He'll be good, right enough.' His nerves were now settling down. 'Why can't I drop him?'

'Because I want O'Loughlin to know where we're heading. I want him to get a report that it's exactly the place to fit what I told him.'

He drove another mile, overtaking a tractor with his off-side wheels up a bank. To Harry's way of thinking, they had accomplished what they'd come for before they'd even stepped into the powerboat. But Virginia, though pale, seemed to know what she was doing. Her calmness was of confidence.

'And where *are* we heading?'

'You know. You know very well. The quarry. The brickworks.' She was half twisted in her seat, eyes to the rear. 'He's still there. Speed up a bit. It's got to look as though we're making a genuine attempt to drop him.'

'That's what I'd rather do.' He glanced at her. 'You *do* know what you're doing, I hope?'

'Of course.'

'Not lost touch with reality? Or somethin' like that.'

'Harry!' There was excitement in her voice now. 'It went better than I could've hoped for.'

'But it was obvious, right from the start, that he didn't have Charlie killed.'

'Of course it was.'

'Then why the hell go to the quarry?'

'Language, Harry.'

'I mean, you didn't *believe* that, did you? This Kieron O'Loughlin story of yours. *Your* story, Virginia. You didn't actually believe he dumped a car with money in it ... don't forget, the money's been found. We *know* where it is. You haven't forgotten that, I hope?' he asked anxiously.

She slapped his knee suddenly, nearly finishing-off a cyclist Harry had been cutting a little close. 'But didn't it fit in a treat, Harry! Oh, it was marvellous. I was making it up as we went along – and he handed it to me on a plate. His son! And it was all there in the background, waiting to be used. The place Charlie *could* have gone, if he'd wanted a quiet place to switch the money to the paint cans. And the place a car *could* have been dumped, in the quarry, where it'd be difficult to recover. It was almost as though it really did happen like that. So what we're going to do is let his ...'

'Minion?' he put in.

'Yes. Let his minion take back a report that it *is* like that.'

He was approaching the crossing by the lay-by. 'Is he still there?'

In her delight she had not looked back for some time. She did so. 'I don't see him.'

'Good,' he said. 'I've had enough of O'Loughlin, and I don't see that this is getting us anywhere.'

She made no answer for the moment. The buildings were in sight before she said, as though it could be an explanation: 'I hate him, Harry. I didn't know I had it in me, this hatred. I would like to see him destroyed.'

'I'm with you there. Where d'you want me to park?'

'In front of the main building. We'll go inside and have a look round. It all helps to establish a background of reality.'

Harry was disturbed. It had shown itself with Angela, this tendency to become confused between the harsh realities of life and fantasy. Angela had lived in a fairy tale life, but inverted. She'd lifted the sordid background of Vic Fletcher's life-style to an unreal level of romance. In Harry's way of thought: she'd been a bit barmy. Now it was reasserting itself in Virginia, who seemed not to realize that O'Loughlin, with whom she was playing tricks, was a vicious and evil distortion of humanity, a man who would enjoy planning the nastiest way for her to die. Yet she'd played with him, even taunted him. And now, when she had the chance to drive as fast as hell out of his orbit, she still played the game.

She was standing beside him, and seemed to be able to read his mind. 'He'll never forget us, Harry,' she said soberly. 'You ought to realize that. We've got to see an end to it, and it's time he stopped calling the tune. Let's go and see what's in here.'

The building was extensive, with high windows, though not high enough to have remained intact, and seemed not to have had any specific purpose. It could have been a storage shed; there was a raised portion suggesting a loading bay. But Harry could not imagine that bricks would need to be stored under cover. Another building, lower and protruding at an angle, had obviously been offices. They walked into the gloom of the larger building through an entrance that would have admitted an airliner.

'What're we looking for?'

'Well . . . Charlie surely did go somewhere to switch the money into the cans. Why not here?'

'After four years . . .'

'We'll look,' she decided.

Vandals and vagrants had scoured it clear. There was barely anything but concrete floor. Their voices echoed. Whispers were taken and enlarged, then hurled back at them.

'It's creepy,' said Virginia.

Rocks had been ricocheted from the walls, and graffiti had been grafted. Cans had been kicked to unrecognizable crumples of metal.

'Cans,' said Harry, walking over to pick one up.

It was unlikely they'd brought their own cans to kick around, particularly ones this size. He picked it up and turned it over, searching for identification in the indentations. And found it. There was the remains of a label. MARTIN'S ACRYLIC . . .

'Heavens,' Virginia whispered, her head close to his. 'It was a wild guess. I didn't think . . . after all this time . . .'

'Not so wild. He had to lie low for a while. He'd bring more cans than he found he needed.' He frowned. 'Informed guess, they call it.'

He threw it away, and followed her out into the daylight, where it seemed they could speak without their voices being broadcast. A wind whipped round the buildings, chasing paper scraps. The sky was low and threatening. Beneath their feet, the surface was soft and slimy. Virginia shook her foot free from a tangle of strip binding steel.

'So that's the third,' she said.

'Let's get away from here, I can feel the eyes on my back.'

'First Freda, then Cynthia, they both said the same.'

'An' fists with guns in 'em.'

'They saw nobody. Nothing and nobody.' She nudged him. 'You're not listening, Harry.'

'I was. They saw nothing and nobody.'

She nodded. 'And now we know Charlie drove up here, and drove away again. It's ridiculous to think he might have headed home along the railway track, and back to Cynthia. It wasn't on his programme. So, as the lane's the only way out, he must have driven within fifty yards of the lay-by. Twice. And *he* saw nothing and nobody. Or he'd have stopped.'

'Maybe . . . perhaps she wasn't . . . sort of, around. We don't know when, do we? The exact time.'

'That's true.'

'Can we stand somewhere else?'

'But think – Angela had phoned. It *must* have been to contact Charlie. Did she see him drive past her, or away from her, in a two-colour car she couldn't have missed?'

'That'd be terrible for her.'

'But he didn't see her, Harry. That's the point.'

He put a paw on her arm. 'I don't wanna worry you, but we're a bit exposed here. Can't we sorta move on?'

'Well, of course. Are you quite sure we're being watched?' She sounded eager to have it confirmed.

'My back's like corrugated cardboard.'

'Then let's give them something to look at.'

She walked over to her car and slid behind the wheel. 'We'll go and pretend we're interested in the quarry.'

'Then keep well clear of the edge. It'll be slippy.'

'Round to the right, wasn't it.' It was not a question; she was already swinging to the right, round the bulk of the office block. 'The advantage of an automatic gearbox,' she explained, 'is that you can trickle along on tickover with your foot hovering over the brake.'

'Let me out here,' he said, as it seemed to him they were already trickling too far.

'If you're scared,' she conceded, her foot touching the brake. 'I'll warn you when you're goin' too far.'

She smiled at him. As though she couldn't tell!

He stood very close to the top edge of the ramp, his eyes on her front wheels, waving her on. The drop to the 45° ramp seemed suddenly very close, the surface too slippy.

'Easy!' he shouted. 'That's far enough. You can walk a yard, can't y'? Stop! For Chrissake stop!'

She did so, and climbed out grinning. He pointed out that if she'd gone an inch too far there was nowhere anybody could stand to push it out. She said she had rope in the back and they could always pull. He said that if she wanted to risk her car for the sake of showing-off, that was all right with him. She laughed and told him he was scared of his own shadow.

'My nerves are on edge.'

'All right. We'll just have a stare down at the water for a minute, as though we *know* there's a car down there, then we'll go home. And this time I'll let you lose him.'

Harry grunted. She was too confident that there was a 'him' to lose. They stood one each side of the car and stared solemnly at the bronze glaze of the water.

'Another couple of inches,' he observed, 'and there *would* have been a car down there.'

That damned water could hypnotize you, he thought, draw you like a magnet. If I stare at it much longer I'll go bloody crazy. He began to turn away from it, and a voice rang out.

'Hold it right there. Hey! You ... you bloody bitch. You hear me? Turn round. You gotta watch this.'

Slowly she moved. This was not on the programme. Theoretically, the watcher should not have revealed himself. It seemed that her body moved without any instructions from her brain. It was also unexpected that the watcher should have been Baldy. He had walked round the end of the office block, and twenty yards into the open. He had acquired another pistol, which he was holding steadily in both hands, and he seemed pleased with the situation.

It had perhaps been a mistake to assume that Baldy's connection with O'Loughlin had been severed. But he was not carrying the gun for self-protection. Every inch of his stance quivered with aggression.

'Don't do anything rash,' she said. Even to herself her voice sounded strange. 'O'Loughlin won't be pleased if you harm me.'

'Keep y'r hands away from your sides, Harry. Tha's dead right. Couldn't be better. Two shots, an' you're both down there, then y'r car after yer. Great, that. Who wants t' go first?'

Harry was feeling desperately for a firm grip beneath his feet, and failing. The only chance was to launch himself forward, fast and low. Even if he was hit, the impetus would carry him forward and take Baldy over. Then she'd have a chance. A small chance . . . if he could only dig a toe in! He was reaching back with his right leg, but there lay the fall-off. Nothing firm there . . .

Baldy, whose leer was failing him, suddenly switched to a snarl. 'Nobody takes a shooter off me.'

Behind him, round the same edge of the same building, stepped Vic Fletcher. He, too, had his pistol, but to Harry it seemed he was moving too slowly, too casually. Unless, of course, he was Baldy's back-up. Why didn't he *do* something?

Fletcher did something. He smiled. The gun was held loosely at his side, and he stopped moving, standing with his legs widely spread. Another clown playing a part, thought Harry. He thinks he's on Main Street in Tucson.

Baldy yelled: 'Why don'tcha say somethin'?'

'I'll say it,' put in Fletcher casually, though with a shake in his voice. He'd suddenly realized where he was and what he was doing. 'Drop that gun, you bald ape.'

Baldy whirled round and shouted: 'Nobody tells me to drop . . .'

Fletcher brought up his gun in a paroxysm of panic, his face twisted with sudden terror because Baldy should have dropped the gun and hadn't. He fired twice, a nervous reaction in case the first one missed. It did not. Baldy collapsed on one knee as it hit him in the right leg. The second bullet Harry heard. He heard it go past his head just as he was about to take advantage of Baldy's distraction. He took a half step back, with the leg on which he'd intended to throw his weight. The intention became fact. The weight was thrown too far back, the rear foot now on the slope. It slipped, he clawed wildly at the front wing of the car, said: 'Yerrr ...' and slid down the ramp on his stomach, feet first, fingers and toes scrabbling for grip on a surface that was red-brown slime.

At his cry, Virginia turned. 'Harry!' she screamed.

He was slowing gradually, spreading himself flat, presenting every possible square inch of his bulk in contact with the surface.

At last he stopped. His feet were a yard above the surface of the water. He stared up at her. She read his lips: 'Can't swim.'

She turned quickly to Fletcher for his help. He had picked up Baldy's new gun and reached back for a long throw, then it flew over her head and she heard it splash behind her. Baldy was trying to drag himself away with only one operative leg. The wound seemed to be in his hip. Fletcher walked up to him and stood with his pistol pointed at Baldy's face. Baldy's wild and furious eyes stared at him. Blood seeped through the fingers spread on his hip.

'No!' Virginia panted.

Fletcher twisted his head, staring back at her with derision. 'He called you names . . .'

'Let him go. Harry's . . .'

'So's he can have another go at yer?'

'Let him go. Come and help me.'

Fletcher straightened. He thrust the barrel of his gun in his waistband and stuck out his chest. 'You heard the lady. Get moving while y' got the chance.' Then he watched as Baldy, impelled by the closeness of his own end, managed to force himself to his feet and hobble away round the corner of the building.

Fletcher walked towards her. 'What seems to be the trouble?' He was locked in a mood that prevented him from inventing his own dialogue.

She realized that he was so tense, so absorbed by the action, that he had little of his mind to spare for speech.

'Harry's down there!'

He came up to the car and looked down. 'So he is.'

Harry was a little closer to the water. His face was expressionless. He was concentrating.

'There's rope in the back,' she said.

'Then get it,' Fletcher advised. 'You all right, Harry?'

175

Harry said nothing. Inflating his chest in order to call out might upset the equilibrium.

She whipped open the boot and fumbled with the rope, nearly dropping it, slammed down the lid, and ran to the edge.

'I hope it's long enough,' said Fletcher.

She tossed down one end. It fell over Harry's face and lay down his back. He stared up at her in agony. It took her several seconds to realize his dilemma. If he lifted one hand to the rope he would lose his grip on the clay surface. First, the rope needed to be fixed.

'Listen to me, Harry,' she called. 'Don't even nod. We'll get this end firm, and when it is I'll shout. Then you can get a hold on it and we'll pull you out.'

'Not me,' said Fletcher.

'What?' She whirled on him in angry disbelief.

'You know what that bastard weighs? More than you'n me together. He'd drag us both in.'

'You spineless . . .' She bit her lip to silence. 'We'll tie it to the car. D'you hear that, Harry? We'll tie it to the car, then I'll tow you out.'

'*You'll* tie it to the car,' said Fletcher. 'You ain't gettin' me lyin' there, that close to the edge.'

For a moment she stared at him. Then, silently, she knelt down to survey the prospects.

There was nothing at the nose of the car to which a rope could be fixed. The nearest usable point that she could see was the wishbone of the front suspension, which was guarded by the wheel. She could not get at it from the front, and from behind the front wheel the ground clearance was too small to allow her head and shoulders to intrude. There was nothing for it but to lie face down, wriggle forward with both arms extended, and feel for it.

From that position, her face an inch from the ground and her fingers blindly fumbling the rope over something metal, she said:

'I suppose that was you, following us?'

'Following Baldy.'

'For which, my thanks. Shout to Harry to hold on.' She was panting with the effort, urgency tangling her fingers.

'Hold on, Harry,' he shouted.

A knot, she told herself, form a knot. 'Why . . . did you . . . follow?' she gasped.

'To see what was goin' on, o' course. Ain't you done it yet?'

Her fingers seemed to have lost all feeling. The knot eluded her, the rope end appearing to be alive. She had no more breath for words. Fletcher filled in the gaps for her.

'Didn' fool me. Oh, I could see what you were up to. Lookin' down in the quarry to make it seem like the money's there. Not likely. Harry wouldn't do anythin' stupid like that. But I've got it sorted out now. I wondered how it'd been done. They met here, didn' they? Charlie an' Harry. An' switched the money. Oh . . . clever. Fooled everybody. O'Loughlin an' me. But Harry didn' dump it here, 'cause he'd never get it back. The point is, where did he hide it?'

She was wriggling free, and turned her head to look up at him. He smiled down at her. She forced herself to her knees, then her feet. She was smeared all down her front, clay on her face. She wiped her hands down her slacks.

'So I was right,' she said in contempt. Then she reached down and jerked on the rope, which seemed reasonably secure, and eased the spare over the edge. Leaning over, she wriggled it until it lay in a straight line beside Harry's right hand.

'It's fastened to the car, Harry. You can grab hold of it now.'

On this he seemed doubtful. From his position he could see the nose of the car protruding just beyond the edge of the ramp. He took a deep breath, and grabbed.

The sudden weight on its nose provoked the car into movement. The front wheels slid three inches. They now rested just over the edge, and were about to angle down the slope.

'Lie still!' she shouted. 'I'll back the car out.'

She ran to the car door, was about to jerk it open, hesitated, then took it very carefully, slid gingerly on to the seat, and left the door swinging.

'Starting the engine, Harry,' she shouted.

'Yeah,' said Fletcher. 'You start the engine.' He was round at the passenger's side, that door open too, staring in. The gun was again in his hand. 'But you ain't goin' anywhere.'

She started the engine. Her foot was on the brake, her hand on the autochange lever. 'I guessed,' she told him. 'It was the money all the while, wasn't it? That was just a blind, pretending you wanted Harry to find out who did the murder. But you're not worried about that. Oh, I grant you, it was all heavy passion at

177

the time, but now it's the money. Four years is too long for your sort of passion. Now take your hand off my car.'

He stood where he was, nodding. 'So right, so right! So now you're gonna slip that lever into drive.' He jerked the gun. 'Into forward drive. Keep y'r foot on the brake. Well, just great. That's real dandy. Now you shout to Harry and tell him you can pull him out if he says where he hid the money.'

She stared straight ahead. She did not even shake her head. The single word was said crisply. 'No.'

'If I shoot you now, you won't be able to stop it.'

'And you'll never know about the money.'

'Shout to him, you bloody bitch!'

'Do it yourself.'

Fletcher turned his head. 'You hearin' this, Harry?'

Harry's choked voice came back. 'Get stuffed.'

Fletcher jerked back. 'I ain't foolin'. Ten seconds you got. Ten seconds, an' I shoot your knee-cap off. *Then* it'll come off the bloody brake.'

She said nothing. She was now pushing on the brake pedal so heavily that her leg was shaking. The gun wavered. His face was crumpled with distress and strain.

'I'm tellin' you . . .'

She said: 'Get away from the car.'

With a scream of fury he ran to the rear. She heard him crying out: 'I'll have y'rover. You hearin' me? I'll shove y'rover.'

She jerked the lever into reverse and banged her foot hard down on the throttle. The tyres whined, and sprayed mud on the underside. For a second the car staggered, then the wide tyres dug in, and it shot backwards. There was a scream from behind, and she banged down on the brake, shot the lever into park, and dived out of the car.

Fletcher was somewhere under the back axle, moaning and howling alternately. She ran to the edge. Harry was halfway up the slope, on his back now because the sudden jerk had twisted him. The rope had one wrist at an awkward angle. The other hand was flailing for a grip. She ran to the back of the car.

'Fletcher . . .'

'Get me outa here!'

'I can't.'

He seemed to be mixed up between the rear suspension and

178

the massive silencer box.

'Ease it . . . Oh Jesus . . . ease it forward . . .'

She went to the driver's door and slowly climbed into the seat. She placed both hands on the wheel, one foot on the brake, and eased the lever into reverse, feeling the power going into the box. Then she sat. Her lips moved.

'Gemme out!' shouted Fletcher.

Deliberately she lifted her foot from the brake and pressed down on the throttle. When his screams became too much to bear, she covered her ears with her hands and let it steer itself, until Harry's head appeared, his shoulders, his knees.

Then she stopped. She cut the engine. When Harry crawled forward and stood over her she was sobbing.

'He's . . . underneath, Harry.'

Harry bent down and looked. He could feel the skin tight over his cheekbones. 'He's not moving.'

She shook her head stubbornly and furiously, trying to free her brain. 'His car. It's somewhere. Find it. The phone.'

He squeezed her shoulder and scrambled away, gradually forcing himself to a run.

After a while she managed to light a cigarette. But she couldn't climb out of the car.

Harry was back before they heard the sirens. He stood beside the open door, and she fumbled her hand into his, where it was lost.

18

Oliver Brent pointed with the walking stick he used only when prowling his gardens.

'It's always been too wet down in that corner. There's a stream, though you can't see it from here. What d'you think about a water garden, Harry?'

Harry glanced back the way they had come. Virginia was still sitting on the bench in the arbour. 'Could be. We might even use the stream and make a decorative waterfall.'

'Good idea. Here. Over here . . . I want you to look at my

179

Michaelmas daisies. They look miserable to me.'

'Probably need parting up. Did you get mildew?'

They chatted on. There had been a complete tour of the gardens, which proved to be more extensive than Harry had expected. He had viewed the rooms above the garage that were to be his, had approved, and there'd been discussion on his salary.

'Could give you an advance,' Brent had murmured.

During all this, until they had reached the bench, Virginia had accompanied them, but had remained silent. For three days she had been unresponsive, polite but distant. Brent had said nothing, but he was clearly worried. They strolled back to where she was seated. She did not turn her head. They took seats each side of her on the rustic bench.

Brent said: 'I always like to sit here. You can relax. The world's out there somewhere . . .'

'Have you decided about Freda Graham, father?' Virginia interrupted.

'She has been charged with the murders of Angela and Cynthia Braine. It now seems doubtful that she'll be fit to plead, in which case it could never come to court.'

She slapped both hands on her knees. 'And Charlie Braine?' There was barely civility in her tone.

'O'Loughlin. His instructions.' Brent's voice was calm. She knew all this . . . but he was patient.

'You'll never get him for it, though.'

'Regrettably, no.'

'Because neither he nor his employees were involved, that's why. Harry can confirm this. From our two conversations with him, it was quite clear he was in no way involved with Charlie Braine's death.'

Harry nodded. He wished she would turn and look at him, look him in the eyes and plead for help or something. He might not know how to handle it if she did, but he wished she would ask, and not try to bear all the misery herself. But at least he could nod and agree. 'He was furious because it wasn't him.'

Brent stared at the rubber tip of his stick, tapped it against his shoe, then spoke carefully.

'It's possible he was too clever for both of you.'

She was stirred to animation. 'Maybe he was. But I'm certain of one thing. He wasn't involved with Charlie's death. As Harry

180

said, he was furious he hadn't been. We knew this before we even met him the second time.'

'I cannot express my disapproval too strongly, Virginia. You should have turned and come away.'

'No!' she said. Her hair tossed as she jerked her head. 'There was something else. I spent most of the second visit establishing a background. For you, father, if you'll use it.'

Brent raised his eyebrows at Harry, who shook his head, implying he was going to say nothing.

'I'll be happy to listen,' said Brent, turning back to her.

'Well ... thank you! Thank you for listening, anyway. The money, father, the money. During the first visit it was clear he wanted to get his hands on it. A matter of saving face. A question of his standing in the foul hierarchy of his profession, which is robbery with violence, if I've got to remind you ...'

'I am quite aware of the sort of scum we are talking about. Don't shout, please.'

'I was not shouting. I was *not*.' She stopped, drew a deep breath, and went on more calmly. 'He wanted that money, in the actual notes that were stolen. He wanted it in his hands, and I worked hard at planting in his mind various doubts about the re-liability of his hired help, to get him round to the mental state where he really did mean his *own hands*. With a bit of luck I managed to use available background to persuade him I knew where that money now lies ... at the bottom of a quarry at the old brickworks. It all fitted together neatly, so that he was con-vinced it was somewhere *he* couldn't get at it and I could. Are you understanding this, father?'

'Completely. Not happy, but understanding.'

'I wondered why you hadn't interrupted, that's all. Where was I? Yes. We – Harry and I – made sure we were followed to that quarry, and by sheer luck we did find evidence that Charlie Braine had been there. But that's not crucial. The point is that we *were* followed, by the one we knew as Baldy.'

'From whom you'd taken the handgun?'

'That one – yes. Baldy, who would no doubt return to tell O'Loughlin what he'd seen, and O'Loughlin would be com-pletely convinced that the money was down in that quarry, inside a car and sealed in empty paint cans. He's perfectly primed. You could have him, father, a present from me.'

181

Brent tapped his pursed lips with the handle of his stick. 'I begin not to like the sound of this.'

'I've told him that *he* couldn't lift that car, and he'll realize that. Although the site's isolated and derelict, it'd be too big an operation to do secretly. But I could do it. Officially. I told him that you would lay on a police team to drag out the car, which I would persuade you was a friend's, and therefore of no official interest to you . . .'

'And he accepted that? Good Lord! You know damned well I can't use members of the force for private . . .'

'I know it. He doesn't. They all think the police are corrupt, and wouldn't hesitate to use public funds for their own purposes. Isn't that right, Harry?'

Two pairs of eyes clamped on his. He'd wanted her to look directly at him, but not so fiercely, not so demandingly. 'Well . . . I'm not in his league . . . but the general idea is that a lot of money sorta leaks into private pockets. Mind you, I, personally . . .'

'There you are then,' said Virginia with satisfaction, beaming suddenly at her father.

'What, exactly, had you in mind?' he asked cautiously.

'You still have the money and the paint cans . . .'

He nodded. 'Evidence.'

'Then I want you to find an old car, any old wreck, and put the cans, with the actual money sealed inside, into that car, and one dark night have it secretly run down the ramp into the quarry.'

'Good Lord!'

'In the meantime I'll see him again and lay it on. I'll persuade him he must come himself to meet me there and collect it.'

'Now hold on!'

She waved him to silence. 'It will be perfectly safe. Harry will be with me.'

Harry stared beyond her at Brent and managed a sickly smile.

'And then,' she said, 'a few days later you mount a large and showy operation with frogmen and cranes and whatever, to drag it out again. He'll be there, be sure of that. I have it firmly planted in his mind that I'd just as soon keep the money myself as exchange it for his diamond. And when it's been rescued, and standing there on the top, your kind superintendent will salute and take his men away, and leave me in possession. O'Loughlin will creep out. I'll let him open the cans himself, feel the money, then your second team of men will close in . . . and we'll have him!'

Her face was now alive, her eyes dancing.

Brent patted his upper lip with the handkerchief from his breast pocket. 'I'm using a lot of resources on this, apparently.'

'But it'll be the first time you've had him away from his little island, and he'll actually be receiving and handling the genuine stolen money. It's lovely. And with my evidence and Harry's, he'll go down for ever.'

Brent got to his feet. Harry thought he was about to walk away, but he was still not treating it as a serious possibility, so that he could smile down at her. 'I think you'd find it would come under the heading of entrapment. The DPP would throw it out.'

'Entrapment, father, as you very well know, consists of persuading someone into committing a crime, and then stepping in.'

'All the same . . .'

'And in any event, it would be *my* trap. Mine!' she said with fierce possessiveness.

'Really, Virginia, you go too far.' He stared down at her with concern. 'And you think he'd admit to the murder of Charles Braine, once we had him inside?'

'Of course not. It wasn't him.'

'I suppose you know who it was, then?'

She nodded. 'I know.'

He was still very grave, then he turned away and began to walk towards the house.

'You might at least discuss it with the Chief Constable,' she called after him.

He stopped and turned. 'I was just about to phone him, my dear.' Then, solemnly, he winked at Harry.

Again she called him to a halt. 'And father – do make sure your second team don't pounce until *after* he's handed me the diamond.'

The corner of Brent's mouth twitched, then he was allowed to proceed to the house. Harry and Virginia looked at each other, and burst into laughter.

'Will he do it?' Harry asked.

'They really want O'Loughlin. I think he will.'

'I'll look forward to it.' He tilted his head. 'That isn't all of it, is it?'

'You tell me,' she teased.

'He knows O'Loughlin'll never forget you. He knows you won't be safe till he's inside.'

She tapped his wrist. 'Clever Harry. I'm counting on it.'

He was still eyeing her suspiciously. 'Why didn't he ask you for a name when you said you knew who'd killed Charlie?'

'Because he knew I had to tell Martin first. It was part of the agreement, before I contacted you. If it succeeded – if *we* succeeded, Harry, you and I – then Martin would know first. Come on, we'll go and tell him.'

The Mercedes was waiting on the drive. He said: 'Just like that? Not even a tararfernow to your old man?'

'He'll know, and it's only fifty miles. I'll drive.'

When they were eventually settled on the motorway, heading north, he said: 'And I haven't succeeded in anything. I still don't know who did Charlie.'

'Just think about it, Harry.'

'Hmm!' He opened his mouth, and closed it. Martin had to be the first to know. Two miles later he ventured: 'And who the hell's Martin?'

'My husband, Harry. My husband.'

Which kept him silent for the rest of the journey.

It was a country mansion set in rolling countryside, unobtrusive and secluded. The gate pillars carried no gates, simply a brass plaque with the words: Marston House. The oval of parking space lay at the foot of seven wide steps, and was flanked by massive cedars. In the distance, water twinkled between trees. A dog barked round the back of the building. A gardener was clipping a bay hedge back to its perfection as a peacock. A peacock strutted, contemptuous of the result.

She led the way in. The lobby was simple, and had been originally the hall. Now it held, to one side, a desk. No one was sitting at it, but a bell invited a visitor's palm. Visitors were rare. There was little for them to visit. Harry worried about the ring of his heels on the patterned stone floor.

The woman who appeared through a side door knew Virginia at once. 'Mrs Reed . . . we weren't expecting you. Never mind. I'll see how he is, if you'd like . . .' She waved vaguely towards two easy chairs that flanked a huge fireplace, now cold and occupied by an artistic crumple of red and black tissue paper, representing a fire. A symbol, Harry decided. The house was so silent that the fireplace contained as much life. They sat one on each side of it, facing each other.

'I owe you an explanation, Harry,' she said, her hands nervous on her shoulder bag. 'I told you a direct lie. I'm not going to apologize, because I think you'll understand. I *am* the daughter of Oliver Brent, but I'm married to Martin Reed. Angela Reed was my step-daughter. I thought that if I told you that, it would weaken my case. People don't accept that any affection exists in that relationship, so I was afraid you'd query my motives.' She paused, but he said nothing. She moved her shoulders, and went on.

'Martin was a solicitor. Still is a solicitor, I suppose. When Angela was killed he took it badly. Blast, that's a stupid thing to say. We both took it, because we had to take it, and it hurt. I loved her, Harry. People said we were alike, but I couldn't see that. She was a rebel, full of life and romanticism, and brought up in such a way that she didn't know what the world was like outside. We could hardly have been more different, but we understood each other.'

Harry smiled gravely. The knobbles round his mouth moved. 'I can understand that.'

'Martin was very sensible. He let her work it out of her system . . . that sort of thing. She had a generous allowance, so we thought she couldn't come to much harm. The harm she came to could hardly have been more tragic. Martin was . . . somebody might have stamped on him. When you were found not guilty, it was the final blow. I *told* him it couldn't be you, but you know about a solicitor's mind – everything has to be set out in phrases that allow for only one meaning. There were no words I could find that gave any meaning to Angela's death. So one night he took the car out and drove into a tree at eighty, they reckoned. Perhaps his mind wasn't on his driving. He suffered terrible injuries to the face and head, and . . . and as far as anybody can tell his mind is a complete blank.'

Harry moved restlessly. The voice in which she was telling it was one he had not heard before. He would have liked to wait in the car, where her other voice had been.

'I come here,' she said softly, 'and talk to him. I don't know if he hears. Then one day I risked something. You . . . you can't talk to nothing, on and on, without wanting to . . . well, shock, I

185

suppose. I promised him I'd find the person who killed Angela, and see that the penalty was paid. And Harry, I thought I saw something – oh, deep down in his eyes. An understanding, I suppose. And of course, doing it was for me too, Harry. You must understand that.'

It seemed to Harry that it was imperative he should understand, and that she should be assured of it.

'Yeah, sure. Well . . . you would.'

She reached over and patted his hand. 'I want you to say nothing, Harry. Whatever I tell him, you'll not say a word. Promise?'

'Promise,' he said, raising his head as the receptionist came down the stairs again.

'He's in the sun lounge, Mrs Reed. I'm sure he'll be glad to see you.'

'Thank you.'

The stairs were dark oak with a hundred years of patina, the corridors panelled, the carpets soft. It was simply an old house, splendidly preserved, but with no evidence of its institutional purpose, until Virginia opened a door and they entered a room with new oak strip flooring and plain colour-washed walls, a few soft chairs, and three silent, empty shells of people. Only the ceiling had escaped. It was still heavily moulded and decorative, still lived.

'Why, hello Jessie. And how are you today? Mr Thomas! I haven't seen you for ages.'

Neither responded to Virginia's greeting. This had been her cheerful voice, the one she was polishing to present to her husband. It shone.

A nurse was standing at the far end of the run of high windows, behind an easy chair. She moved forward.

'Here's your wife to see you, Mr Reed.' Then, in the same tone: 'No change, I'm afraid. I'll leave you with him now.'

Harry watched her go, young and attractive, efficiency in every movement of her limbs. How can they work here? he wondered. And not go insane.

Virginia was standing, looking down at her husband with a smile. 'Pull up a couple of chairs, Harry,' she said, not looking round.

Martin Reed did not turn his head. He was sitting with his knees together and raised, his left hand lax on the chair's arm, the other spread on his chest. He had been a fine man, Harry could tell, tall and distinguished, though now the clothes were empty on him, his collar gaping at a gaunt neck. His moustache was trimmed, and his face so clean and shining that it did not seem to be flesh at all. Then Harry realized that he was looking at a reconstruction of a face.

As they took their seats, Virginia said: 'I am going to tell you what happened that day, Martin, and what has happened since, so that you'll understand. This is my good friend Harry, who's been helping me. Without Harry, I would never have got to the truth.'

She then went on to tell him what she thought to be the truth. Her voice was steady, not a monotone but enlivened by emphasis and modulation. She did not take her eyes from his face, which registered nothing. The hand at his chest might simply have fallen there by accident. He did not move it, even by so much as an inch.

When she had laid on the background, had detailed her and Harry's adventures with O'Loughlin, and the Freda–Cynthia relationship, she finished:

'So you see, Martin, the police believe O'Loughlin had Charlie killed because he double-crossed him over the money, but I can't believe his men would have killed him and then missed the money in the paint cans. The police also believe Freda Graham killed both Angela and Cynthia. I do not believe this to be true. I'll tell you what I think happened.'

Martin Reed stared at her and through her. He was looking at her face only because she had placed her chair so that he would be doing so.

'Angela and Charlie were intending to go away together. He hadn't told his wife about this plan, naturally, and he hoped if all went well that he'd have the haul from the bank robbery, and what he could get from the stuff from the jeweller's shop, to give them a good start. Angela . . . well, you know Angela . . . it was just another adventure that may or may not have come off, so she said nothing to Vic Fletcher, though they'd been living together as man and wife for six months. She was leaving it open so that she could return if it all went wrong. Now . . . there are two strange circumstances about Angela's movements that day, after Harry left her at the lay-by. One: she made a phone call – actually

187

made it, otherwise she wouldn't have used the money. And two: she became apparently invisible.'

Harry cleared his throat, but she touched his knee and he was silent.

'Freda Graham said she didn't see Angela when she drove to pick her up. This isn't remarkable. Angela, as you know, was basically a law-abiding citizen, though she was doing her best to get out of the habit.' She smiled, and one of Martin's fingers moved. When she went on, her voice was uncertain. 'The first thing she did – and this would be instinct – was to dial 999 and report her car stolen. She was told to stay where she was. At that point she would realize she had made a mistake. She was now going to get herself tied up with police procedures, when she ought to be trying to reach Charlie. It's obvious where their meeting place was . . . the derelict petrol station, where Charlie was intending to clean his car back to plain black.'

Harry realized that she was laying this out as simply and plainly as possible, as a solicitor would appreciate.

'So what would she do? She would hide, of course. There were hedges. There was a gate only a few yards from the lay-by. She could hide there and wait. Later, Cynthia drove there, and said she saw nothing. Angela was hiding. She was obviously waiting for a specific car to come for her, a black Escort XR3, as Charlie would have told her, which she'd last seen as a red and green one. And she'd be waiting for it because she'd phoned to say where she was. But at the time she phoned, Charlie could not possibly have reached his car wash. So . . . the very fact that she was hiding means that she had left a message.'

Harry stirred again. She did not even notice, being so concentrated on what she was saying.

'Charlie Braine was obviously a clever man, having made his plans so carefully. He had water laid on . . . in fact, it's still connected. He would have had to have electricity connected, to power the car wash. He wouldn't forget to have a phone installed. For emergencies. As Angela's was – an emergency. She knew where to phone. She did so. And waited. But it meant that Charlie must have had one more person involved in his scheme, somebody he was paying for the simple duty of sitting by the phone in case, and probably to report that everything was quiet before Charlie drove to the car wash. The tragic thing about it is that, during the time she was waiting – nearly two hours – Charlie probably drove past her twice in the car, still in its red and green state, the first time taking the road to the abandoned brick-works. I wonder whether she thought he was taking the back way home, back to his wife. In any event, he'd be past before she could get out on the road. And later, when he'd switched the money to his paint cans, he might simply have turned right, and she'd get no more than a flicker of colour. She was hiding. Waiting for the car to park in the lay-by. As a black one.'

She looked abruptly away from Martin's eyes, as though she had become hypnotized by them. Quickly, she fumbled in her bag and found her brown cigarettes, lit one, and turned her head to blow smoke away from Martin's eyes.

'Having worked that out,' she continued, more relaxed now that she could distract her attention to the cigarette from time to time, 'it seemed clear to me who was the person waiting at the phone for messages. In practice, he confirmed my guess himself. Just consider the facts surrounding Charlie's death. He should have arrived at the car wash with the money in the back of his car, in canvas bags. It was not there . . . it was in paint cans in the boot. The murderer missed that, possibly because of panic, poss-ibly because he assumed the cans were full of paint. For whatever reason, he believed the money had changed hands, and later, when there had been time for thought, it must have seemed that the only person it could have been passed to was Harry, who had probably hidden it himself.'

A tear appeared in the corner of Martin's left eye. Perhaps this was normal, thought Harry, because Virginia reached a tissue from the box beside him and wiped it away gently.

'But Harry went out of circulation for four years, so he wasn't around to ask. By that time, my dear, everybody assumed O'Loughlin had the money, or, because Charlie had disap-peared, that he'd got the money with him. Only the murderer would believe that Harry had the money hidden somewhere, knowing that Charlie hadn't taken it somewhere, and knowing that O'Loughlin hadn't been involved with Charlie's death. It was Vic Fletcher himself who told me he was after the money, and it had been Fletcher who'd been haunting Harry, pretending he believed Harry had killed Angela. He was hoping Harry's nerve would break and he'd go for the hidden money, and make

189

a run for it.'

On his knees, Harry's fingers closed to fists. He said nothing. She stubbed out her cigarette and went on: 'If you consider Fletcher in that context, it all falls into place. To Charlie, he was a man he'd paid in the past for stolen vehicle documents, so he was a man he'd possibly use as a contact, to sit over the phone at the petrol station. Not a man he'd confide in, to whom he'd mention the name of the woman he was intending to go away with. And Angela, it's obvious she couldn't have told Charlie that the man she was living with was Fletcher. It only needed one spark for the situation to explode, and that spark was her phone call to the petrol station. She was speaking to Fletcher. Perhaps she didn't recognize his voice in that setting. Perhaps he recognized hers, and disguised his own. In any event, she told him, without realizing, that she was the woman Charlie was intending to go away with. And she told him exactly where she was waiting.'

She took a breath. 'I don't think I can go on, Harry,' she said softly.

'You're doing fine.'

She touched her brow with her fingers, then looked up again.

'After four years, it was the money he wanted. On *that* day . . . well, perhaps he felt something special for Angela. I don't know. But when Charlie did arrive, and drove straight into the car wash, Fletcher would be waiting, and hating him. And he shot him and left him there, while he took the car, now black, to the lay-by. It was what she'd been waiting for. She ran out to it. Oh, I've waited hours . . . And Fletcher got out and said: he isn't coming, he's dead, I shot the bastard dead. Or words to that effect. And she, in fury, went at him with her shoe, which he'd be able to take from her easily, probably laughing at her, and you know how wild she always became when people laughed at her, so she'd go at him with everything, and he'd strike back with what he had – short of producing his gun – which was the shoe. So I suppose . . .' She sighed. 'I reckon that in law it might be called self-defence.'

She was silent. In the dull eyes there had been something, but it was not recognition.

Harry whispered: 'Cynthia.'

It was to him she explained, but still for Martin's ears. 'In the shed, to us, she shouted that she'd driven to the lay-by and seen nothing. It was loud enough for Fletcher to have heard, if he'd been hanging around. So she was killed, in case she was lying, and *had* seen something. Just in case.'

Silence again. Martin blinked. She went on, a catch in her voice, in case the blink had been intentional.

'Fletcher gave me the vital information – that all the while he'd been after the money – while I was involved with trying to rescue Harry. As I've told you, Martin, Harry was in desperate trouble. He couldn't possibly have climbed the rope, because he was plastered with slippy clay. I didn't think he could even hold on much longer. So I had to back up the car, and Fletcher was trapped beneath it. I killed Fletcher, Martin. He's dead . . . the man who took Angela's life.'

Martin's lower lip quivered. A bubble of saliva appeared on it. For a second, intelligence awoke in his eyes, but the effort depleted him.

'I know what you're going to say,' she told him huskily. 'But I've already been informed that it'll be treated as justifiable homicide. Otherwise . . .' She reached forward, smiling, and placed her hand on his knee. 'Otherwise I'd have had to ask you to appear for my defence.'

Then she straightened her skirt and got to her feet. 'It was very pleasant speaking to you again, Martin, particularly as I had this news for you. Let Angela rest now. I'll come again soon.'

Harry rose with her. Solicitor, she'd said. Perhaps she'd meant barrister. He couldn't think of anything to say, but as he moved past Martin's chair the hand rose from his chest, hovered, and slowly moved towards Harry. The head turned to monitor its progress. It clawed at Harry's hand, then caught his wrist. Harry felt the pressure, then it fell to Martin's knee.

When Harry turned, Virginia had run from the room.

19

They were ten miles nearer home when Harry next spoke. He was driving, his mind still engaged with the scene between Virginia and her husband.

'Will your father accept all that?'

'It wasn't invented just for Martin.'

He had wondered how much, in his situation, Martin had warranted the truth. 'There's not a scrap of evidence,' he pointed out.

'True,' she conceded. 'But I think it'll persuade him to withdraw the charge against Freda.'

'Hmm!' he said, and accelerated down the slip road to join the motorway. Then he was silent for a few miles.

He now had an elusive thought captured and analysed. She had been honest with him in finally revealing her true reasons for approaching Harry at the beginning. But she could have been doing no more than freeing her conscience, in which case it could signal the end of their relationship. Harry had to know the truth, which was all bound up in the question: did they now fully enjoy each other's confidence? If she could lie to her husband, as he was sure she had, if only by implication, then she could still be prepared to lie to Harry. Would she dare to repeat it?

All this he finally forced his brain to comprehend. He wasn't sure how to broach the question. He stalled.

'Your father'll never authorize that trick with O'Loughlin.'

'Want a bet?' She stretched, seeming to relax. 'It could be fun, though.'

'I can't wait.'

She patted his knee in approval. It was clear she saw a continuation in their partnership. He plunged. 'I could have . . .' Then he sidestepped it at the last second.

'I could've . . . sworn he'd refuse.'

She shook her head. 'And have you thought, Harry . . . if it comes off, and O'Loughlin actually gives me the diamond, there'll be half of its value for you.'

It sounded a little dishonest to Harry. 'Me? It's *your* diamond.'

'It was your finger it stuck to,' she reminded him severely.

It was in considering the peculiar pathways of her logic that he found himself saying it.

'I could've climbed that rope, you know. I had a good grip.'

'Do you imagine I didn't realize that, Harry?'

Smiling, relaxed, he drove on, letting the car have its head.

STACK 1195

BETTWS

0353465